Mace and Jenny

Becky remembered her
years ago, when she had suggested kind of
hopefully that maybe Jenny could divorce Mace
and marry Taggart.

Jenny would make a good stepmother. She didn't
yell. Much. She tolerated mud better than most
women. And she made really good apple pie.

Then when Becky finally grew up, Mace could
marry her. He was the cowboy she'd fallen in love
with when she was five years old.

She didn't say that part out loud, of course. But
when she suggested that Jenny would make him a
good wife, Taggart had said, "Won't happen, pard.
Jenny and Mace have been a pair long as I can
remember. I believe it'd take an atom bomb to split
'em apart."

Turns out her dad didn't know everything after all.

Dear Reader,

The hustle and bustle of the holiday season is just around the corner—and Special Edition's November lineup promises to provide the perfect diversion!

This month's THAT SPECIAL WOMAN! title is brought to you by veteran author Lindsay McKenna. *White Wolf* takes you on a stirring, spiritual journey with a mystical Native American medicine woman who falls helplessly in love with the hardened hero she's destined to heal!

Not to be missed is *The Ranger and the Schoolmarm* by Penny Richards—the first book in the SWITCHED AT BIRTH miniseries. A collaborative effort with Suzannah Davis, this compelling series is about four men…switched at birth!

And bestselling author Anne McAllister delivers book six in the CODE OF THE WEST series with *A Cowboy's Tears*—a heartfelt, deeply emotional tale. The first five books in the series were Silhouette Desire titles.

The romance continues with *The Paternity Test* by Pamela Toth when a well-meaning nanny succumbs to the irresistible charms of her boss—and discovers she's pregnant! And Laurie Paige serves up a rollicking marriage-of-convenience story that will leave you on the edge of your seat in *Husband: Bought and Paid For.*

Finally, *Mountain Man* by Silhouette newcomer Doris Rangel transports you to a rugged mountaintop where man, woman and child learn the meaning of trust—and discover unexpected happiness!

I hope you enjoy all that we have in store for you this November. Happy Thanksgiving Day—and all of us at Silhouette would like to wish you a joyous holiday season!

Sincerely,

Tara Gavin
Senior Editor

Please address questions and book requests to:
Silhouette Reader Service
U.S.: 3010 Walden Ave., P.O. Box 1325, Buffalo, NY 14269
Canadian: P.O. Box 609, Fort Erie, Ont. L2A 5X3

ANNE McALLISTER

A COWBOY'S TEARS

Silhouette®

SPECIAL EDITION®

Published by Silhouette Books

America's Publisher of Contemporary Romance

For Peter
with love and thanks for thirty wonderful years

For Courtney, David, Joseph, Patrick and James
our children

and most especially for AJ
who really did "improve the quality of life around here"

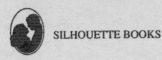 SILHOUETTE BOOKS

ISBN 0-373-24137-2

A COWBOY'S TEARS

Copyright © 1997 by Barbara Schenck

Printed in U.S.A.

Books by Anne McAllister

Silhouette Special Edition

*A Cowboy's Tears #1137

Silhouette Desire

*Cowboys Don't Cry #907
*Cowboys Don't Quit #944
*Cowboys Don't Stay #969
*The Cowboy and the Kid #1009
*Cowboy Pride #1034

*Code of the West

ANNE McALLISTER

was born and raised in California, land of surfers, swimmers and beach-volleyball players. She spent her teenage years researching them in hopes of finding the perfect hero. It turned out, however, that a few summer weeks spent at her grandparents' in Colorado and all those hours in junior high spent watching Robert Fuller playing Jess Harper on "Laramie" were formative. She was fixated on dark, handsome, intense, lone-wolf types. Twenty-nine years ago she found the perfect one prowling the stacks of the university library and married him. They now have four children, three dogs, a fat cat and live in the Midwest (as in "Is this heaven?" "No, it's Iowa.") in a reasonable facsimile of semiperfect wedded bliss to which she always returns—even though the last time she was in California she had lunch with Robert Fuller.

Dear Diary

I'm worried. Something's the matter with MACE. He doesn't smile any more and I can't remember the last time he called me Shadow. Of course I don't trail after him like I used to, but I'm ten now and I got a life too—sorta.

My dad says to mind my own business. He says I worry too much and people can solve their own problems. Like he's doing such a great job with the Twins! HA!

The thing is I've loved MACE as long as I can remember. And even though I know I'm not ever going to get to marry him (on account of him already being married and 23 years older than me) I still want what's best for him. Felicity, my mom, says love is like that. I just wish I knew what to do!

                                        Becky

Prologue

Mace Nichols was on his own.

He stood in the doorway of the tiny two-room log cabin, where he'd just dumped his gear, and stared out across the valley toward the Crazies.

He was alone.

The cabin echoed with emptiness. No one had lived there since Jed McCall and his nephew had moved out the year before.

Originally it had been a settler's cabin, then a line shack, then the place Mace and Jed and Taggart Jones had come to as teenagers whenever they'd wanted to get away from nosy adults. Here they had drunk beer, looked at pictures of naked women and indulged their youthful dreams.

In fact, Mace had indulged in a little more than dreaming the first few times he'd brought Jenny up here. But he had never told anyone about that.

Later, after they were married, well, it was no secret what they were doing!

Same thing Taggart had done when he'd brought his new bride, Julie, to live in the cabin eleven years ago. Unlike Jenny, though, Julie had hated the cabin. She'd thrown a fit and insisted they get an apartment in Bozeman. Taggart had, but even so, the marriage hadn't lasted a year.

After Taggart and Julie's brief stay, the cabin had gone back to line shack status until five years ago when Jed had taken it over.

And now it was Mace's turn again.

Only this time he was alone.

Because—for the first time in fourteen years—there was no Jenny.

No Jenny.

He shook his head and rearranged the thought. *No Jenny* was the negative way of looking at it.

He tried to focus on the positive: he was on his own. He was his own man, answerable to no one. No one at all.

He'd never been on his own before. Ever.

He'd fallen in love with Jenny Fitzpatrick at the age of seventeen. He'd married her not quite two years later. They'd spent over fourteen years as two halves of a whole.

No longer.

He was on his own. The thought opened up the horizons. Gave him new scope. He tried to imagine it—all the places he could go, people he could see, adventures he could pursue.

He wanted Jenny.

"Grow up, for God's sake," he told himself sharply.

The words echoed around the cabin like bullets in a hatbox. "You don't always get what you want."

A hard adage when it came to you so late in life. In his thirty-three years, Mace had pretty much become accustomed to problems being somebody else's. His own life had always been charmed.

How could he not feel that way?

He'd been so loved and had come so far. A humble ranch hand's son, he'd scrimped and saved and worked and slaved until he'd managed to become a rancher himself. A small-scale rancher, true enough—one of those men who lived daily on the edge of potential disaster from beef prices or governmental meddling or city-slicker politics or the freak Montana blizzard—but a rancher nonetheless.

And blessed, because it was the only thing he'd ever wanted to do. The land was in his blood.

And he'd been blessed, too, for having Jenny.

Sweet, funny Jenny. Jenny, who'd tickled and teased him, laughed and squeezed him since they were seventeen years old. She'd had her eye on him since they were eight, she'd told him once. He hadn't noticed her until their senior year in high school.

"What a late bloomer," Jenny had scoffed.

Well, yes, he'd admitted. But when he fell, he fell like a ton of bricks.

His father had said he wasn't good for anything but digging postholes when he was thinking about Jenny.

"Reckon I'll just keep you on the ground," his old man had said, shaking his head in disgust. "Leastways there you won't fall off."

Mace hadn't cared. He'd brushed off all comments about his love of Jenny. He ignored Taggart's speculative remarks and Jed's silently raised eyebrows.

Now there was a pair of late bloomers, he'd thought at the time.

But he didn't spend much time thinking about them. He had other things on his mind—*one* thing—Jenny.

They got married right out of high school, when she was just barely eighteen and he was not quite nineteen.

"You're lucky you didn't have to marry her sooner," Taggart muttered.

Taggart had eyes in his head. Jed had thought so, too.

Even if they didn't talk about what Mace and Jenny did when they went up to the cabin, they knew.

And Mace knew they were right. That was one of the reasons he considered himself blessed.

He'd loved Jenny too young and too fully—and yet they escaped the consequences of that love. There had been no weeping mother or shotgun-waving father forcing them to the alter. Thank heavens.

Not that Mace had anything against kids. But he'd been barely more than a kid himself. So he'd been just as glad he wasn't going to be a father right away.

When they were older, he'd told Jenny, there would be plenty of time for that.

Besides, he was too much in love with her to want to share their universe with anyone else just yet.

Even if he had wanted to, they couldn't have afforded it. Working flat out, cowboying on Taggart's dad's spread, Mace barely made enough for them to live on.

"I can work, too," Jenny said.

"Doing what?" Mace scoffed. "Slinging hash? Waiting tables?"

He knew Jenny wasn't that kind of girl.

Hell, she'd wanted to be a schoolteacher all her life. She was always the brainy one at school, the one who got straight As and barely cracked a book. She'd made being valedictorian of their class look easy.

All the teachers thought it was a damn shame she gave up going to college to marry a dead-end cowboy like Mace Nichols. Oh, they hadn't said so. But he knew it.

Mace might not have been the student she was, but he could read the dismayed looks they gave her as well as anyone. They wondered what she saw in him.

Sometimes Mace wondered himself. But he didn't question his blessings very long. He just thanked God for Jenny and vowed to be the man she needed, no matter what anyone else thought.

In fact, all those pitying looks Jenny got made him furious. They made him want to show everybody that marrying him wasn't a dead end, that he could provide for Jenny just fine.

"I don't want you working," he told her flatly when she suggested it.

So she hadn't. But being home all day, while he was out cowboying for Will Jones, had given Jenny lots of time to think about what she was missing.

A baby.

A baby?

"God, you got babies on the brain," Mace complained whenever she brought it up. "I told you, we can't afford one."

"We could if I worked," Jenny said reasonably.

"But then you wouldn't have time for it."

Jenny smiled ruefully. "Catch-22."

"I guess." Mace figured that was out of one of the books she was always reading, but he didn't know for sure. He didn't have time to read.

What little time he had, he wanted to spend doing more interesting things—like taking his wife into his arms and nuzzling her neck. Like kissing her senseless. Like giving her something else to think about besides having kids.

"There's lots of time left for babies, Jenn," he assured her between kisses. "We're only twenty. We got years and years."

"I know that," she answered with a sigh. And then she smiled against his mouth, then succumbed to the touch of his lips, kissing him back.

The kissing led to touching. The touching led to the bedroom. The babies were forgotten.

And Mace got what he wanted. Again.

The following year, though, the issue came up again when Taggart married Julie, and within a month there was a baby on the way.

Mace saw the yearning in Jenny's eyes when she found out Julie was pregnant, but he pretended not to notice. He was only dragged into discussing it when she brought it up.

"Of course, I'd like a baby, too," he said when she mentioned it. "But first I'd like to get us some land."

They'd been lying in bed in this very cabin, Will Jones's version of "married cowboy's housing," when they'd talked.

The cabin was small, it was leaky, but for the time being at least, it was theirs. Still, Mace knew, as he lay staring up at the tin roof, listening to the rain come down—and in—that he wanted better than this.

"Land?" Jenny mused. She was on her stomach beside him, naked and soft, and if he hadn't just finished making love with her, he knew he'd be making love to her again.

He nodded. "Yep. Land. You don't get anywhere workin' for somebody else."

His dad had always told him that, and his dad's example more than his dad's words had shown the truth of the matter. The Nicholses had never, as far as Mace knew, owned the land they'd worked on. They'd always come too late, left too early. And when times got tight, they were the first let go. It wasn't going to happen to him. To *them*. Not if he could help it.

"Will would sell me some up above Flathead, I reckon. Or maybe ol' man Galbraith will sell out."

"A ranch, you mean?"

He nodded. "It'd take a heck of a lot of work to get the down payment, but we could do it. Will would let me run cattle with him in the meantime. I know it."

"You're serious?"

He pushed himself up on his elbows to meet her gaze.

"You bet. But," he felt compelled to be honest, "it's a long haul, Jenny. It'd mean...puttin' things off."

"Babies, you mean?" She was looking right at him, her hazel eyes unflinching.

He ran his tongue over his lips. "I know Taggart and Julie are having a kid. I know I said we'd start thinkin' about a family. And I am thinkin', believe me. But what I'm thinkin' is that Taggart's got the ranch coming to him someday. And I'm thinkin' I got nothing. I want better for our kids than that. I want better than my dad was able to do for us. He tried, but hell, we up and moved so many times before we came here an' Mr. Jamison took him on..."

The first eight years of Mace's life had been spent moving from one ranch to another where his dad had worked his tail off and then got let go because the rancher decided to cut back.

Only Otis Jamison, because his spread covered half the valley, could afford to take on a good man and keep him through the hard times as well as good.

But even then, there'd been no getting ahead.

Mace's mother had worked just as hard as her husband, trying to make ends meet. It was hard work as much as pneumonia that killed her when Mace was fifteen.

He wanted better for Jenny.

"What do you say?" he'd said to her then, nuzzling her ear, nibbling her jawline, beginning to want inside her once more.

Her hazel eyes smiled at him. Then she wrapped her arms around him and giggled. "I say 'Just keep thinking, Mace.' You're so good at it."

"You think so, huh?" he said, rolling her in his arms until he slid on top of her, then into her. "I'm also good at this."

And then he'd loved her.

He'd moved slowly, leisurely, fitting his body to hers, savoring the miracle of how well they fit together, how attuned they were to each other's rhythms. They'd come a long way since their first fumbling attempts at lovemaking. In those days it had all been hot, fevered gropings and eager desperate efforts that had, as often as not, left them breathless and frustrated. Certainly they'd left Jenny frustrated.

He wasn't much good at holding back in those days, hadn't really figured out yet the real meaning of "ladies first."

But Jenny had never complained.

She'd wrapped her arms around him and moved with him, meeting his urgency with her own. And over time he'd got better at their loving. He'd been less frantic, more leisurely. He'd spent more time stroking and touching and kissing, enjoying that, letting the anticipation grow.

"Along with other things," Jenny had said, giggling, when he'd told her that one night. She'd reached a hand down between them and touched him where another part of his anticipation was "growing."

Mace had trembled under her touch. His breath had hissed out between his teeth, and his whole body tensed.

"You're playing with fire," he'd warned her.

Anticipation was fine as long as he could control it, but when Jenny took over—watch out!

"Fire, hmm?" She'd smiled and brushed a kiss across his lips. She moved above him then, bolder than she had been when they'd first begun making love together. Her hand moved more insistently. "What is it they say about starting fires with friction?"

"Jenn!"

But she didn't let him go. She feathered kisses along his jaw, then dropped them on his breastbone. She touched his nipples with her tongue. She made him squirm.

Jenny could always make him squirm—and make him

love every minute of it. And he always took great pleasure in returning the favor.

He *had* taken pleasure.

Had. Past tense.

Mace's fists clenched tightly at his sides. He swallowed against the ache in his throat and closed his stinging eyes to shut out the sight of the cabin to which he'd brought her fourteen years ago, the cabin in which he'd loved her the first night of their married life. Just hours before he'd vowed to love her for a lifetime.

He still did.

He loved Jenny—but he would never be able to show her how much. Not in that way again.

Chapter One

Jenny opened the door carefully, as if she were expecting at any moment for a bomb to go off in her face.

She could almost hear it ticking in the silence of the ranch house kitchen. No, it was only the clock above the stove, and she was being fanciful.

She didn't feel fanciful. She felt worried.

She looked around for signs of Mace.

His boots weren't by the back door. His hat wasn't on the hook. She hadn't seen his truck, but she'd assumed he'd parked it behind the barn. Maybe he wasn't back yet. She glanced at the clock. Only five-thirty.

Yes, it was possible that he wasn't home yet.

If he'd had to go above the creek to move cattle, he might be late. Jenny rarely knew exactly when to expect him. It was just that somehow—today—she'd expected him to be here.

So they could talk.

They needed to talk.

Yesterday, when they'd got the news, neither of them had said much. It was too new, too hard. She, at least, hadn't known what to say.

Mace, normally far more taciturn than she, had been the one to blurt out, "I don't believe it," when the doctor had given them the test results.

His normally darkly tanned face had drained of color, and he shook his head angrily. "That's bull," he'd said.

The doctor had smiled sympathetically, but his sympathy didn't change his words.

"I'm afraid it is," he'd said gently. "On this test, at least, the results are pretty conclusive. You aren't producing any live sperm."

Jenny had seen her husband floored in a fight. She'd seen him kicked by a horse. She'd seen him gored by a bull.

But she'd never seen Mace as white as death.

He sat in the chair next to her, absolutely rigid. He opened his mouth, then closed it again. His lips pressed together in a tight line—so tight a muscle in his jaw ticked.

So tight she thought he'd shatter. His whole body seemed to clench.

She wanted to reach out to him, to touch him. But she knew as sure as she knew Mace that if she did, he would crack right there.

The air in the room seemed to sizzle with electricity, to grow hot and close, as if a storm were brewing right there in the office. For what seemed an eternity no one moved.

Not Mace. Not Jenny. Not even the doctor.

He sat quietly and let his words sink in. He looked at them with quiet commiseration, but he didn't qualify anything. He didn't offer any hope. He wasn't going to deny what he'd just so baldly said.

Finally when the silence went on and on, he said, "I wish I could give you better news."

"Maybe they just died! Right then!"

At Mace's outburst, the doctor looked startled. He raised his gaze to watch as Mace seemed almost to erupt from the chair.

He paced the length of the small office, then spun and stalked back. "I mean, maybe *those* sperm were dead!" he said. "That once. That one time we—you…!" He couldn't say the words. She knew how much he'd hated the experience. "Who could blame 'em?" he said bitterly. "Prob'ly scared 'em to death."

He didn't look at Jenny as he spoke. He didn't have to; she knew what he meant.

They'd argued about his going to the doctor at all.

Jenny had been there more times than she wanted to count. She'd been trying to get pregnant for over three years. At first it had been no big deal.

Sometimes when you stopped trying to prevent pregnancies, you didn't get pregnant right away. Jenny knew that. She was philosophical.

Then she thought maybe she was nervous, maybe she was trying too hard. Maybe that was the problem.

But after two years had gone by with no results at all, she'd begun to think maybe it was more than that.

She started reading everything she could about conception. She talked to her doctor, she took her temperature. She took thyroid pills. Eventually she'd had tests. And more tests.

Everything seemed fine. She asked the doctor about fertility drugs. He said he didn't think she needed them.

"But I'm not conceiving," she argued.

"Maybe it's your husband. Maybe we should check."

It wasn't something Jenny had wanted to bring up to Mace. There had been very little in their marriage that she'd been reluctant to talk about. But somehow, asking Mace to do this wasn't easy.

Maybe because she knew how he'd react.

"Fertility tests?" He was aghast. "Like I'm some damned bull?"

"It's just to check, Mace," she said. "To rule out the possibility."

Mace grunted. It didn't make sense, he'd told her. He had a healthy sex drive, for heaven's sake! There was certainly no question about him being able to get it up, to put it crudely.

He put it that crudely.

But when Jenny sighed and turned away, he relented.

"Fine," he said gruffly. "You want me to do it in some damned cup, I'll do it in some damned cup. But I don't know what it will prove."

Now he knew.

Now they both knew.

Jenny felt cold. She felt sick.

"Of course it's just one test," the doctor said. "I never like to base everything on one test. But if it does prove out, it's probably the result of some viral infection you had as a young man. Mumps or—"

"I never had mumps!"

"—or some other infection that really didn't even bother you significantly," the doctor continued firmly. "One that you might barely have noticed. You'd have run a fever and—"

"I've always been perfectly healthy!"

"I know." The doctor smiled at Mace, but he still didn't back off. He didn't give them any hope at all.

"So give me another test." Mace's fists were clenched against his knees. He hunched forward in the chair, his chin thrust out, defying the doctor, denying the diagnosis.

"All right." The doctor pulled out a form and picked up his pen. "We can set up a time, then, and—"

"Now."

The doctor blinked. He looked at Mace. He looked at Jenny.

"Now," Mace said again. He stood up and held out his hand. "Give me your damned little cup again and let me do it now."

Jenny knew how much Mace had hated that "damned little cup." He'd told her after he came home last week that using it had been the most humiliating experience of his life.

He stood in their bedroom with his back to her, scowling out into the darkness, saying, "They *know* what you're doing! They hand you this little cup and send you into this room with a pile of skin mags and *they know!*"

When he turned around, she'd seen the color high against his cheekbones.

Jenny had felt a tremendous wave of love for him at that moment. To a man who valued his privacy as much as she knew Mace did, that hadn't been easy to take.

She went to him then, putting her arms around him. She tugged his shirt out of his waistband and had run her fingers up his back, then down his chest. She'd eased open the button on his jeans.

"No one knows now," she whispered against his lips.

He'd groaned. "Ah, Jenny," as he'd borne her back on the bed.

But in the doctor's office, he didn't even look at her. He waited, hand outstretched. Finally the doctor got up and went to the door. "Come with me."

Mace followed him out.

Jenny half rose to go after him, but the door shut firmly.

She sank back into the chair. What was she going to do? Offer to help?

"Oh, Mace," she murmured.

Her fingers knotted. Her eyes shut. It didn't matter. In

her mind she could still see the stricken look on his face. *Oh, Mace.*

The door opened, and the doctor came back in and cleared his throat. "If you'd, um, like to have a seat in the waiting room, Mrs. Nichols..."

Numbly Jenny nodded. Clenching her purse against her middle, she went out into the corridor and walked toward the waiting room. Past three closed doors, behind one of which Mace was...

All the nurses seemed to glance in her direction as she went by. But not one of them would hold her gaze.

Jenny's own gaze dropped to focus on the floor. She went into the waiting room and sat down. She picked up a magazine and tried to act calm, indifferent, as if her world wasn't falling apart, as if her husband wasn't doing what he was doing, as if this was just another doctor's appointment.

She waited a long, long time.

When the doctor had called her back in, Mace was already sitting in the consulting room, staring out the window. His jaw was locked.

The doctor motioned her into the chair next to Mace's. She moved to sit down. Mace shifted his knee away so they didn't touch. Jenny looked at him, then back at the doctor.

He folded his hands on top of his desk. "I'm sorry. I'm afraid the results are the same." He gave her the same sad, sympathetic smile.

Jenny mustered a smile, too. A small one. A wooden one. But the best she could do.

He knew how much she wanted a family. He knew how willing she'd been to try whatever she could. She didn't have to ask to know there was nothing left to try. "Thank you."

Mace shoved himself up out of the chair. His jaw was still clenched.

He did get the one word *thanks* beyond his lips.

Jenny could only guess what it cost him.

"There are other ways to have a family," the doctor said, rising, too, as Mace opened the door and headed out into the corridor. "Adoption. Artificial insemination."

Not now, Jenny wanted to tell him. *We can't talk about that. We can't even think about that now.*

She gave him a tight, wan smile and said, "Thank you. We'll give it some thought."

She could see Mace's back disappearing into the waiting room. "We'll be in touch."

"I'm so sorry, my dear," the doctor said.

Not half as sorry as I am, Jenny thought.

And not a hundredth as sorry as Mace was. She knew her husband well enough to see how badly the doctor's words had rocked him. And she knew he'd looked instantly—even while pretending not to—to see how badly they'd rocked her.

There was no use pretending they hadn't. Even though she'd thought she was prepared for anything, she knew she hadn't been able to hide her devastation at the doctor's blunt diagnosis.

They would never have children.

The family she had hoped and prayed for as long as she could remember—the children she and Mace had scrimped and saved and planned for since they were barely more than children themselves—would never be.

Not the way they'd always assumed it would be, at least.

Yes, they could have a family. Jenny understood that. A part of her had been considering other options ever since she'd been disappointed for the third month in a row. But now wasn't the time to think about options.

Now she had to think about Mace.

He wasn't waiting for her in the corridor. By the time she got outside he was already sitting in the truck, the engine running.

She clambered in wordlessly, and she barely got the door closed before he gunned it, burning rubber on the asphalt parking lot.

They'd planned to go out to eat after the appointment. Neither of them got to Bozeman regularly, and they always had to make a special effort to get there together.

"We'll make it a date," Jenny had said, grinning at him as she went out the door to work that morning. "We can go to Girardi's for supper. Pick me up after school."

Now the thought of eating made her ill. There seemed to be a bowling ball where her stomach used to be. Thinking about her favorite fettucine with pesto on top of it was actually painful. She didn't say so, though. She would leave it up to Mace to decide what they did.

Wordlessly he drove to the small Italian restaurant near the university that had been their favorite place. He pulled into a parking place and cut the engine, then dropped his hands into his lap. Jenny saw his fingers clench.

One of her hands stole out to touch his, to curl around it. He pulled away.

"Mace. It's all right, Mace," she said softly.

His head jerked around, and his eyes flashed fire at her. "The hell it is!"

The paleness was gone from his face now. She could see the dark flush across his cheekbones even beneath the darkness of his tan. "Didn't you hear what he said, for God's sake?"

"Yes, Mace, I heard." She tried to keep her voice even. Mace didn't. He was practically shouting at her.

"Then don't try to tell me it's all right!" The look he gave her was so anguished, she turned her head. His fingers clenched around the steering wheel, and he sat unmoving, staring straight ahead.

Jenny looked at him out of the corner of her eye, wishing she could say something that would help, not having the faintest idea what to say.

There was no help.

Oh, Mace.

He sucked in a sharp breath, then shoved open the door of the pickup. "Come on." He was out of the truck and headed into the restaurant before Jenny could get her door open.

She didn't order the fettucine. She knew she'd never be able to get it down, so she ordered a salad instead. She didn't even know if Mace noticed.

He ordered what he always did—lasagna—then sat staring out the window. He drummed his fingers on the tabletop. He cracked his knuckles. He didn't say a word.

He still hadn't by the time the waitress brought their meals. Then he bent over his and ate with a vengeance.

Jenny could barely touch hers. She buried a tomato beneath the lettuce. She stabbed a mushroom cap. She nibbled a crouton. She had hardly made a dent in her meal when Mace shoved back his plate.

"Are you going to eat that or just play with it?"

Her head jerked up at his harsh words—the first he'd spoken to her since he got out of the truck.

She dropped her fork. "Play with it, I guess." There was no use lying about it. She gave him a faint smile, which he didn't return.

"Let's go, then," he said, and was already shoving back his chair.

Relieved, Jenny tossed her napkin on the table and followed him. She caught up with him outside, grabbing his arm and slowing him down. He tensed beneath her touch and glanced her way for just a moment, but he didn't lace his fingers through hers. He just kept on walking.

When they got to the truck, though, he opened the door for her and waited until she got in before he went around to the driver's side.

He didn't burn rubber leaving the parking lot this time, either. In fact, he drove carefully, steadily, through Bozeman and up onto the interstate, heading home. He still didn't speak.

At least he didn't speak to her.

Jenny was fairly certain there was plenty of conversation going on inside his head. She watched him out of the corner of her eye, wishing she dared to reach out and touch him again. But there was a shield between her and Mace right now, and she knew that for the moment, at least, she wasn't going to be able to reach him.

He needed time.

Maybe they both did.

A lot of years' worth of hopes had been dashed in the space of a few words that afternoon. It would take more than a few minutes—or even a few hours—for them to come to terms with this new reality.

It would be hard for her. It would be harder by far for Mace.

He was a proud man. A private man.

And for her he'd given up his privacy and had his pride ground into the dust. She loved him for it. Loved him more deeply and more fully than she'd ever loved before.

Her hand crept out and touched his knee. He flinched. She didn't move it. She edged closer to him. "I love you, Mace," she whispered.

His jaw bunched. His fingers strangled the steering wheel. "Yeah," he said. His voice was gruff, his eyes never left the road. His fingers never left the steering wheel. He didn't touch her in return.

She hoped that once they got inside they would talk.

There in their own snug house, the one Mace and she and their friends, Jed and Taggart, had built with their own hands, she thought they would begin to come to terms with the hand they had been dealt.

But when she got to the porch, Mace wasn't with her. He was heading toward the barn.

"Mace?"

He turned his head, but he didn't stop walking. "Got some chores to do." And he disappeared around the corner of the barn.

Jenny had plenty of chores of her own. Working full-time at Elmer's small elementary school kept her busy all day. There were always things to be done at home at night. Washing to be put in the machine. Clean clothes to be folded and put away. Vacuuming. Dusting. Holes to be mended in Mace's jeans. He wore them until they were white in the seat from riding, and across the thighs from where he balanced the hay bales he lugged.

"We could buy you a pair of new ones," she suggested often enough.

But he always shook his head. "Too stiff," he said. "Too much trouble to break 'em in. You can patch 'em once more, can't you?"

So after she put the laundry in, she turned on the lamp by the rocking chair and pulled a pair of Mace's threadbare jeans into her lap and began once more to patch them.

And to wait.

It was mundane, mindless work. Not enough to distract her. Not enough to keep her sitting there. She kept putting them aside and getting up to pace around, to go into the kitchen and look out toward the barn, to try to catch a glimpse of Mace.

It was late when he finally came in. He was dusty and

dirty and barely looked her way as he headed for the bathroom. "Gotta take a shower."

Jenny put the last of the mending aside and followed him. He was standing by the closet in their bedroom, stripping off his shirt. "Want me to scrub your back?" she asked softly.

Another night she knew he would have given her that sexy, lopsided grin of his and drawled, "Well, now, why didn't I think of that?"

He didn't even glance at her. Just said, "I can do it myself," and, grabbing clean underwear out of the drawer, he padded barefoot into the bathroom and shut the door.

She supposed she shouldn't have said anything so light-hearted. She hadn't meant to tease. Only to show him that some things hadn't changed. Never would change: she would always love Mace Nichols no matter what.

She got into her nightgown while Mace was in the shower, then brushed out her long dark hair and shut off the light.

Perhaps it would be easier to talk in the dark, she thought as she slipped into bed to wait for him there.

He took a long shower. She knew he was avoiding her. But avoiding her wasn't going to help. They had to talk about it sometime. They had to hold each other and comfort each other and love each other. And then decide where to go from here.

At last the door opened and he came into the darkened room.

She heard the clink of his belt as he set it on the dresser, heard the sound of his jeans settling in the dirty clothes basket behind the door. She heard his footsteps creaking around the room. They stopped. He wasn't by the bed.

"Mace?"

She heard a weary exhalation of breath. "What?"

She pushed herself up on one elbow, then didn't know what to say. "I've...just been...waiting for you."

"Why?" There was a wealth of self-deprecation in just that one word.

She sat up. "Because I love you, Mace. Because I know you're hurting." She hesitated. "Because I'm hurting, too."

The floorboards creaked beneath his feet as he came closer to the bed. "I know that." His voice was so low she barely heard the words. But they made her sit up and reach out to him.

"Come to bed, Mace."

There was only silence then. No floorboards. No footsteps. Only silence. So much silence that she thought she could hear him take a breath. It seemed an eternity until he let it out again.

Then, slowly, he came to bed.

The mattress sagged beneath his weight. He stretched out carefully, the way he did sometimes when he'd pulled a muscle or taken a spill, as if all his muscles hurt. He lay flat on his back and folded his arms under his head.

Carefully, as if his pain was physical, Jenny rolled onto her side and put her arm across his chest, snuggled into his side.

Any other night one of his arms would have come around her and pulled her even closer. One of his legs would have tangled with hers.

He didn't move.

She edged up and pressed her lips to his jaw. But he didn't turn his face to touch his mouth to hers.

He didn't do anything at all.

She sighed and nestled closer, hugged him tighter. "I love you, Mace," she whispered.

He didn't say a word.

He didn't say anything at breakfast the next morning,

either. He had already shaved by the time she got up. He came out of the bathroom as she was rubbing the sleep out of her eyes.

"Morning." She smiled at him.

It was still too dark to see if she got one in return.

He had the oatmeal cooking by the time she finished in the bathroom. There were two bowls on the table, and he was putting slices of bread in the toaster. The orange juice was already poured. Breakfast as usual.

Jenny breathed a sigh of relief.

They would cope.

They would get through this day—Mace on the range and she at school. They would find their bearings in the commonplace activities of every day—and then tonight they would be able to talk about this blow fate had dealt them.

It would be easier by then. They would each have had a chance to get used to the idea. They would each have space. Mace needed more than she did, but she was willing to wait for him. And then they would figure out together what to do about the family they had wanted so long.

At least that was the plan.

But Mace wasn't home.

He wasn't there when she got back from school that afternoon. Of course it was barely more than midday the way the sun stayed so high for so long in June. And Mace had cattle to move, others to check. Some field work to do.

Fine, Jenny thought. She dropped her bag from school and set to work making a pot of green chile stew.

It was Mace's favorite, and she figured he might think she was trying too hard, but she didn't care. She loved him. She wanted him to know that.

The stew took two hours to cook and simmer. After two more hours Mace still hadn't come.

Jenny went out onto the porch and looked around. The

sun had dropped well below the northern Bridgers now. Twilight was upon them. She went over to turn on the light by the barn.

Mace was such a good horseman that, over the years, she had learned not to fret about accidents when he didn't show up.

Of course things could happen, but Mace was careful, not a man to take unnecessary chances. And when he was riding Chug, his sorrel gelding, she knew he was on the best possible mount.

So she stirred the stew once more, turned the flame under it even lower and told herself he'd be along.

By ten, though, she was sure something was wrong. She wished he'd said if he was going to be working their own land today or helping Jed or Taggart on theirs.

But Mace had said nothing this morning.

Jenny sighed and glanced at the phone.

She paced the small kitchen and living room, then went out once more to the barn, to make sure it was Chug that Mace had ridden out this morning.

Chug was, in fact, gone.

So were the trailer and the truck.

Jenny sighed and ran a hand through her hair, relieved. He had to be with Taggart or Jed. If he'd been on their own land, he wouldn't have needed to trailer Chug anywhere before riding out.

She grained their other two horses and went back to the house, gave the stew one more stir, then picked up the phone and called the Joneses to ask Felicity where they were and when they'd be done.

Taggart answered the phone.

Startled, Jenny demanded, "What are you doing there?"

"Jenn? What do you mean, what'm I doing here? I live here." She could hear the smile in Taggart's voice.

"I thought..." She squelched the worry in her voice as best she could. "Where's Mace? Is he with you?"

"Nope. Haven't seen him."

"All day?"

"Nope. I got a school starting tomorrow morning. I've been here all day getting ready." Taggart taught bull riding to rodeo rough-stock hopefuls. "Sorry. Maybe he's at Jed's."

"Maybe," Jenny echoed. "Thanks." Slowly she put the receiver down.

She opened the door and stared out into the darkness, willing a pair of headlights to appear over the rise. "Damn it, Mace. Where are you?"

The phone rang.

She practically ran to answer it. "Hello?"

"I just went into the den," Taggart told her, "and said you were looking for Mace. Becky said she and Tuck saw his truck up by the cabin this afternoon."

"Our cabin?" The one she and Mace had lived in when they were first married? The one Mace and Jed and Taggart had hung out in when they were kids? The one Jed and Tuck had lived in until last year?

"Yep. Reckon maybe he was making a circle up above the creek," Taggart said. "If he's not back yet he's probably planning to stay the night."

"Probably," Jenny agreed.

"He'll have food and firewood up there. I'm sure he's fine."

"I'm sure, too," Jenny said, though it wasn't food or firewood she was worried about. "Thanks, Taggart," she said.

Of course he was fine. He just wasn't ready to talk.

If he'd decided to make a circle up above the creek today of all days, he still had some thinking on his own to do.

She dished up a bowl of the stew and picked at it, but

she wasn't hungry. She was lonely. Worried. She wanted to put her arms around him. She wanted him to put his arms around her.

She did up the dishes, then turned on the television. But there wasn't anything worth watching. She tried reading, but that was even harder. The blanket she'd been knitting sat waiting in the bag beside the sofa. She couldn't face it tonight.

She left on the porch light just in case, then went in to go to bed.

It looked like Mace had cleaned the bedroom. There was less stuff on the dresser. No comb. No spare change. No loose socks on the floor.

She kicked off her shoes and unbuttoned her shirt, then opened the closet.

Mace's shirts weren't there.

Jenny stared.

Then she turned and yanked open his dresser drawers. His shorts and undershirts were gone, too. A vise gripped her throat, disbelief choking her.

"Mace?" She could barely get his name past her lips. Her palms were suddenly wet, her breathing quick.

She hurried into the bathroom and jerked open the medicine chest. Hers was the only toothbrush there.

"No." *No!*

She ran back to the bedroom, then to the living room, scanning desperately, seeking futilely for some word, some note. He couldn't simply have picked up and walked out of her life!

She flipped through the bills on the desk, riffled through the magazines on the coffee table, fanned yesterday's unread mail.

Nothing.

She went back into the bedroom, checked the dresser, the top of the chest. The bed.

Still nothing.

Then, with a growing sense of certainty, she turned and went into the bedroom across the hall. "The spare room," they called it, when other people came to stay. Mace's brother, Shane, or her sister, Teresa, were known to use it on occasion. Taggart's daughter, Becky, spent a week or a weekend with them now and then.

But in private, to Mace and Jenny, it had always been "the baby's room," where they would put "Butch and Sundance," as Mace was wont to call their unborn children.

She turned on the light.

The note was on the bed.

Jenny, she read, but her hands shook so badly she had to press the paper flat to continue. *I know how much you want a family, and you deserve to have one. You won't as long as you're married to me. We'll get a divorce soon as we can. I'll take care of it, unless you want to. If you do, that's okay. I won't stand in your way. Mace.*

Chapter Two

The sound of a shot jerked Mace out of a fitful sleep.

A light blinded him.

It took a moment, but when at last his muddled brain began working, he realized he hadn't heard a shot at all.

The door had banged open. And Jenny loomed over his bed.

"How dare you?"

He blinked up at her, trying to shield his eyes with one hand and grope for the edge of his sleeping bag with the other. It wasn't that she hadn't seen every bit of him a million times. It was that being naked in the face of fury, even Jenny's—*especially* Jenny's at the moment—seemed like a pretty dangerous idea. "What?"

"Don't 'what' me, Mace Nichols! How dare you walk out on me? How dare you write this sniveling little note and run away?"

He didn't have to read the paper she shook in his face.

He remembered it. He'd worked on it hard enough. "I wasn't 'running away.'" Though God knew he'd like to have. Trouble was, it wouldn't matter how long and far he ran—what he was running from would always be there.

The injustice of her accusation infuriated him. He shoved himself back against the rough log wall of the cabin, glanced at his watch, then scowled up at her. "For God's sake, Jenn, it's almost one in the morning!"

"I know what time it is! What I don't know is what you're doing up here!" The color was high in her cheeks. Her hair was loose, curling around her head, the way it did when he made love to her.

He shoved that thought away.

"You know what I'm doing," he said tightly. He jerked his chin toward the note in her hand. "I told you."

She crumpled the paper and threw it at him. It hit his cheek and fell onto the bed. "But I didn't believe it! You're moving out. We're getting a divorce. Just like that. Honest to God, Mace, how could you do such a stupid thing?"

He glared at her, stung. "Stupid? Like hell it is. It's the only thing that makes sense!"

"Walking out on me after fourteen years of marriage makes sense?"

He wasn't going to argue with her. He'd never won an argument with Jenny in his life. He wasn't good at them—wasn't good with words.

And in this case it wouldn't matter, anyway. Whichever way it went, he lost.

Mace clenched his jaw and looked away, digging down deep inside for every ounce of strength he had. Then, when he had all he knew he was going to get and what he desperately hoped was enough, he turned back to her.

"Yes," he said through his teeth.

There was total silence.

He couldn't even hear her breathe. Outside a coyote howled. Nearer at hand, Chug whickered in the barn.

But inside the cabin the silence went on. And on.

Mace looked away again. He didn't want to see her distress, didn't want to face her pity. He locked his jaw and stared at the wall and wished to God she'd go away. Didn't she know how hard it had been to walk out?

Didn't she know how hard it still was, pushing her away like this?

Go, damn it. Just go.

But Jenny stayed.

"So," she said finally with a deceptively conversational lightness, "are we finished, then, Mace? Is that it? Is it over? All we had? All we worked for? Fourteen years down the drain. Poof." Out of the corner of his eye he saw her blow a puff of air. "Gone. Worth nothing."

Goaded, he couldn't remain silent. "You know it wasn't worth nothing!"

"You're acting like it was worth nothing!"

"You want a family," he said stubbornly.

"I want you."

"You want a child," he corrected her. "Children. You've wanted them for years! *Years,* damn it! That's all you could talk about. All you hoped and planned for. You know it. And—" he enunciated each word clearly "—I can't give them to you."

"There's more than one way to have a family!"

His fists clenched on his sleeping bag. He stared down at his white knuckles and shook his head. "It's not the same."

"No, it's not. I agree." Her voice was quieter now, more reasonable. "But—"

"No." He cut her off firmly, flatly. There was no being reasonable here. His whole world, his whole understanding of himself as a man, had been cut from under him. He wasn't going to talk about "other methods."

There might be other ways to give her a family. But nothing else was going to make him a man.

The test results were conclusive. Final. He was sterile.

He would learn to live with it.

But he would live with it by himself.

He wasn't going to go through life living on her pity. And he wasn't going to make her suffer for something that was none of her fault. It wasn't his fault, either, but it was his life.

He *had* to deal with it.

"Go home, Jenny," he said heavily, still looking down. "Just go home."

She moved closer. Her hands, her jeans were in his field of vision. "Mace..."

"No." He closed his eyes.

"I know it hurts. It hurts me, too. But if we talk—"

"Talk doesn't make sperm!"

"No, but—"

"Nothing makes sperm, Jenny. I'm never going to give you a child. So just let it go. Let *me* go!"

"No."

"That's what you should have said that day fourteen years ago."

"Don't be an ass."

"I'm not. Asses aren't sterile."

"Mace!"

He knew the argument was going to go on—the argument he didn't want, couldn't win. And so he did the only thing he could.

"In some ways," he lied, "it's a relief."

Jenny blinked. Her mouth shut like a trap. She looked at him closely. "What's that supposed to mean?"

He braced himself against the wall and drew a breath. "I mean you're the one wanted the kids, not me."

Jenny's eyes widened. Her mouth opened, but no words came out. Only air—as if it had been punched from her. The flame in her eyes faded, then flickered to life again.

"That's not true. You wanted kids, too!" she argued. "You know you did! That wasn't you all those nights, talking about taking Butch and Sundance—" he couldn't quite suppress the wince at the names with which they'd always jokingly referred to their kids "—about camping up by the lake with them? That wasn't you who bought that little Stetson last fall down in Bozeman? That wasn't you I found putting new wood in my old family cradle? That wasn't you—"

"Stop it!" The words were wrung out of him. His fists strangled the sleeping bag. "Just stop," he said, his voice harsh and as ragged as if he'd run miles and miles. Even his breath came hard.

He could hear it, could hear his heart hammering.

There was silence again. Long. Deafening. Silence that seemed to vibrate throughout the room.

"You wanted kids, Mace," Jenny said softly.

Yes, all right, he had. But however much he might want them, he couldn't have them.

And that was the truth—the whole truth.

"It's past. Go away, Jenny," he said, his voice low. When she didn't move, he forced himself to look at her, to meet her gaze unflinchingly. "Go on. Get out. Now."

He didn't think she was going to. He wondered for a minute if he might have to get out of the bed, after all, if he might have to march naked across the room, grab her and put her out the door, shutting it behind her.

He wondered if he could.

And then he heard her take a breath. "All right," she said, and her voice was firm now, strong. "I'll go. And you

just sit up here and sulk. Feel sorry for yourself. Have yourself a wonderful pity party, Mace, if that's what you want.
But don't bother to invite me. I wouldn't come if you did!"

Then she turned and stalked out, her footsteps loud on
the bare floor.

The front door opened and shut. This time there was no
bang.

But that didn't make the feeling any less fatal.

She should be shot.

Jenny didn't know what ever had possessed her!

How could she have been so insensitive? How could she,
of all people, have thrown Mace's feelings in his face?

She would have to apologize.

Tomorrow.

There was no way she was going back up there tonight.

It had taken her almost an hour to get there the first time.
Used to finding the cabin easily in the daylight on horseback, she hadn't driven the narrow mountain track in years.

She'd missed it in the dark and had bumped around
barely visible ruts, trying to gauge where she was for ages
before she'd realized she'd taken the wrong turn. The delay
hadn't improved her disposition any. By the time she got
there, she'd been fuming.

And Mace had borne the brunt of it.

She'd seen the suffering in his face the moment she'd
flicked on the light. Even though he'd tried not to show it,
she'd seen the telltale bunching of muscle when his jaw
had tightened and the way his knuckles had gone white as
they'd clenched the sleeping bag. But she'd been too angry
to stop and think at that point.

And now?

"Oh, Mace."

She turned onto her side and reached out her hand to

touch the pillow where for fourteen years her husband had laid his head.

Jenny drew his pillow into her arms and pressed her face into it.

She found the scent of him there in the cotton against her cheek—that trace of soap and shampoo and shaving cream, the tantalizing scent of leather and lime and, always, the faint hint of horses, all of it combining indefinably into a scent that was purely Mace—but not all of Mace.

She had thought last night was the worst night of her life.

Tonight she knew better.

She pressed her face into the pillow and cried.

He was there again today.

Becky was surprised. She hadn't expected it. She knew as well as anybody that cowboys never stayed in one place for long, especially when they ought to be moving the herd to summer pasture. But Mace's truck had been parked by the old cabin yesterday when she and Tuck had ridden out to get away from "the baby brigade"—which was what they called the sudden explosion of infants in their respective households—and it was there again today.

Becky thought that was sort of odd.

But lately she thought the whole world was a pretty odd place.

She used to think that once she got her dad married off, things would settle down and she would have a normal life. She didn't expect to have all her problems solved in half an hour like they did on television. But she did expect that they wouldn't keep getting worse.

Now she wasn't so sure.

Nothing in her life seemed to quite fit anymore.

Least of all her.

Her whole life she'd been "Taggart Jones's kid." They'd been a twosome—just she and her dad.

Now there was Felicity, of course. Becky wasn't sorry at all that her dad had married Felicity.

But she hadn't figured on it changing who she was. It had. She wasn't the only one who was "Taggart Jones's kid" these days. Now there were two more. Twins.

It wasn't that she didn't like her new brother and sister. She did. Most of the time she thought they were pretty amazing creatures. Like puppies or newborn lambs. Kind of cute and sort of cuddly—when they weren't crying or spitting up on her.

But they had changed everything. Nobody had any time anymore. Felicity was constantly changing them or feeding them or walking them around or rocking them in the rocking chair or reading in one of those stupid books that tell you you're doing everything wrong.

She really seemed to be afraid she was doing everything wrong. And even Taggart, who had managed *one* baby all right when it was Becky, seemed to be over his head in infants every time she looked at him.

There didn't seem to be any hands—or time—left over for her.

Every time she thought that, though, Becky felt crummy. Like she was a bad person for thinking it.

Probably she was a bad person for thinking it. She didn't know anyone else who resented two helpless little kids.

Susannah, her best friend, seemed to cope with her two little brothers all right. She played chopsticks on the piano with them and didn't care if they just banged their fists on the keys. She played ball with Clay, the older one, and didn't try to strike him out. She built towers with Scott, and usually didn't get mad when he knocked them over before she was done. She even baby-sat them sometimes when her mom and dad went out.

The very thought terrified Becky.

Puppies she could handle. Lambs were okay. Colts were actually fun. Even calves weren't too bad. They were interesting—and sturdy.

Becky liked sturdy. Nobody ever yelled at you to be sure you held its head up when you gave a leppie calf a bottle.

Tuck, who had been her friend forever, said not to worry, that the twins were close to three months old and pretty soon would be able to hold their heads up on their own.

It couldn't happen soon enough for Becky.

It seemed to her that even Tuck coped better than she did—and Neile wasn't even his real half sister. He even lugged her around in a backpack sometimes.

"Gotta show 'er the ropes," he'd say.

And he never got mad at all—except when Neile broke the points of his pencils and put his drawing charcoal in her mouth.

Becky looked forward to the day when Willy and Abby were old enough to toddle around and put things in their mouths.

It would be nice when they stopped waking up ten times a night and let people get some sleep for a change.

She'd be glad when her dad heard her the first time she asked him a question, and when Felicity didn't fall asleep at the dinner table, and when she remembered to buy ponytail fasteners like she promised when she went to the store.

But Becky didn't say any of that. Not to Susannah. Not even to Tuck.

She just thought it—and felt guilty for thinking it. And went on long rides after school to try to sort things out.

But she wasn't doing a very good job of it.

It seemed to her as if she was the only thing out of sync in the whole world—until she rode up over the ridge and looked down on the cabin and saw Mace's truck there again today.

It was parked exactly where it had been the day before, as if he hadn't gone home at all.

Sometimes, she knew, cowboys and ranchers didn't get home at night if they couldn't find all the cattle or they had trouble moving them. Maybe that was what happened to Mace. Maybe he was so late getting down last night that, if he still had more to do, he wouldn't want to bother driving all the way home only to come back again today.

She was surprised, though, that he hadn't bothered to take a cellular phone along to call Jenny. But, then, maybe he didn't have one. Mace didn't have a lot of money. A cellular phone might be a luxury. Becky's dad, Taggart, had thought it was for years.

But now that Becky rode out alone and Felicity had to drive to Bozeman in the winter, he made sure they had one along.

Mace obviously hadn't.

It was a good thing Becky had seen his truck yesterday so she could tell her dad where he was. Then Jenny wouldn't worry.

Unless she should have been worrying! Becky thought, pulling up her horse so sharply, that he tossed his head and almost bucked her off.

"Sorry. Sorry," she soothed him, patting his neck.

But really, what if Mace's truck was still there because he'd had an accident? What if he was up on the range hurt and alone?

Becky put her spurs lightly to Blaze's sides.

If Mace was hurt, she would have to find him!

"Don't overlook the obvious," her father always told her. So she banged on the door and even opened it and called his name, but he wasn't there. There were some cattle behind the cabin in a field Mace was obviously using as a holding pen.

She rode Blaze down there, studying the ground as she went. You had to look at the way the grass was flattened or twigs were bent to see which way they'd come from or gone, her father told her. She dismounted and knelt to scowl at the grass and the hoofprints. There were a dozen steers in the pasture already, and they hadn't exactly tiptoed in.

"Playin' scout?"

Becky's head jerked up.

Mace was sitting on horseback grinning down at her.

Some scout, she thought, disgruntled, cheeks flaming. She hadn't even heard him coming!

Straightening up, she stuck her hands in her pockets and gave a little shrug, feeling self-conscious. "I was going to come rescue you. I thought you were hurt."

"Hurt?" Mace's brows drew down beneath the cowboy hat that shaded his eyes. "Why would you think that?"

"I saw your truck here yesterday. An' it was still here today."

"You were here yesterday?" He sounded as if he was accusing her of something.

Becky frowned. It was one thing if her dad and Felicity got mad and yelled at her sometimes. They were her parents, and even if she didn't think they were being reasonable, she figured it was their right to yell if they wanted.

But Mace wasn't supposed to. He was her friend.

More than her friend, actually.

She dropped her gaze and dug the toe of her boot into the dirt. He was the cowboy she'd fallen in love with when she was five years old.

Not that he knew.

It'd embarrass him to death if he knew a thing like that. It would embarrass *her!* And anyhow, it wasn't like she'd ever had a chance with him. Mace had been married to Jenny since way before Becky was born.

They had a good marriage, too.

She remembered her dad saying that, years ago, when Becky had suggested kind of hopefully that maybe Jenny could divorce Mace and marry Taggart and become her stepmother.

Becky thought Jenny would make a good stepmother. She didn't yell. Much. She tolerated mud better than most women. And she made really good apple pie.

Besides, Becky had thought, if Jenny divorced Mace and married Taggart, when she finally grew up, Mace could marry her.

She didn't say that part out loud, of course. But when she'd suggested that Jenny would make a good stepmother, Taggart had said, "Won't happen, Pard. Jenny and Mace have been a pair long as I can remember. I believe it'd take an atom bomb to split 'em apart."

It was just as well. Becky didn't need another grouch in her life. Not even a drop-dead handsome one like Mace Nichols.

She turned her back on him, put her boot in the stirrup and swung back onto Blaze's back. Giving him a nudge with her heels, she started to ride away.

"Hey!"

Becky hesitated at the sound of Mace's voice, then kept going

He caught up with her. "I didn't mean to growl at you." There was a sort of hesitancy in his voice that she'd never heard before. "I was surprised. That's all. I didn't see you up here yesterday. You didn't stop."

Mollified, Becky said, "Me 'n' Tuck came up riding. I saw your truck. I told Dad last night when Jenny called looking for you."

"Jenny called you?" There was no hesitancy now, only

sharpness, and Becky wondered if he was mad because she'd told.

"She was worried. You know moms worry," she explained.

It was something she'd just begun to understand since her dad had married Felicity.

It wasn't that her dad didn't care, just that Felicity was more obvious about it. It was kind of nice most of the time, but Becky was looking forward to the twins getting old enough so that Felicity could worry about them, too.

"Jenny's not a mom."

Becky blinked at his harsh tone, then shrugged. "Guess not. But you know what I mean."

"Yeah." Chug sidestepped and Mace reined the horse in sharply.

Becky cocked her head. "Are you mad at Jenny?" she ventured after a moment.

Keeping his eye on his horse, Mace shook his head. "Of course not."

"You sound mad."

"I'm not mad, damn it!" His voice quieted. "I'm not mad." He pulled a bandanna out of his pocket and rubbed it over his face. "It's hot and I'm tired, that's all. You want some lemonade?"

Becky brightened. "You got some?"

He turned his horse and headed toward the cabin. "Come on." Becky followed on Blaze, dismounting and tying him next to Chug and loosening his cinch. Then she hurried to catch up.

She thought he'd have an ice chest. Her dad always brought one when he was going to be up here for a day or two. But Mace went in and opened the small refrigerator, then took out a bottle of lemonade.

Becky got the glasses out of the cupboard and set them

on the table. Then she stepped back and looked around while he poured.

Nobody had used the little cabin much since Tuck and Jed had lived there last year. All the things that had made it homey then were gone now. But there were dirty dishes soaking in a pan of soapy water in the sink, and through the open door to the small bedroom, she saw an open duffel bag on the soft pine floor.

Mace cleared his throat.

Becky turned quickly to see him holding out a glass to her. She grabbed it and gulped, coughing her head off when it went down the wrong way.

Mace slapped her on the back. "You okay?"

"F-fine," she croaked as soon as she could. "Must've just gone down the wrong pipe." Her gaze drifted back toward the open duffel.

Mace stepped into her line of vision. "How come you're up here two days in a row?"

Becky shifted uncomfortably from one foot to the other. "Oh, you know, just, um, sorta riding around."

"Riding around?" She heard the doubt in his voice.

She just looked at her boots and didn't answer.

"Riding around," Mace mused after a moment. Then he said shrewdly, "Guess things must be pretty hectic at your house."

Becky dug her toe in the rug underfoot. "Yeah."

"Willy and Abby givin' you trouble, are they?"

"Course not," she lied. She should have known better than to try any such thing in front of Mace Nichols. He knew her far too well.

"How come you're livin' here?" she asked, hoping to distract him.

"Who says I'm living here?" The sharpness of his tone rocked Becky back on the heels of her boots.

"Nobody. I just...saw the duffel bag." She craned her neck to look toward the bedroom door as she spoke.

Mace's gaze followed hers. A muscle in his jaw ticked. "I had some fence work to do out this way after I moved the cattle. And I told Taggart I'd fix the roof on this place. Figured it'd take me a few days, so I brought some gear."

"Oh."

Mace tipped his glass and drained the lemonade, then set the glass down on the counter with a thump. "It's gettin' late. You better get a move on or you're gonna miss supper."

Becky blinked. It was bad enough that her dad and stepmother didn't seem to have any time for her—was Mace trying to get rid of her now, too? Hurt, she looked away.

"I've had enough," she said, and put the glass down next to Mace's, then wiped her mouth on her sleeve.

Mace sighed, took off his hat and raked a hand through his short black hair, lifting it in spikes on his head. Then he jammed the hat back down. "I'm sorry, Beck. I'm not trying to throw you out. Go ahead and finish."

"I'm done," Becky said stubbornly. "Really." And she headed for the door.

Mace followed her out. He tightened the cinch for her and stood there while she mounted. Then, before she could go, he caught Blaze's bridle.

"Thanks," he said, "for caring enough to come looking."

Becky's eyes widened. Her heart flip-flopped in her chest. She swallowed hard and nodded her head.

A faint grin touched Mace's mouth for the first time that day. "Hang in there, shadow," he said, calling her by the pet name he'd given her when she was five and had followed him everywhere.

Then the grin faded and his eyes got inexplicably bleak. "Don't let the rug rats get you down."

* * *

It was the second night of the rest of his life.

The way he felt, Mace hoped his life was short.

He lay on his back on the bed that, in the first days of his marriage, he had shared with Jenny. It was lumpier now. The mattress thinner. A spring poked him. If he rolled over to avoid it, he knew from experience that he'd keep right on rolling into the middle of the bed.

If Jenny had been there to meet him, to wrap her arms and legs around him and take him home, he'd have rolled over in an instant.

But Jenny wasn't there.

And tonight she wouldn't come banging in the door to curse and yell at him.

She'd done her yelling, spent her fury last night. She wouldn't be back.

Good. The worst was over. He'd survived.

He stretched and shifted his shoulders against the mattress, feeling the tension still in them, trying to ease it, telling himself it was just tired muscles, no more, no less. That they ached only proved he was getting lazy, that he'd needed a hard day's work.

Well, he'd had one. He'd worked his horses and dogs—and himself—far harder than usual. Harder, maybe, than he'd ever worked in his life.

It was good for him. He'd been getting lazy.

He'd spent too many nights making love to Jenny, getting a later start on his chores than he ought to have. He'd spent too many afternoons coming in early so he could spend time with her before dinner, talking, laughing, making plans.

Plans. He snorted now.

Hell of a lot of good plans ever did anyone!

He, of all people, ought to have known that.

His old man was a great example. Reese Nichols had had more plans than any man alive.

He planned to get rich ranching. He planned to make his fortune panning gold. He planned to catch a mustang herd and find a horse that could run faster than Secretariat. Plans, oh, Lord, the man had had plans!

They'd as good as killed his wife. She'd known them for the pipe dreams that they were, but she'd stood by him, anyway—working, scraping, saving, hoping—when all reason for hope was gone.

The way Jenny would stand by him—now that all their hope was gone.

Unless he stopped her.

He was right to have stopped her.

He couldn't bear to see the sadness on her face day after day when she faced the room where they would never be able to put the child they would never conceive. He couldn't bear to have her put her arms around him and make love with him when he couldn't give her the fruits of what that love should bring.

He thought about Becky with her twin troubles. He knew what she was going through. He'd seen Felicity, tired and frazzled. He'd heard Taggart, grumbling, his patience worn thin.

If they only knew the alternative, he thought bitterly.

He knew the alternative. He was going to live with it every day of his life.

But Jenny wasn't. At least he could spare her that.

He shut his eyes and tried to go to sleep. To dream. To forget. But he couldn't erase the memory of her face— radiant and hopeful as it had been on their wedding day, dazed and delighted at the passion of their lovemaking, warm and tender, as she kissed his shoulder, then curled against him in the night.

No one curled against him this night.

He wondered if anyone would ever curl in his arms again.

Chapter Three

Jenny didn't tell a soul.

What was she going to say, after all?

"Oh, by the way, Mace walked out on me two weeks ago. After almost fifteen years of a wonderful marriage, we're getting a divorce."

Not hardly.

At first, of course, she didn't say anything because she didn't believe it was true. The whole thing seemed like a bad dream.

Even when she went back to the cabin the next evening to apologize and he paid more attention to the tack he was mending than to her, and refused to discuss anything at all, she still couldn't believe that it was over between them.

She told herself that Mace needed space. He needed time. But in the end, he would need her.

She couldn't imagine that she'd go to bed alone every night for the rest of her life. She couldn't accept the fact

that every dinnertime would pass without the sound of
Mace's truck rumbling up the road or Mace's footfalls on
the back porch steps. She couldn't believe she would never
again brush his hair off his forehead or hear his voice calling her darlin' or feel the rough brush of his cheek against
hers.

It wasn't true, she told herself.

But two weeks after he walked out, she came home from
the last day of school to find a stiff ivory-colored envelope
in the mailbox.

Hollis and Son, Attorneys at Law, it said in the upper
left-hand corner. Jenny looked at it curiously.

Were they the lawyers who had handled the section of
Otis Jamison's land that Mace had arranged to buy?

If so, in the morning she could take the letter up to him.
Tonight she had agreed to go to a movie with Felicity.

"Girls' night out," Felicity had said. "I need it. Desperately. Don't say no."

Jenny hadn't. She had told herself she could use a night
out herself. She had been home alone too much. She had
spent too long fretting about Mace.

If this letter confirmed the results of the land survey, it
would be something less volatile that they could discuss.
An opening, a chance to show Mace that there was more
to their life and their marriage than his inability to have
children.

She slit it open as she walked back to the car, wondering
idly why they'd addressed it only to her.

She unfolded it, then stared at it, disbelieving.

Mace was filing for divorce.

She stopped dead still. She tried to swallow and could
not. She tried to breathe and couldn't seem to do that, either. She looked at the paper again, but couldn't read it at
all now; it was shaking too hard.

At first just the paper shook. Then she realized it wasn't

the paper. It was her hand, then her arm and finally her whole body.

Her fingers clamped on the stark white sheet, steadying. But there was no steadying her mind. It reeled.

He didn't mean it. It was wrong! A mistake.

Please God, it was a mistake.

But there it was in black-and-white legalese: Mason Joseph Nichols was advising Jennifer Anne Nichols that he was seeking a dissolution of their marriage.

The sun beat down on Jenny's back but failed to warm her. From the inside out, she was ice. Frozen and shattered at the same time. A million tiny ice chips, held together only by nerves.

And then she felt a trickle of heat on her cheek. The only warmth in the universe. A tear.

She didn't know how she made it back up the road to the house. She didn't remember parking her car by the back porch. She didn't remember bringing in the groceries or throwing the rest of the mail on the table. She didn't remember crawling under the covers of their bed.

She never remembered the phone ringing.

But it rang.

And rang.

And rang again.

And then there was nothing. Silence. Pain. Tears.

And finally a hand on her shoulder, tentative, yet firm, jarred her back into awareness.

Hours had passed. She didn't know how many. Didn't care.

"Jenny? Are you all right?" The hand shook her again. The voice, at first soft and concerned, became urgent now. *"Jenny?"*

She rolled over, blinked. Felicity stood over her, a desperately worried look on her face.

"Are you sick? I've been calling and calling! I thought

we'd agreed to go to the movie in Bozeman tonight. What's wrong? Where's Mace?''

Where's Mace? Jenny took a ragged breath, tried to find the words.

Failing, she shook her head. Her face was stiff, masklike, and, scrubbing at it, she realized it was from dried tears she didn't even remember having shed.

Felicity crouched beside the bed. "Jenny, tell me what's wrong. Why didn't you answer the phone? I called to tell you when the movie started, but you didn't answer. So I called again. And again. I thought you'd gone somewhere with Mace, but Becky said she didn't think so. And then I thought the worst. I *still* think the worst! *What's going on?*''

The paper was still crumpled in Jenny's fist. Wordlessly she pulled it out.

Felicity spread it out and read it, then looked up, shocked. "It's not true," she said. "It's a joke. A sick joke. I wonder who would do a thing like that.''

"Mace," Jenny said. It was a sick joke, all right. But it was Mace's sick joke. Jenny knew that.

"It doesn't make sense. You two have the best marriage I know! *Why* does he want a divorce?''

Jenny couldn't answer that.

If Mace chose to tell people, he could. But she didn't think it was likely. Mace was an intensely private man. He had allowed doctors and nurses to invade that privacy for Jenny's sake. She owed him the respect of what he had left. She shook her head.

"It's insane," Felicity said.

"Yes." Jenny could agree with that.

"It doesn't make sense.''

"To him it does.''

"But—''

"I'm sorry I didn't answer the phone," Jenny said. "I was...upset."

"An understatement, I think," Felicity said gently. "Where is Mace?"

"He moved out two weeks ago."

Felicity's eyes widened. "Moved out? So it's not a surprise? The letter?"

"It is," Jenny said. "Moving out isn't the same as wanting a divorce. He talked about it...but I didn't believe he'd go through with it." She pressed her lips together and swallowed. "I should have known."

That was nothing but the truth. She should have realized how strongly Mace felt about this.

It was exactly what an idealistic idiot like Mace would do. He knew how badly she wanted a family. It was all she'd talked about. He was right. It had been her dream, her hope, her plan—the way the ranch had been his.

But not at the cost of her marriage, damn it!

"What can I do?" Felicity asked her. "Can I help? Can Taggart help? Do you want Taggart to talk to him?"

"No."

"They've been friends for years."

"We've all been friends for years," Jenny said dully. "That's why I know. Taggart can't help."

"But—"

"No."

"You mean you're just going to let him do it?" Felicity was indignant.

"I don't know what I'm going to do."

"You ought to hit him upside the head. He's got the best wife in the world. What's he throwing it all away for?" She stalked across the room, then whirled and confronted Jenny. "Don't tell me he found someone else?"

"No." Jenny could defend him from that accusation, at least.

"Well, thank God for that." Felicity breathed a sigh of relief. "I thought he had more sense," she said, justified.

"Oh, yes. Mace is very big on sense." He thought what he was doing was eminently sensible—even though it was cutting out her heart.

"Then *why*—?" The words were almost a wail. Then Felicity clamped her mouth shut. "Never mind. It's none of my business. I know it's none of my business! Taggart would say I'm poking my nose in where it has no right to be and that's true. But I care, damn it! I care about you. And," she added, "as much as I might like to punch his lights out right now, I care about Mace."

Jenny believed her. She was even grateful—for all the good it would do. She smiled wanly. "Thanks."

"So what I can do to help?"

Jenny shook her head. This wasn't like their ranching operation where you could solve your infertility problems with a straw of sperm. Men were not interchangeable. Men had egos. Pride. Determination. And this man was more stubborn than any bull.

Felicity, disgusted at Jenny's lack of initiative, slapped her hands on her hips. "So, that's it? You're just going to let him go?"

Was she?

Was she just going to knuckle under and join Mace in the petition?

Or was she going to try to salvage their marriage? Try to get through to him?

"No," she said, sitting up straighter, "I'm not just going to let him go."

"A divorce?"

"Shh, Taggart! Stop shouting! You'll wake the children!"

One of them was already awake, thanks very much.

Awake and sitting scrunched at the top of the stairs where they couldn't see her but she could hear them.

But Becky knew they didn't mean her, in any case.

They meant Willy and Abby, who had both been colicky all evening and had yelled so much she'd slammed her book down and put her hands over her ears.

Her father, pacing with a frantic Willy against his shoulder, had shot her a hard glare. "If you don't want to listen, leave!"

She wasn't used to her dad being impatient. Not *that* impatient. It wasn't as if she was the one doing the yelling, after all!

She'd dropped her hands, hunched her shoulders and said, "All right. I will."

She went out without looking back, determined to sit on the fence and wait until the noise was over and he came to tell her to come in.

From the fence she could still hear Willy wailing, but it wasn't so loud. She sat and watched the sun set and wondered if Willy would stop, by the time it got dark. If he did, maybe her dad would come and sit on the fence with her the way they used to, just the two of them, looking for the first star.

They hadn't done that since the babies were born. It was one of a lot of things they hadn't done since the babies were born. She shot a quick glance over her shoulder to see if he might be coming. He wasn't.

She waited...and waited. The sun went down. The stars came out. It got dark. He didn't even seem to remember that she was gone.

She stayed out until ten—past her bedtime, even for summer. And when she finally came back in—she found him asleep on the sofa.

There was the sound of clinking dishes in the kitchen. Becky supposed she ought to offer to help. Felicity had to be as tired as Taggart, and Becky knew she would smile and give her a hug. Felicity gave good hugs.

But she didn't want one of Felicity's hugs right then.

She wanted her dad's.

She sat in Grandpa's old overstuffed chair where Taggart would see her when he woke up.

He did, half an hour later. He blinked and frowned at her as he hauled himself to a sitting position and glanced at his watch. "What are you still doing up? Go to bed."

So she'd gone to bed.

But not to sleep.

She'd fumed silently until she was sure they'd forgotten her, though she doubted it would take that long. And then she slipped out of bed and went to sit at the top of the stairs to listen.

She didn't know what she expected to hear. She knew what she *hoped* to hear. She wanted to hear her father say he regretted snapping at her this evening. She wanted to hear him say what a good kid she was.

But they weren't talking about her at all.

"A *divorce*? Mace and Jenny?" Taggart lowered his voice, but not much. "I don't believe it!"

Neither did Becky. She felt like she'd been punched in the belly.

"I didn't believe it, either," Felicity said. "But apparently he moved out a couple of weeks ago."

Becky's jaw dropped. Then Mace hadn't been just staying at the cabin for a few days.

"Moved out?" Taggart's voice rose again.

"That's what Jenny said. She didn't say where."

"Question is why," Taggart muttered.

Amen, Becky thought. She tried to remember anything Mace might have said that would answer it. Nothing came to mind. He'd been short-tempered, she remembered. He'd almost sent her away.

"Jenny didn't say," Felicity was saying.

"She wouldn't."

He was pacing now. Becky could hear him. She unfolded enough to lean around and peek past the banister to try to see his face.

Taggart raked a hand through his hair. "Maybe they just had a fight. Maybe he just left to cool off."

"For two weeks? He got a lawyer."

"A lawyer? *Mace?*" Taggart was incredulous.

So was Becky. Mace wasn't a lawyer sort of guy. As far as Becky knew, he never turned to anyone else for anything. And he always tackled things head-on.

Old-fashioned, her grandpa called it. It was a compliment.

Becky could go along with that. Of course as far as she was concerned, Mace Nichols could do no wrong.

So, if he and Jenny had problems, how come he wasn't solving them by himself?

How come he was getting a lawyer—and a divorce?

She edged forward, hoping her father had the answer to that.

"I asked her if she wanted you to talk to Mace, but she said no," Felicity was saying. "It wouldn't do any good."

"It wouldn't," Taggart agreed. "He's as stubborn as Aunt Harry's mule." He scowled and hooked his thumbs in his belt loops. "What the hell's wrong with him? He's been in love with Jenny since he was wet behind the ears." He sounded angry now, as if Mace was letting him down, too, and he stalked to the other end of the room.

Becky wondered if anyone had considered that maybe it was Jenny's fault. She opened her mouth, then closed it again. There was no way she could point that out.

She wrapped her arms around her knees tightly and rocked forward to see where her father was.

A mistake.

Before she could stop herself, she tumbled like a bowling ball all the way down the stairs!

"What the—" Taggart barked.

"Oh, heavens, Becky! Are you all right?" Felicity cried.

When Becky stopped bouncing, she lay there a minute and wondered if she could pretend not to breathe until they gave her up for dead and buried her.

Probably not.

Reluctantly she opened her eyes. Felicity looked worried. Taggart looked, well, just short of murderous.

Felicity crouched beside her, patting her. "Where does it hurt, honey?"

"I can tell you where it's going to hurt," her father said ominously. "Get up."

Felicity shot him a hard look. "For goodness' sake, Taggart. She might have broken something."

Taggart's gaze met Becky's. If she thought he'd barely seen her earlier this evening, she was under no such illusion now.

She wiggled experimentally, as Felicity patted her all over. Nothing hurt that much. She struggled to sit up.

"I'm okay. I just...tripped." Her gaze slid away from her father's.

"Tripped?" It was hard to believe a man could get that much disbelief in one word.

Maybe, she thought glumly, it was because she gave him so much practice.

"Um," she said. She got to her feet, trying to smile at Felicity to reassure her.

Felicity didn't look reassured.

All of a sudden there was a wail from upstairs. Felicity looked up. The first wail was joined by another one. And followed by the sound of Taggart gritting his teeth. He said a rude word under his breath and nailed Becky with a glare.

She did her best to sidle out of reach.

"You get one. I'll get the other," Felicity said to Taggart.

Becky thought she was the one her father wanted to get.

Taggart stood there, indecisive, his gaze still fixed on Becky. The wails grew louder and more insistent.

"Oh, hell," he muttered. "Get to bed. But we're not finished, Rebecca. Believe me." Then he followed Felicity up the steps.

Becky waited until they were both busy with Willy and Abby before she went after them. She climbed the stairs slowly and edged past the twins' room.

She could hear the creak of the old rocker her grandma had rocked her in when she was little. She could hear the soft murmur of Felicity's voice as she soothed the baby she was nursing. She could hear her father's footsteps as he paced and jiggled and tried to distract the other twin. He was singing softly. It was a song she remembered him singing to her when she was little.

Nobody heard her.

It was just as well.

Becky got to bed and slid between the covers.

Then she lay there and tried to feel relieved that her dad hadn't yelled more or swatted her bottom. In the old days he wouldn't have been so easily distracted. She supposed she ought to be grateful to Willy and Abby for yelling their heads off.

She twisted against the sheets, hoping to settle in. She tried to feel tired and content, the way she used to feel right after her dad and Felicity got married—as if finally things were all right in her world.

But things weren't all right.

Nothing was all right. And she didn't know what to do.

It didn't seem as easy as the last time she'd had to fix things. Then it had been obvious what the problem was—

and how to fix it. All she'd had to do was find her father a wife.

She'd done that. Now they were supposed to live happily ever after. That was the way it worked.

Wasn't it?

Becky folded her hands and stared at the ceiling. "If this is happily ever after," she told God, "You've got a little work to do."

It was the middle of the night and she was still awake and no nearer figuring out how to help God sort things out, when Becky remembered what Felicity had said about Mace and Jenny getting a divorce.

Becky's eyes shot wide open as the implications hit.

Her stomach clenched. So did her toes and fists.

Did that mean God had been listening to all those childish ramblings she'd shared with Him all those years ago?

Back then—she must have been five or maybe six—she'd wanted to marry Mace. But Mace was already married. Becky wasn't sure how to dispose of Jenny until she came up with the idea of them getting a divorce so Jenny could marry her dad.

Once or twice she might have even prayed for it to happen. Well, all right, she *had* prayed for it to happen. But that was before she got older and knew better and figured out that just as Felicity was the right woman for her dad, Jenny was the right woman for Mace.

Then she'd stopped praying for it, though she'd never stopped loving Mace.

So, what was this?

Some sort of delayed reaction? An incubation period, like when she got the chicken pox a couple of weeks after she'd been exposed to Tuck's?

Did God have some sort of divine in-box where her request kind of got shoved to the back for a few years and just now came to His attention?

And if so, did that make Mace and Jenny's divorce *her* fault? The thought made her stomach hurt.

"I didn't mean it," she told God. "I was just a little kid."

If that made any difference to God, He didn't say. Becky waited, eyes on the ceiling, wishing He'd answer. But all she heard was silence.

Finally she turned onto her side and curved herself around her pillow with the bronc rider pillowcase and tried to sleep.

Then she remembered all the nights she'd pretended the pillow was Mace.

She sat up and deliberately shoved it away.

She could see it still, though, out of the corner of her eye. Her stomach didn't hurt now, but it felt hollow and cold where the warmth of the pillow had been. She tried hugging her arms across her chest. It didn't help.

She couldn't go to sleep without her pillow.

Was Mace sleeping alone tonight wishing he was holding Jenny?

Becky sat up again and picked up the pillow. She tugged the pillowcase off and set it on the nightstand next to her bed. The pillow looked lumpy and old and sort of forlorn without it. She knew how it felt.

The ticking scratched her cheek. She didn't care. She laid it down and settled next to it, curving her body around it once more.

That felt a little better.

She could still see the pillowcase. Putting out her hand, she touched the edge of it, rubbed it between her fingers, then closed them over it.

"It'll be all right, Mace," she said softly, hoping it was true.

She still had it twined between her fingers when she fell asleep.

Life went on.

Wasn't that what the sitcoms said?

Of course it did. Jenny knew that.

"There is life after divorce," her friend Mary Alice at the beauty parlor, who'd had five husbands, told her.

Of course there was.

But Jenny didn't want to find out. "I'm not getting a divorce," she told Mary Alice.

"Maybe not," Mary Alice said. "But Mace is."

"Not if I don't agree."

Mary Alice made a tsking noise. "That's where you're wrong, kiddo. Doesn't matter whether you want it or not. This is a no-fault state."

Jenny knew there was no fault in the split between Mace and her—unless you counted his pigheadedness.

She found out a couple of days later that by *no-fault,* a lack of pigheadedness wasn't what the Montana legislature had in mind.

What they meant, Jenny learned by going down to the courthouse in Livingston and reading the laws, was that if Mace could prove he and his wife had lived apart for 180 days, he could get a divorce from her whether she wanted him to or not.

"Damn it!" She slammed the book shut.

Three clerks and a patron jumped.

"Sorry," Jenny muttered. She gathered up her things and left, still fuming. How dare legislators mess up her life this way? What did they know about the vagaries of marriages? What did they know about pigheaded, stubborn cowboys who were too damn noble for their own good?

Nothing, obviously.

Well, if that was the law, that was the law. She wasn't going to be able to get it changed.

So she had—she calculated as she hurried back to her car—164 days to change her misguided husband's mind.

Even for a man as stubborn as Mace, surely that would be enough.

Chapter Four

On Saturday morning when Mace showed up at Taggart's to help out with the bull-riding school, he could tell they knew.

Not about his infertility—he still could barely make himself think the word—he knew Jenny wouldn't have betrayed his privacy about that.

But she had obviously told people they were getting a divorce.

He could see disapproval in the hard stares Taggart and Noah gave him when he got out of his truck.

He could feel the censure in Jed's narrow gaze.

He tried to ignore it. He knew they wouldn't challenge him directly. He'd have told them to mind their own business if they had.

He hoped they'd be polite, tolerant. They were simply silent.

"Want some help with the bulls?" he asked Jed, doing his best to sound everyday natural.

Jed shrugged and looked away.

But if he thought the men were hostile, their reaction was nothing compared to their wives'.

Tess and Felicity and Brenna pointedly turned their backs on him when he looked their way. It was so noticeable that he could see Taggart's bull-riding students look twice in his direction.

He felt heat rise on his neck and turned away, pretending extreme interest in fixing a buckle on his bullfighting vest.

The moment he did, he could feel the women's eyes on him, and he heard the mutters and whispers as he moved away.

A muscle ticked in his temple. Tension knotted in his neck. His fingers fumbled with the buckle. He cursed under his breath. But he told himself he didn't care.

They didn't understand—any of them! If they did, they'd applaud him for his selflessness.

But he wasn't going to tell them. No way was he going to admit such a thing to his friends and their wives.

It was between him and Jenny. It wasn't anyone else's business at all!

So he kept his chin up and his gaze firm. He fixed the buckle on the vest, then went about checking the chutes and sorting the bulls the way he always did. He was cool and efficient. Steady and dependable. They didn't need to talk to him. He didn't need to talk to them.

There was none of the usual camaraderie that made him look forward to Taggart's weekend schools. There wasn't a hint of the habitual needling and easy teasing that he and Mace and Jed and Noah shared.

So, who cared? He'd survive.

He was surviving now. Surviving without something—without some*one*—that hurt a lot worse.

It was easy enough to ignore the silence until lunchtime. But when he went to get a hot dog and some chili from the pot that Brenna was ladling out of, she was always serving somebody else. At first he thought that in the crush of hungry cowboys, she just didn't see him standing there with an empty plate. But then the crowd thinned out and still he stood there, and she didn't even look at him.

He understood then, felt the lead settle in the pit of his stomach. But he didn't move away.

"I'd like a hot dog, please." He kept his voice even, tried to make it sound casual, as if it wasn't choking him to have to ask for something so simple.

She slapped a hot dog and a bun on his plate and never once looked his way.

"Thanks."

But she had already left.

At least the spoon was in the chili crock. He helped himself to that. Then he carried his plate to the table with the condiments and took his time putting mustard and ketchup on the bun. No reason to hurry. No one was waiting for his company.

Taggart, his back turned, was deep in conversation with two students. Three or four others were talking to Noah. Jed, standing a little to one side, eating, glanced Mace's way, then moved deliberately to join Noah's conversation.

Jaw set, Mace carried his plate to his truck and sat on the tailgate. He took a bite of the hot dog. He hadn't eaten anything since yesterday evening.

"El hambre es la mejor salsa," he remembered from high school Spanish. Hunger is the best sauce.

The hot dog tasted like sawdust. He chewed it, anyway.

Conversations went on around him, past him, over him—never once included him. Tess and Felicity came down from the house, each carrying one of the twins. Brenna followed with Neile, her baby. Taggart stopped his conversation to take a twin in his arms and, grinning, jiggle it up and down. Jed came across and took Neile away from her mother.

"How's my baby?" Jed asked, and nuzzled his nose against Neile's rose petal cheek.

Mace looked away.

"I brought you some lemonade this time." The voice at his elbow made him jerk.

Becky was holding out a paper cup.

A corner of his mouth lifted. At least Becky hadn't abandoned him. He took the cup she offered and drained it in one gulp. "Thanks."

"Want more?"

He glanced toward the table where the coffee urn and the lemonade cooler sat. He'd have to walk past Jed and Taggart and their wives to get to it. He'd had too much pointed snubbing for one day. He shook his head. "I've had enough."

Becky followed his gaze. "I'll get it," she said.

She took the cup and marched across the yard. He watched her go, surprised at how she'd taken charge, surprised, too, at how tall she seemed. It was just yesterday she'd had to crane her neck to look up at him.

"Time flies when you're havin' fun," he muttered under his breath.

She came back with two cups, handed him one, then set hers down on the tailgate and boosted herself up to sit alongside him.

"I wasn't sure you'd come today," she said. She was staring straight ahead, not looking at him.

He shot a quick glance in her direction. "I always come. When have I ever missed a school?"

"You haven't." She took a swallow of lemonade. "But you haven't ever got a divorce before, either."

She looked up at him then, and her green eyes were dark with worry.

Of course she knew. Why had he figured she didn't? He turned his head to stare across the yard at the corral. "Not the same thing. One has nothing to do with the other."

Becky didn't say anything to that. Out of the corner of his eye he could see her booted feet swing back and forth.

He could feel the questions she wasn't asking. *What* does *it have to do with? Why are you getting a divorce?*

But she didn't say a word.

He took off his hat and shoved a hand through his hair. "Look," he said, "sometimes things happen. Things you don't count on. Things you don't plan. Things you don't want! But they do and then...you got to deal with them."

Becky's boots stopped swinging.

"Yeah," she said, her gaze settling on her father and stepmother and the babies they held. Then, in a voice that sounded like it had to work its way up from China, she said, "I know."

The 164 days dwindled to 155, and Jenny hadn't made any headway at all.

How could she when every time she even caught a glimpse of her stubborn husband, he headed in the other direction?

She was determined to do her share of the summer field work, figuring that it would bring her together with him. It didn't. If she went to help with the irrigation, he stayed on the other side of the field. If she ventured to ride along a fence line and discovered him there, too, he said, "I'll do this," and waved her away.

The one time she did actually get to exchange words with him—when the letter finally came about the land they'd been trying to buy and she went up to the cabin with it— he met her at the door and said tersely, "Obviously we won't be buying it now."

She thought he looked like hell. He was thinner than

she'd ever seen him. Wearier looking. There were dark circles under his eyes. She wanted to put her arms around him and couldn't stop herself from taking a step forward.

He immediately stepped back behind the half-closed door, holding his hand out for the letter at the same time. "I'll take care of it."

"Mace, please don't do this."

He shook his head. "I've got to."

He'll come to his senses, Jenny told herself. She knew he would.

At least she prayed he would.

In the meantime, she didn't know what else to do.

"You think I should *what?*" Jenny stared at Felicity, certain she had heard wrong. Of course she was preoccupied and missed half the things that were said to her these days.

But had Felicity really suggested she—

"Go out on a date."

She *had* heard right. She stared at her friend. "You're joking of course."

"Actually, I'm not." Felicity grimaced as she eased a strand of hair out of a nursing Willy's eager grasp. "Though I would have hated anyone who suggested it to me," she admitted, forestalling Jenny's next protest. "I *did* hate people who suggested it to me when I was still getting over Dirk's death."

"So why are you suggesting it now?"

"Mace isn't dead."

"I know that." But sometimes these days she wanted to kill him!

It would be a damn sight easier than living with the pieces of her life that he had so determinedly shattered, then thrown away.

She'd called his lawyer and tried to get him to talk some

sense into Mace. But Anthony Hollis was just as pompous an ass as he'd been in high school. You couldn't talk to him then, and Jenny couldn't get him to listen to her now.

"I can't talk my client out of a divorce that he deems in his best interest, Mrs. Nichols," Anthony had said in his most patronizing voice.

"His best interest!" Jenny had sputtered. "Do you know *why* he wants this divorce, Tony?"

She heard Anthony's teeth come together with a snap and she remembered he did not like to be called Tony. Tough.

"He doesn't need a reason beyond irreconcilable differences," Anthony said.

"We can reconcile them, damn it, if he'd sit down and talk to me."

"Sometimes it's better to let the lawyers do the talking," Anthony said in his stuffy voice.

"Are you telling me to get a lawyer?"

He was.

And now Felicity was suggesting she get a date!

The world was conspiring against her.

"I think, under the circumstances, a date would be a wonderful thing," Felicity continued doggedly. "It would take your mind off you-know-who. It would show you that there are other fish in the sea."

"I don't care if there are other fish in the sea."

"And—" Felicity continued just as if Jenny hadn't spoken "—if Mace found out, it just might wake him up."

"Wake him up?"

"Make him jealous."

"Mace? *Jealous?*"

Mace had never been jealous in his life!

He'd never had reason to be. Since the day she'd laid eyes on him, Jenny had never looked at another man.

"Why not Mace?" Felicity said. "He still loves you."

Jenny wondered how everyone knew that.

Most of the time when people got divorces, at least one person had fallen out of love. She pointed that out, but Felicity wasn't convinced.

"Not in this case," she said.

Why did they think she and Mace were getting a divorce, then? She didn't ask. "I don't want to go out on a date," she said.

"Neither did I," Felicity said complacently. "But I went, anyway."

"And did you have a good time?" Jenny asked with more than the tiniest bit of sarcasm.

"No. But I'm not sorry I went. It made me aware of how dead I felt. And how alive I became around Taggart."

"Mmm." Trouble was Jenny already knew how alive she was—around Mace.

"Besides," Felicity said smugly, "I've got the perfect date for you."

Jenny groaned. "Some pie-eyed doughboy who eats garlic sandwiches?"

"Close," Felicity said. "My brother."

"What brother? I didn't mean—" She broke off, embarrassed now.

Felicity laughed. "His name is Tom. He teaches English and Literature at a college in Iowa."

"I think Iowa's a bit far to go for a date."

"Ah, but he's coming here." Felicity shifted Willy to the other side, then smiled up at Jenny. "Tomorrow."

Jenny froze. She shook her head quickly. "No. I can't."

"You could...."

"No." She was backing toward the door.

"Relax," Felicity said easily. "I won't make you do it. I just thought—" she gave a faint shrug "—maybe it would help."

Jenny knew that all their friends wanted to help.

She knew they were all poised to do anything they could. For her. For Mace. For both of them.

If they only knew what to do.

But there was nothing anyone could do. She smiled a little wistfully. "Thanks for the thought."

"Tom's a nice guy. He's divorced. Has a five-year-old daughter, Katie. He was going to come out for a couple of weeks and bring Katie, but his ex-wife just got remarried and so Tom is coming on his own."

"I see." She wasn't sure she saw, actually. But she didn't see what it had to do with her, in any case. No matter how nice Felicity's brother was, he wasn't Mace. She wasn't interested.

"Think about it," Felicity said.

Becky had been doing a lot of thinking.

About what was going on at her house. About what was happening to Mace and Jenny.

It felt like the world was coming apart. Like nothing was working anymore at all. She didn't much like it—any of it—but she didn't know how to fix it.

She thought about discussing it with Susannah. But she was embarrassed. She didn't like admitting that things were less than perfect at home.

After all the work she and Susannah had done to get her father and Felicity together, it would seem like she'd failed if she had to admit that things weren't super.

They had been—until Willy and Abby.

But there wasn't much she could do about Willy and Abby. It wasn't like anyone had asked her if she wanted twins! They'd simply told her.

She could still remember how happy her dad and Felicity had looked when they'd given her the news.

She remembered how grouchy her dad was these days

and how distracted Felicity was, and she wondered if they were still so thrilled.

It wasn't something she thought she could ask.

She didn't have anybody to ask about Mace and Jenny, either.

It was true—about the divorce. Before she'd gone to sit by Mace on the tailgate of his truck at bull-riding school, she'd hoped Felicity was wrong, that she'd made a mistake. But one look at Mace had told her Felicity was right.

Why? she wanted to ask him. *What happened?*

But she couldn't. When she looked at Mace that day, he'd reminded her of her dog, Digger, the day he'd been shot by that hunter.

He'd hurt so much he even bit her dad who was trying to help him. The good news was that Digger eventually recovered.

She wasn't so sure about Mace.

She would have liked to ask Susannah's opinion about that, at least, but there wasn't time, and anyway, Susannah had her own problems.

She had to leave the Monday after bull-riding school to go to her aunt Maggie's mother's funeral down in Wyoming.

And even if she'd been there, Becky wasn't sure what she could have said. There was stuff about Mace Susannah didn't know.

She didn't know about those talks Becky used to have with God, for one thing. The ones where she sort of said she wouldn't mind having Mace for her own.

She wasn't sure she wanted to tell Susannah that.

Susannah didn't know that Becky's pillowcase had a lot in common with Mace, either. Susannah's pillowcase had flowers on it, and the hem wasn't frayed.

Becky had never told Susannah that she felt wobbly in the knees sometimes when Mace grinned at her, either. And she'd never told *anyone* whose lock of hair she kept in the envelope in the trick box on her dresser!

One time when she was staying at Mace and Jenny's for the weekend, Jenny cut Mace's hair, and Becky had volunteered to sweep up after.

"Your grandma trained you right," Jenny had laughed, handing her the broom.

Becky swept. And when she was dumping it, she just happened to hang on to one shiny, black lock for her own.

No one knew whose it was—not even her father.

He thought it belonged to Digger. "What do you need the hair for when you've got the whole dog?" he'd asked her.

"I like it," Becky had answered with a shrug. It wasn't exactly a lie.

But Susannah would know right off it wasn't Digger's hair. She'd want to know whose it was.

And Becky had never been ready to talk about that.

So she couldn't talk to Susannah, even when she came back from Wyoming.

Later she wondered if maybe God sent her Tuck.

She and Tuck McCall had been friends as long as she could remember. Tuck had been with her, watching on television when Taggart won the National Finals Rodeo. And he'd been there the next day when Taggart and Noah were badly hurt.

Becky was the first person he'd told when Brenna, his uncle Jed's new wife, decided they were going to exhibit his sketches along with her watercolors at her New York opening. Three years earlier she had been the one he'd told when his mother, Marcy, was dying. They'd cried together at her death.

She hadn't spent as much time with Tuck recently. Maybe it was because she had Susannah now, or maybe it was because Tuck was older and had bigger fish to fry and more important things to do.

But she was glad when Brenna called and asked Taggart if Tuck could spend the weekend with them while she and Jed went down to Jackson Hole for an opening of one of her art shows.

He'd been with her that day they'd seen Mace's truck at the cabin. And he'd known Mace and Jenny all his life, too. Plus he was pretty smart. He didn't talk much, but he saw a lot.

He'd probably know if it was her fault that they were getting a divorce—if she could figure out how to ask him.

It turned out to be easier than she thought.

Saturday afternoon they were sitting by the creek, skipping rocks, counting how many splashes they could make.

Tuck was usually better at it than she was, but she'd done a lot of practicing lately. The creek was one of the places she could go where she couldn't hear crying babies.

She asked him where Neile was, because she was actually sort of surprised that her parents didn't have Neile, too—though how they could possibly have managed a third baby she didn't know!

"Jenny's got her," Tuck replied absently. He was searching out rocks and piling them up in front of him.

The rock Becky had been about to skip dropped from her fingers. "Jenny?"

"Yeah. Brenna reckoned it'd give her something else to think about."

"Other than...the divorce, you mean?" Becky said carefully.

Tuck picked a blade of grass and stuck it in the corner of her mouth. "Yep."

Becky wrapped her arms around her knees. "Do you know why?" she asked cautiously. "Why they're getting the divorce, that is?"

"Nope." He studied the rocks he had collected, then looked over at Becky's to see if any of hers looked more promising.

"No idea?" Becky persisted.

Tuck frowned. "Why? What difference does it make?"

Becky shrugged. "I was just...wondering. My dad always said they were meant for each other. Always had been. So I was sorta surprised."

Tuck slanted her a glance. "I'd've thought you'd be all for it."

"What do you mean by that?"

He grinned. "You were always followin' Mace around."

Becky felt her face burn. She picked up a rock and flung it hard. "I didn't follow Mace around."

Tuck's brows lifted. He looked at her for a long moment, unblinking, until she was the one who looked away.

"Much," Becky muttered, head down.

Tuck grunted. He looked over at her rocks again, hopefully this time.

She sighed. "Go ahead."

He selected one and, taking careful aim, he sidearmed it across the water. They both watched it skip, skip, skip, skip, then sink.

Then they sat silently.

"You don't think I caused it, do you?" she asked finally.

Tuck cocked his head, his hazel eyes meeting hers. "Them gettin' a divorce?"

Becky nodded gravely, then drew her knees up and wrapped her arms around them. "I sorta used to ask God for, um, Mace."

She heard Tuck suck in his breath.

"I was little," she said quickly. "I didn't know any better. But I wondered. What if—"

"Naw."

"Naw?" she said hopefully.

"Naw," Tuck repeated firmly. "God don't work like that."

"How do you know?"

"'Cause I used to pray sometimes that Scotty Lindstrom would break his arm."

Becky's eyes widened. She thought Scotty had been Tuck's friend. "You did? Why?"

Tuck tossed her a scornful look. "So's I could be the best pitcher. Why d'you think?"

"Ah." She nodded, understanding. Besides his drawing, Tuck liked baseball best.

"It never happened, you notice," Tuck said gruffly.

"No." She paused. "He's pretty good."

Tuck snorted. "Just gets better 'n' better."

"Yeah." She tried not to sound too admiring for fear Tuck would think she didn't respect his pitching. "So, prayin' for bad stuff to happen to other people doesn't work? Ever?" Becky pressed, just to be sure.

"Nope. Jed says God don't play favorites."

Becky loosed her knees and took a deep breath. She stretched out her legs and tipped her head back and looked up at the deep blue Montana sky. Something that had been tight and knotted inside her eased a little. She took another breath and felt it shudder out of her.

"You gonna use all those rocks?" Tuck asked.

She smiled. "You go ahead."

Jenny should have said no. She should have said she was busy, that her life was too full, too complicated, too...too anything.

She should never have said she would take Jed and Brenna's baby!

"For the weekend," Brenna said apologetically. "We want to go to Jackson. Just the two of us." She blushed a little, then hurried on. "We could take the kids, but—"

But they didn't want to. They wanted each other. Jenny had no trouble seeing that. She understood it, all too well.

"And we thought maybe you'd like—I mean, I suppose you might not—but if you're not too busy...."

And Jenny couldn't lie and say she was.

Everyone knew she wasn't busy now that school was out. She was going crazy on her own.

They felt sorry for her. They wanted to distract her. Make her look outside herself, take an interest in life. And they knew she loved kids.

It was natural.

They didn't know why Mace had left.

She didn't tell them. She just said, "Yes."

And so she had Neile.

She'd never had a baby before. Had wished. Had dreamed. But never...

She and Mace had taken care of Becky occasionally, before Taggart remarried. They would invite her out to spend the occasional weekend with them, realizing that Taggart needed a break and that his parents couldn't be counted on to do it all. Plus, they genuinely liked having her around.

Jenny thought the little girl could use a mother's touch now and then. A steady diet of rodeo cowboys could leave a girl a little unbalanced.

So she and Becky baked cookies. They did jigsaw puzzles. They'd planted a garden and picked wildflowers. Becky lapped it up, enjoying every moment Jenny spent with her.

But Jenny had never kidded herself: the person Becky adored was Mace.

"You're her hero," Jenny had said to her husband more than once after one of Becky's weekends with them. "If she was a little older, I'd have some real competition."

Mace had grinned the "aw shucks" grin that had melted

Jenny's knees back in junior high, the grin she was equally sure was melting Becky's.

"You think so?" he said, as pleased as he was embarrassed.

Becky, of course, never said so. For a little kid, she had admirable restraint, Jenny thought. She'd just followed Mace wherever he went.

Jenny didn't mind. It showed that the little girl had good taste.

Besides, she'd always told herself, it was good for Mace. It gave him experience with kids. Experience they'd need when they had their own.

At least that was what she'd hoped.

The feelings were bittersweet when Brenna and Jed brought the baby Friday afternoon.

"I don't want to impose," Brenna said for the thirtieth time, lingering on the doorstep to adjust Neile's playsuit. "But I couldn't ask Taggart and Felicity. They've got their hands full. And Tess really doesn't have time with her brood. So I thought, you know..."

"Did Jenny say yes when you asked her?" Jed asked his wife.

"Of course," Brenna replied indignantly.

"Then trust her. She knows what she's doing. Come on." He steered Brenna toward the car, then looked back to give Jenny a wink. "See you Sunday. Have fun."

Jenny smiled gamely and snuggled the little girl against her shoulder to wave goodbye. Fortunately it wasn't until they had disappeared around the bend that she felt the first renegade tear fall.

She wiped her eyes on her sleeve and sniffled. "Sorry about that," she said to the baby as briskly as she could. Her voice only broke a little. Neile looked at her curiously, her lower lip trembled.

"Oh, now," Jenny whispered. "Don't you cry, too." She took a deep breath. "Come on, young lady. I'll show you around."

Jed had set up a portable crib in "the spare room," before he and Brenna had left. Now Jenny carried the baby into the room, aware that she'd almost never set foot in here since Mace had left. It was stupid, she knew, to avoid a room. But she couldn't help it. She tried to sound cheery now.

"This is where you're going to sleep," she told Neile, "in that snug little bed your daddy brought. And I'll be right next door."

She carried the little girl out of one room and into the other. "See? Not far at all. And if you want anything, all you have to do is cry." She dropped a kiss on the baby's fair hair. "Which I'm sure you will."

At least the lip had retracted. Now Neile gummed her fist and looked up curiously into Jenny's eyes as if to say, "Who are you and why are you talking a thousand words a minute?"

"It's just that I'm nervous," Jenny explained.

Being the sole person responsible for a child who couldn't even say, "I'm hungry" or "I need to go to the bathroom," was a daunting prospect.

Neile screwed up her face and started to whimper.

"Shh, now. Shh. It's all right." Jenny hoped, even as she said the words, that they weren't a lie. After all her desperation for a family, what if she wasn't cut out for motherhood?

What if she had put Mace through all that for nothing?

Had she destroyed her marriage over a desire to be something for which she had no talent?

She hadn't destroyed their marriage, she reminded herself. It was Mace who had walked out.

She could have learned to live without having children.

But she did love the warm weight of Jed and Brenna's baby snug against her breasts. She did relish the fresh laundry smell and soft, rosy cheeks of little Neile McCall.

And she knew Mace would have, too.

"Oh, Mace." She buried the words in Neile's silky hair. Then, because the little girl whimpered, Jenny did a desperate little two-step into the hallway, dancing the baby in a circle, humming softly.

"Shh, Neile. Shh, little baby." She nuzzled the baby's soft hair, nibbled the side of her neck, then blew lightly against her cheek.

Neile pulled back and blinked. Her whimper died. Her eyes widened. She looked at Jenny.

Jenny touched the petal-soft cheek with one finger. "Like that?" she asked, and blew again.

A sound came out. A gurgle? A chuckle?

Then Neile smiled. It was a tentative smile, a wary smile. But still—a smile.

And for the first time in weeks Jenny felt a smile touch her face, too.

On Sunday mornings Jenny went to church.

She fully intended to go this morning, except she didn't realize how long it would take to get a baby ready.

Saturday morning she'd awakened at five and lain there in anxious anticipation of Neile's first murmur. This morning, however, she was experienced enough—or tired enough—that Neile was in full-throated roar by the time Jenny managed to pry open her eyes.

"Coming," she called, stumbling out of bed and groping her way into her robe. "I'll be right there."

She fed Neile and bathed and changed her, then deposited her on a blanket in the middle of the living room while she got herself fed and dressed. By the time she was done, it was late, but they still could make it. She scooped the baby up off the rug and heard a faint squishing sound. There was a definite feel of dampness against her fingers.

"Uh-oh."

Neile gurgled.

Jenny carried her into the bedroom. By the time the second change had been accomplished, Neile was gnawing her fist and looking around hopefully.

"You're hungry?" Jenny had figured out the meaning of that particular look the day before when it had been followed almost immediately by a much more demanding cry.

She supposed she could take the baby and a bottle and hope that Neile cooperated during the thirty-minute drive into Elmer.

But then Neile yawned and jammed her fist into her mouth and began to gnaw. Her brow puckered. Her hopeful look faded. A sniffle was fast turning into a sob.

"I guess we're not going today," Jenny said to her charge. She yawned and carried the baby to the kitchen.

With luck, she thought, after Neile had her bottle, she would go down for a morning nap. Perhaps she could get one as well.

She was beginning to understand those dark circles under Jed's and Brenna's eyes. She wondered how, with *two* babies, Taggart and Felicity ever managed to cope.

Neile was frantic by the time Jenny got the bottle ready and carried the little girl to the rocking chair. Neile glommed on at once, wrapping fat fists around the bottle and staring up at Jenny unblinkingly.

Jenny trailed a finger along the baby's cheek. "Better?"

At first Neile's sucking came hard and fast. But gradually the tension in her small limbs lessened. The rhythm of Jenny's rocking soothed her. Her grip on the bottle loosened. She blinked. Her eyelids drooped.

Jenny smiled. With one finger she touched Neile's small hand.

It let go of the bottle and latched on to Jenny's finger with a strong grip. Jenny rubbed her thumb lightly over the baby's tiny fingers...and wished...

For Mace. For the love they'd lost, for the children they'd never have, for the hopes and dreams that had once seemed so possible and which were forever out of her grasp.

It wasn't only Mace who could have a pity party, she thought wryly.

But even as she thought it, her eyes blurred, and she had to tip her head back and close them against sudden tears.

The door opened.

Jenny's head jerked up.

Her eyes flew open—to see Mace standing there.

Chapter Five

"Mace." Jenny's bare whisper sounded shocked.

No more than he was. Mace stood rooted to the floor, one hand on the doorknob, staring at her. He could almost feel the blood draining out of his darkly tanned face at the sight of Jenny sitting in the rocker holding a child!

He began to back out the door.

She started to get up, but the baby made a sound of protest, and she sank back to rock it some more.

Mace felt a muscle tick in his cheek.

This was not something he wanted to see. He had come now because he was sure she wouldn't be here! He had come because he was sure he could get in, gather up the rest of his gear, get the book work he needed and be gone before she got home from church.

He'd been counting on it.

The certainty of her absence was the only thing that had got him out of his truck and up the steps.

And now here she was—with a baby in her arms.

Abruptly he turned away.

"Mace! Wait!"

The rocker creaked again as Jenny half rose, then, at the child's whimper, sank back once more. "Mace! Come back here. If I get up, I'll wake her. Please!"

He didn't want to stop. He didn't want to go back. He didn't want to think about Jenny with a baby in her arms.

"Mace!"

The baby was crying now, and Jenny was following him.

He turned and glared at her. "What, damn it?" His voice was harsh, ragged. "For God's sake, sit down. You're making it cry."

Jenny eased back and sat down in the chair and began rocking again. The wailing stopped. "Her," she corrected. "It's Neile. I'm baby-sitting Neile for the weekend."

"Good for you." His voice was still harsh.

It didn't matter whose child it was; it wasn't theirs.

He'd thought he would be over it by now. He'd thought the steady normal everyday ranch work that had sustained him his whole life would sustain him now.

Think again, he told himself savagely.

In the three weeks since he'd walked out, things had gone from bad to worse. He'd had too much time to think, too much time alone.

Too little Jenny.

He'd hoped that talking to Anthony would settle things. Once the legal proceedings were underway, he had told himself, there would be no changing his mind. No going back.

Great theory. He just wished his head—and his heart— would get with the plan.

They hadn't. They wanted Jenny.

So badly that he'd finally made himself an appointment in Billings with another doctor. Maybe the local one had spermicide in his stupid little cups. Maybe he was a quack. Maybe, Mace desperately hoped, he was wrong.

Friday he'd found out that the second opinion confirmed the first.

"No sperm," the doctor had told him, shaking his head sympathetically. "I'm sorry."

Mace didn't need—or want—sympathy. He wanted sperm.

"Can't you do something? Isn't there some way? What are we putting all this money into medical research for?"

"Perhaps a donor?" the doctor suggested.

"No." He wasn't having some other guy's sperm swimming around inside Jenny!

"I'm sorry," the doctor said again. "We can often help if the count is simply low. But when there are none..." He spread his hands helplessly.

And Mace had driven home feeling, if possible, even worse than he had three weeks before. On the drive down he'd dared to entertain the faint hope that he could drive back to the ranch tonight and take Jenny in his arms and tell her that the nightmare was over.

It seemed to him now that the nightmare had just begun.

"Jed and Brenna went down to Jackson," Jenny was explaining. "She's opening a show there. More cowboy hero paintings and a new series on children of the West. That was the official excuse." She smiled a little nervously as she talked, as if Mace were some sort of wild animal that she might spook at any moment. It wasn't far from the truth. "I think they wanted a second honeymoon."

"They had their first less than a year ago," Mace muttered.

But he understood. He remembered that desire. He remembered weeks—months—when he didn't think he could take Jenny to bed often enough.

He *still* felt that way, God help him.

"Yes, but they haven't had much time to themselves," Jenny reminded him. "They've had a houseful, with Tuck and the baby and Brenna's dad."

"I know what their problem is," Mace said tightly. It was nothing compared to his own—the big unsolvable one and the smaller more immediate one: how was he going to get out of here with Jenny smiling at him like that?

"I'm glad you're back."

"I'm not back," he said. "I just came to get some stuff. I didn't think you'd be here," he added bluntly.

As he hoped, her smile faded. His last words had been cruel and unnecessary, and he knew it. He watched as the hurt flickered across her face.

He expected it—*hell, he'd caused it*—but still he had to steel himself against it. Hurting Jenny was like hurting himself. And even being prepared for it didn't help.

He shoved himself away from the door. "I'll come back another time."

"No!" She leaped up this time, not caring whether she woke Neile or not. "You're not going to walk out on me again, Mace Nichols!"

He tried. She came after him, bouncing the baby as she hurried across the room and onto the porch. Neile, obviously unused to such treatment, dropped her bottle and began to wail. Jenny kept coming.

Mace made it all the way to his truck, feeling as if all the devils in hell were on his tail. He had the door open when she caught up to him and grabbed it to stop him from getting in and closing it. She almost dropped the child.

Mace saved the baby—and ended up holding her himself. "Here." He tried to thrust Neile back into Jenny's arms.

But Jenny was having none of it. She folded her arms across her chest and shook her head. "You hold her, and we'll talk."

"We have nothing to talk about."

"What about the little matter of that petition to dissolve our marriage?"

"What about it?"

"I don't want to dissolve our marriage."

"Maybe not now. You will."

The stubborn Jenny Fitzpatrick chin he remembered from childhood lifted now. "You think so, do you?" she challenged.

"Yes." The word came through his teeth as a hiss. Neile wailed in his arms. "Damn it, Jenny!"

He couldn't take this! Jenny kept her arms folded as he fumbled with the crying child. "Shh," he muttered to her, jiggling her against his chest. "Hey now, shh. Jenny," he pleaded. "Take her. She's your responsibility."

"Interesting that you're so big on responsibility," Jenny said, "when you've just walked out on me."

"For your own good," Mace countered, stung.

"The hell it is!"

"It is," he insisted. "You'll thank me someday."

She gaped at him. "I'll thank you? Oh, sure. Maybe you expect me to even name my first-born son after you?"

He felt the blood drain from his face.

He shoved Neile at Jenny so firmly this time that she had no choice but to open her arms. Then he jumped in the truck, slammed the door and gunned the engine.

"Mace! I'm sorry. I didn't mean that, Mace. Don't go. Don't! Damn it, Mace."

But the thought of Jenny with a first-born son that was someone else's was more than he could take.

Jenny told herself she was foolish. She told herself she wasn't ready for this. She told herself that she'd be sorry.

But there was just so long you could bang your head

against a wall—or against the hardheaded stubbornness of your husband—and get nowhere.

She had to do something.

So Jenny took Felicity's suggestion: she was going on a date.

Well, it wasn't precisely a date. It was dinner at Felicity and Taggart's with Becky and the twins and Felicity's newly arrived brother, Tom.

"I can't believe I'm doing this," she told Felicity.

"Relax. It will be good for you."

"But I'm not interested in another man!"

"Maybe it's time you get interested." Felicity's tone was sympathetic, but firm. She was more of a realist than Jenny.

Still, it turned out better than she'd expected. Maybe it was because Felicity's judgment was generally to be trusted. Maybe it was because, when she met Tom Morrison, he didn't seem threatening to her peace of mind.

Mostly it was because he was nothing like Mace.

Tom Morrison had warm brown eyes and shaggy blond locks that were as different from Mace's sea blue eyes and short-cropped black hair as day was from night. He was lean, but not hard. His conversation had more to do with books, politics and National Public Radio than it did a bull's breeding line or the price of feed this coming winter.

Jenny began to relax.

While Felicity put dinner on the table and Taggart juggled a fussy baby, Tom lounged in the porch swing and, bouncing a happy baby on his knee, talked about a book he was assigning for a course in African literature he was teaching in the fall.

Jenny sipped her margarita and listened, letting Tom's conversation wash over her. It was so pleasant. So nondemanding.

She found herself surprisingly interested in the book he was talking about, which she'd never heard of. Not surprising. There were always too many chores to be done for her to settle down with a book. The most she ever got to read, it seemed, was the newspaper.

Now he piqued her interest. The course he was teaching sounded interesting, too. Once upon a time she'd have liked to take a course like that. She said so.

Tom smiled. "They probably have a similar course at Montana State. Why don't you look into it?"

"I've never taken any college courses," Jenny confessed. "We never had time...or the money."

She felt a little like she was betraying Mace when she said that, so she added quickly, "I never minded, really. I like being a teacher's aide."

"You can still be a teacher's aide if you take classes," Tom said.

"Yes," Felicity said, coming out onto the porch. "Why don't you check it out, Jenn? You could start work on a degree."

"Oh, no," Jenny said. "I couldn't. I have no time." Then she stopped, and felt her face flush.

The fact was, this summer she did have time. This summer she wasn't working with Mace because he made it so obviously clear he didn't want her to. She'd tried to help, but his determined cold shoulder had made her mad. If he thought he could handle the ranch on his own, fine, she thought. Let him.

Since then she hadn't saddled a horse.

Now, though she had some time, the thought of taking a class at the university was daunting.

"I haven't taken classes in years," she protested. "And I've never taken any in college. I'd probably fail."

"Lots of nontraditional students feel that way," Tom said easily. "In fact, most of them do better than the kids. They're motivated. Professional. Adult." He gave her an encouraging smile over the top of his margarita glass.

His faith in her was surprisingly touching. Jenny found herself smiling back. "I wouldn't know where to start."

"All colleges have admissions counselors. Why don't you go see one?"

"I don't know...." Jenny nibbled at the salt on the rim of the glass, then ran her tongue over her lips. It seemed like a huge departure from her real life. See a counselor? Think about college?

What would Mace say?

Would Mace even *know?* Or care?

She took another sip of her drink. "Maybe I will."

The next morning Jenny was convinced her brave statement had been the margarita talking. She wasn't seriously thinking about going back to college, was she?

She looked around the small ranch house she and Mace and their friends had built. In it she saw the embodiment of Mace's dreams, Mace's hopes.

She had taken them on, had been very happy with them, but they hadn't been hers. Not to begin with.

Her dream had been a college education. A job teaching, not just being an aide to someone else who taught. She'd had the grades for it. As valedictorian of their small high school, she'd had offers of plenty of scholarships and grants.

But she hadn't wanted scholarships or grants or the college education as much as she'd wanted Mace.

And now?

She didn't have Mace.

She briefly entertained the possibility that she wouldn't win out, that she might never have Mace again. She didn't really believe it. But...

Go see an admissions counselor?

Maybe she would.

*   *   *

He didn't let himself dwell on Jenny's first-born son.

He didn't let himself dwell on Jenny.

Every day when he got up, it took Mace less time to remember where he was and why Jenny was no longer beside him, shove the thought away and force himself out of bed to get on with his life.

Every night when he came back to the cabin, exhausted from a day riding the range, moving the herd, doctoring cattle or fixing fences, it didn't take him long to find something else to do to keep from thinking about her.

Pretty soon he'd be fine, he promised himself. Before long he wouldn't miss her at all.

But there was no comfort in knowing it.

No comfort at all.

It might have helped a little if he'd had a friend or two. A little camaraderie. A bit of distraction.

But his friends were Jenny's friends. And that weekend at Taggart's school, it had been all too obvious who they were giving their allegiance to.

And anyway, if someone did come by, there was always the chance that the conversation would come around to Jenny—and why he was divorcing her. He had no doubt speculation was rife.

And he had nothing to say.

The knowledge of his infertility shamed him and embarrassed him still. Every time he thought about what he wasn't capable of doing, he felt like less than a man.

It was better that they think him a surly, selfish son of a bitch. He didn't want them thinking he was less than a man, too.

So he stayed by himself.

When he needed groceries or gasoline, he drove to Livingston. When he needed blackleg medicine or a new cinch for his horse, he drove to Bozeman. When he needed to talk to his lawyer, he used his newly purchased cellular phone.

The last time he called, Anthony had told him that Jenny had a lawyer and was asking for half the property.

"Half the property? What's she going to do with half the property?" he yelped. "She won't stay on the ranch."

"No, but by law she's entitled to a share," Anthony said.

Of course she was, Mace knew that. But he just thought of her as moving to town or something. He wanted her to have plenty to live on. She deserved plenty. Trouble was, even in the best of times they'd never had plenty between the two of them.

And now they were going to have to divide the ranch?

"I'll have to buy her out," he told Anthony.

Though how he was going to do that, he didn't know. They barely broke even now. Maybe she'd let him pay her over time. A long time.

Or, he wondered, was she insisting on half just so he'd drop the petition?

He didn't know.

"I'll talk to her lawyer," Anthony said. "I'll see what we can work out. Don't worry."

Yeah, right.

Mace hung up and worried all night.

There was only one really good thing in his life now, and that was that his herd had never looked better.

It was because he spent hours with them, checking on them, doctoring them, moving them to better grass, catching problems before they had a chance to develop. Doing things the way they ought to be done.

It just went to show, Mace assured himself, that he didn't need Jenny. And he didn't need his friends.

But he couldn't suppress the surge of pleasure he felt when he came over the rise above the cabin one afternoon and saw Becky riding toward him.

He grinned and waved at her.

"Hey, shadow, haven't seen you in a while," he said when they got close enough for his voice to carry.

She shrugged. "Been busy," she replied, her voice a monotone. She didn't smile. She looked worried.

Mace dismounted by the barn and started to take his saddle off while he waited for more explanation. It wouldn't take long. Becky usually talked his ear off.

But she didn't today. She sat there looking unhappy, and he wondered if things were all right at home.

"Twins still keepin' you awake all night?"

"Huh?" She looked almost startled, then shook her head vaguely. "Not really. They're...getting better. A little better," she qualified. She still didn't smile.

Mace slung his saddle over the fence rail and looked up at her. "You gettin' down or just passin' through?"

"Um..." For a moment she seemed almost indecisive. Then she said, "Getting down, I guess."

She dismounted and loosened the cinch, then stuffed her hands in her pockets and stared distractedly at her feet and then out across the valley.

This was not Becky.

He studied her downbent head for a moment, then said, "How about a cup of coffee?"

"Coffee?" She looked at him, astonished.

He didn't blame her. He'd never offered her a cup of coffee in her life! She was a kid, for heaven's sake!

But then she said, "Yeah. All right."

He led the way into the cabin and put the coffeepot on the stove. Becky followed, but she didn't perch on one of the chairs and tip it back and forth the way she usually did.

Instead she went to the window and stood still, staring out across the valley. She ran a finger in the dust along the windowsill.

Mace wondered if living with Felicity had taught her to

be critical of his housekeeping skills. He was pretty sure he didn't live up to Felicity's standards, but Becky didn't say anything, just doodled in the dust.

"So," he said as they waited for the coffee to boil. "What's new at your house?"

He expected to hear some grumbling about the twins. But Becky turned, her back against the windowsill and said, "Jenny's goin' out on a date with my uncle Tom."

"*What!* I mean, what?" His brows drew down. "What Uncle Tom? You don't have an uncle Tom. You've only got an aunt."

Erin. Taggart's sister. He knew that. She was three years younger than Taggart, lived in Paris, and the last Mace had heard she wasn't married.

"What the hell are you talking about?" He knew he was scowling at her, but Becky stood her ground.

"My 'new' uncle Tom," she qualified. "Felicity's brother. He's visiting us for the summer. From Iowa."

Iowa?

Jenny was going on a *date* with some guy from Iowa?

Already? Talk about a fast worker. Hell, the ink was barely dry on the divorce petition!

He felt like he'd been punched in the gut. His fists clenched, and he had to consciously ease them, flex them, try to keep from strangling something.

"Coffee's boiling," Becky noted.

Mace reached over and shut it off. Automatically he got two mugs down off the shelf and filled them—or tried to. His hand trembled so much he spilled the liquid all over the counter.

Wordlessly Becky mopped it up.

He tried again. His mind was whirling.

Of course he'd known Jenny would date other men. How was she ever going to meet one to father her children and give her a family if she didn't?

But he hadn't expected her to jump into it so eagerly—or so soon!

Wasn't it just a few days ago that she had chased him clear out to his truck to tell him she didn't want a divorce?

Obviously she'd changed her mind.

This Uncle Tom person, Mace thought savagely, must be a hell of a stud!

"He's a nice guy, my uncle Tom," he heard Becky say. She seemed to be almost apologetic. "He's a teacher. A professor really, at a college. He teaches English."

"Good for him," Mace said through his teeth. He doubted that was what Jenny saw in him.

She probably saw sperm.

"He doesn't know as many cowboy stories as you," Becky continued hurriedly. "An' he can't play the harmonica like you can. But he knows a lot about pirates, an' African folktales an' he tells pretty good jokes. He's pretty cool."

"Swell." Mace's fingers strangled the coffee mug.

Becky looked at him warily. Then, as if she thought it might be a good idea to change the subject, she said, "We got a lot of company. Susannah's uncle's here, too."

Mace frowned. "What uncle? Just her uncle?"

Had Tanner left his wife? Had Luke left his? If either had, it wasn't for the reason Mace had left. Tanner had three kids and Luke, two, at last count.

Maybe Jenny could go after them, too.

"Not her real uncle. Her aunt Maggie's dad." Becky's forehead scrunched with the effort of trying to get it straight. "A great uncle removed or something, Dad says. He's really nice, too, except he's kinda sad. His wife just died."

Mace supposed he would be a little old, but perhaps Jenny would get around to him if this Tom character didn't work out.

His fingers tightened on the coffee mug. "So, where are they going on this date?" he asked as casually as he could. "Jenny and your, er, uncle."

"Dunno for sure. Prob'ly a movie. Felicity was reading him the movie schedule last night."

"Felicity's helping the romance along, huh?" Traitor, Mace thought.

Becky shrugged uneasily. "It's not exactly a romance. Yet. They've only been out a couple a times and—"

"This isn't the first time?" Mace demanded.

"Well, th'others weren't dates really. Monday they went to Bozeman...to the college, I think. Jenny might take classes."

"Classes? At MSU?"

Becky nodded. "She got a catalog, and she and Uncle Tom have been going over it, and she said she's thinking about it."

It seemed to Mace she was thinking about a hell of a lot. And she wasn't letting the grass grow under her feet, either!

Classes! Men! What next?

"I wasn't sure I shoulda told you," Becky said. "About Jenny an' Uncle Tom an' all. I mean, it might be nothing." She held the mug of coffee against her lips so she could breathe the aroma as she watched him over the top.

Mace flattened his hands on the countertop and stared out the window, at the same time giving his best imitation of a nonchalant shrug. "Doesn't matter if it is something," he lied. "It's not my business."

"You don't care?"

"We're getting a divorce, you know that."

"I know, but—"

"So it's not my business what she does."

"It is if you want it to be. You could ask her not to go," Becky argued.

He wished. His fingers curled into fists. He stared straight ahead and shook his head slowly. "No."

"You could," Becky insisted. "If you don't want her to go out with him, tell her so. You're still married! If you wanted, you could get back together."

"No!" It was almost a shout. "No," he said more quietly but just as forcefully. "We can't. We won't. So Jenny can date—" he couldn't quite keep his voice even when he said the words "—anybody she wants. Your uncle. Susannah's uncle. Anybody's damned uncle. It isn't up to me. I told you that."

"But—"

"No *buts!* Damn it, Becky. No." He slapped his palms on the countertop, then turned and glared at her. "Leave it. Thanks for tellin' me. It's very interesting. But it's none of my business anymore. Now just leave well enough alone."

He picked up his mug, drained the rest of his coffee, then thumped it down again. "I've got work to do. Come on," he said roughly. "You better go on home."

For a long moment Becky didn't move. She just looked at him, and the look in her eyes was one of such profound hurt that he felt as if he'd kicked a pup. Then, her expression grew shuttered. Her gaze became remote.

Macc cursed under his breath. "I'm sorry. I didn't mean to yell at you. It's just…not something you'd understand."

Becky dumped the rest of her coffee into the sink and walked past him out the door. "I understand," she said. "I shouldn't have come. I'll go."

Chapter Six

So she'd blown it.

She'd been torn all week about whether she should tell Mace about Jenny and Uncle Tom.

Susannah had said that if Jenny dated Uncle Tom—if she *married* Uncle Tom!—it would serve stupid old Mace right. Tuck said if Mace was the one trying to get the divorce, why should he care what Jenny did?

But Becky hadn't been sure.

She would have liked to ask her stepmother, but Felicity was distracted because Willy had an earache and had kept her up all night, and when Becky asked, "Do you think Jenny likes Uncle Tom?" she didn't even know what Becky really meant.

So what else was new? Becky thought.

But even if she had known, Felicity wasn't exactly a disinterested bystander. As Uncle Tom's sister, she might very well think it was better to have Jenny married to her brother than to Mace.

Becky knew better than to ask her dad.

Taggart would tell her to mind her own business—in no uncertain terms—and that would be that!

But Taggart hadn't talked to Mace that day at the bull-riding school. No one had. They'd all ignored him, turned their backs on him.

Only Becky had talked to him, had heard the pain in his voice and had seen the lonely look in his eyes.

She was almost certain he still loved Jenny—even if he was asking her for a divorce—and so she'd stuck her nose in—tried to help.

For all the good it had done...

Now she had Mace mad at her, too.

But this dating business wasn't just a one-off.

Becky wouldn't have gone running to tell Mace if she'd only seen them together once. The night that Jenny had come over for dinner, well, even if she did spend most of it listening to Uncle Tom and hanging on his every word, it was no big deal.

But then two days later they'd gone to Bozeman together. Uncle Tom had taken Jenny to talk to someone at the university, Felicity said.

"So she'll feel more comfortable when she signs up for a class."

"A class?" Becky couldn't imagine anyone Jenny's age voluntarily taking classes. She personally could hardly wait to stop.

"Mmm-hmm." Felicity sounded pleased. She was humming as she mashed a banana for Willy who was over his earache. "It will be good for her, going back to school. Give her something positive to think about."

Becky said, "I guess."

She seemed to think about it and talk about it—to Uncle Tom—a lot. Becky didn't tell Mace that just two days ago she'd seen them having coffee together at the Busy Bee. And that last Sunday after church Jenny had borrowed one of their horses and she and Uncle Tom had gone out riding.

He'd wanted to see a small mountain lake Taggart had been telling him about, and Felicity had suggested Jenny show it to him.

None of those were really "dates," technically, Becky didn't suppose. But she thought the line was getting pretty blurred.

The one coming up on Saturday night, though, was perfectly clear.

It was a date. She'd even heard Felicity call it that.

"I'm glad you're taking Jenny out on a date," Felicity had said to Uncle Tom last night when they were sitting in the kitchen after dinner. Taggart was out feeding stock, and the twins were, for once, both asleep at the same time.

Becky was on the porch, brushing burrs out of Digger's coat and, though they couldn't see her, and she didn't really mean to be spying, she could hear every word.

"She needs a little bit of fun," her stepmother continued. "And so do you."

"Matchmaking?" Uncle Tom had asked.

Becky stopped brushing the dog and edged closer to the window. Digger turned his head and nosed at the brush in her hand.

"What if I am?" Felicity replied. "People did it to me. After Dirk died."

Dirk had been Felicity's first husband. Becky had seen his picture. She didn't think he was nearly as handsome as her dad, but he looked nice enough, and she knew Felicity had loved him.

"Her husband is alive and well," Uncle Tom reminded her.

"And divorcing her, the idiot." Felicity thumped something on the table.

"Why?"

"God only knows," she grumbled. "Midlife crisis, no doubt. They've been married forever. Since they just got out of high school. Never dated anyone else. Maybe now he wants to sow his wild oats. Well, Jenny's too nice to have to put up with that."

"Yeah, but—"

"And she wants a family. She's always wanted a family, and obviously Mace doesn't."

Becky moved a little closer to the window.

"And you've got a family," Felicity continued.

"I have Katie," Uncle Tom qualified. "Sometimes."

"Well, if you had a wife you might be able to convince Lottie to share her more often. And you and Jenny could have kids, too. You wouldn't mind more, I daresay."

"No, but—"

"There. See. It'd be perfect. Don't you think?"

"I think you have my life all figured out," Uncle Tom said with a laugh. But he didn't sound discouraging.

He actually had sounded pretty interested—as if he thought Jenny might be right for him, too.

And that was why Becky had gone up the mountain to tell Mace.

This one really was a date.

Jenny had called the other times she'd been places with Tom "dates" because saying the word made her feel a little daring and alive. And, to be honest, because if she thought of them that way, perhaps Mace would, too, and then he'd come roaring down the mountain to reclaim her.

But he didn't.

And now, after a pleasant evening with Tom at Felicity and Taggart's house, an afternoon spent checking out classes in Bozeman, a cup of coffee at the Busy Bee and a Sunday afternoon horseback ride, she was going out with

Tom, not just because she was feeling reckless and hoping to goad Mace, but because she found him interesting and entertaining and likable.

So it was a date.

And she was nervous.

She'd never been on a date before. Not with anyone besides Mace, at least. Unless, of course, you counted their senior year, when Taggart had taken her to the homecoming dance after she and Mace had briefly broken up. Taggart had got a black eye for his trouble, and she and Mace had made up the next week.

But clearly Mace wasn't interested in giving her other suitors black eyes these days.

In fact, he seemed infuriatingly willing to pass her on to another man. Wasn't that the reason he was divorcing her?

She tried not to think about him. She focused instead on Tom. But thinking about Tom—and his expectations—simply increased her nervousness.

She had paced a rut in the living room by the time Tom's car came over the hill, and she didn't wait for him to knock on the door so she could be demure and proper. She went out to meet him.

He was as easy to talk to and listen to as he had been on the other occasions. As they drove over the pass toward Bozeman to the movie they had chosen to see, he told her about helping Taggart move some bulls to another pasture that afternoon, emphasizing his own lack of experience with cowboy skills and making her laugh.

But even to her ears, her laugh sounded strained. She knotted her fingers in her lap.

"Nervous?" Tom asked, slanting a smile in her direction.

"No," Jenny lied. Then, "Yes," she admitted. "I haven't done this in years. And never with anyone but my—but Mace."

"Takes some getting used to," Tom said easily. He flexed his fingers on the steering wheel. Jenny watched them with some apprehension, wondering if he would take one of them off and reach down to take her hand.

Should she let him?

Oh, Jenny, she thought, smothering an inward groan. *You are a moron. An idiot. Grow up, for heaven's sake. Holding your hand can hardly be considered "making an advance."*

All the same, she was glad when his fingers settled lightly once more against the wheel, and she felt free to breathe again.

They arrived just as the movie was going to start. And as it was an arty British film, based on one of the books he was teaching this coming fall, she imagined he'd be too engrossed in it to pay any attention to her.

Maybe he was. He laughed a lot and once or twice looked her way to see if she was enjoying it.

She tried to. It was full of witty dialogue and meaningful glances, and she knew she wouldn't have been able to drag Mace to it in a hundred years. Mostly, though, she ended up trying not to notice every time Tom's shoulder or elbow touched hers.

They were accidental touches, after all. They meant nothing. She was just being hypersensitive.

And if her shoulders felt cool, it was because she was used to going to movies with Mace. He'd have had his arm around her. He'd have pulled her as close as their separate seats would allow, and when the hero was kissing the heroine, there was a good chance that Mace, even after fourteen years of marriage, would have been stealing a kiss from her.

Jenny felt a hollow, desperate ache expand somewhere deep inside her—the same hollow, desperate ache she felt every time she let herself think about Mace. A shudder ran through her.

Warm fingers closed quite suddenly over her own. She looked over at Tom, startled.

In the light from the screen she could see him looking back at her, his mouth touched by a gentle smile—as if he knew.

Did he?

As if in answer, his fingers squeezed hers lightly. Then, leaving his hand where it was, Tom turned back to watch the film.

Jenny turned her head and tried to watch it, too. But she didn't see anything at all—only felt her fingers curved inside his.

For the first time in her life she was holding hands with a man other than Mace.

She was out on a date. And all she wanted to do was cry.

"So, what'd you think?" Tom asked her as they left the theater. His fingers were still wrapped around hers as they walked to the car, a casual, but deliberate connection.

Jenny considered breaking it, then decided not to. He wasn't overstepping any bounds. He had a right to this much. It was something she would have to get used to. If not from Tom, then from someone else.

Somehow. Someday.

"I liked it," she said with as much heartiness as she could manage. "A lot."

"They weren't as faithful to the book as I'd have liked." Tom opened the door for her and closed it after she got in, then went around and got behind the wheel. "But I suppose if they were going to be absolutely faithful, we'd have been sitting there a few more hours."

"I haven't read the book," Jenny admitted. "I'm afraid my education is pretty dismal."

"They might use it in that lit survey class you're signing up for."

He had gone with her last week down to Bozeman where she'd met with an academic advisor. She'd been reluctant, convinced that she would be biting off more than she could chew. But Tom hadn't seen it that way at all.

"Most professors love to have nontraditional students," he assured her. "They bring a lot of experience to the class, and they're serious about learning."

Jenny was serious, but she was also scared. She hadn't been in school for fifteen years. A few years back she had all but given up the idea of ever getting a college education. There seemed to be no point—and no time. Her life was taken up with Mace and her job and the ranch and—she hoped, someday a family.

She still had her job as a school aide, of course. But it was a mere shadow of the job she'd once wished to have.

And there would be no family now. There wouldn't even be Mace. He had walked out, taking her hopes and dreams with him.

So she let herself be persuaded to sign up for two courses—a survey of British literature and an introductory psychology class.

"Good choices." Tom had approved.

Back in high school, English had been her favorite class, and once she'd committed herself to doing it, this course seemed like a good place to start. The psych class was a general education requirement.

"A good thing to have if you go on for your degree," Tom said.

"I can't get a degree. That would take years," Jenny protested.

"So?"

It was a fair question. She signed up for the psych class.

It would be one requirement out of the way. It also—she hoped, though she didn't tell Tom—might give her some insight into what made Mace tick.

If they had offered a course called Introduction to the Intricacies of the Minds of Stupid Men, she would have taken that in a minute!

"I'm glad we went," she said now. "Even if it doesn't end up being on my reading list. I'm glad I saw it." She turned and gave Tom a determined smile. She wouldn't let herself think about Mace anymore tonight.

He wasn't thinking about her.

"Me, too." Tom reached over and took one of her hands in his, wrapping warm fingers around hers and giving a gentle squeeze.

Jenny squeezed back.

"Feeling better?"

Jenny nodded. "Yes."

It was almost the truth.

It was all right that Jenny went out on a date.

It was only to be expected.

That was the idea, wasn't it? Mace asked himself. She was supposed to meet someone else, *marry* someone else.

She couldn't do that if she didn't go out with him first.

All the same, the very notion drove him nuts.

What did Jenny know about dating, for heaven's sake? She hadn't dated in years! She hadn't dated anyone—*ever*—except him! Unless you counted the time she went to homecoming with Taggart.

Mace rubbed his fingers over his fist, remembering that incident.

Then he took a deep breath and told himself he wasn't about to do anything that stupid anymore. He was grown up now.

And this wasn't Taggart, who'd taken Jenny out just to rile him.

Besides, like he'd told Becky...who Jenny dated wasn't his business.

He wasn't very convincing.

Who the hell was this uncle Tom, anyway? The very sound of the name set his teeth on edge. What would a college professor want with a salt-of-the-earth woman like Jenny?

And what—besides sperm—would she see in him?

Mace wore a rut in the pine plank floorboards of the cabin before he took his fretting outside. There, without really thinking about what he was doing, he saddled Chug.

He'd ride off his frustration and his concern. It wouldn't be the first time. And he could check on the cattle down the valley while he was at it. And if he had to pass the ranch house to check on those particular cows, and it just happened to be getting close to suppertime on Saturday night, well, too damn bad.

He kept to the tree line when he came within sight of the house. The last thing he wanted was Jenny to see him and think he was checking up on her. He wasn't, damn it.

But he couldn't deny that he felt an odd sort of relief wash over him when he saw that her car was there.

He settled more easily in the saddle then, breathing deeply, glad that she'd come to her senses.

There would be time for all that dating business. Later. After the divorce was final.

Well after.

She wasn't over him yet. Was she?

His brows drew down. No, of course not. She was the one who'd run after him when he'd come down to the house and she'd had Neile there.

He'd been the one to walk out!

So maybe she got the message that he meant it.

The thought wasn't as satisfying as it ought to have been.

But she was there. Or was she?

Maybe only her car was there. Maybe Tom had come and picked her up. That was the way it was supposed to happen, wasn't it?

He wasn't exactly familiar with the ins and outs of proper dating behavior. When he and Jenny had been dating, he hadn't had a truck of his own, so they'd had to double with Taggart or Jed, or sometimes, he remembered with chagrin, Jenny had borrowed her dad's truck and had come to get him!

He edged a little closer to the house, hoping to tell if she was there or not by the way the shades were hanging. He touched his spurs lightly to his horse's sides, moving farther down.

The place was totally quiet. Door closed. Lights off.

But it wasn't really early enough for her to turn the lights on yet. She might be in the kitchen cooking.

And all she'd have to do was look out the window and she'd see him lurking there.

Quickly he urged Chug back up into the trees and headed toward the pasture. On his way back he stopped to clean out an irrigation ditch he'd just cleaned out last week. Then, because it was still a little bit light, he moseyed along the fence line. No sense in heading back to the cabin yet, he thought righteously. Not when he could get all this work done down here.

He checked fence until it was too dark to see his hand in front of his face. Then he rode back toward their house. He could, of course, have gone over the hill. It would have been closer to the cabin to take that route. But the trail was easier along the trees. No sense in putting Chug in a situation where he might stumble in the dark.

There wasn't a single light on in the house.

"Damn it," Mace muttered under his breath.

The horse, picking up on his tension, sidestepped, and he rubbed his hand along its neck.

"'S all right," he said in a low tone. "'S okay."

But it wasn't all right at all.

What the hell did Jenny think she was doing, going off and not even leaving a lamp on? Didn't she know better than to come home to a dark house?

Of course she did, unless...

Unless she didn't intend to come home that night.

Visions of his wife naked in some hotel room bed with—

Mace inhaled sharply. No! He wasn't even going to let himself think about that.

He rode all the way into the yard this time. Since she wasn't home, it didn't matter. He dismounted, then left his horse by the barn and crossed the yard to the house, clumping up the steps and rattling the door handle.

At least she'd had the brains to lock it.

They had rarely locked their doors when they were here together. But it was different for a woman alone. He was glad she wasn't taking any chances since he'd left.

He stared at the door, wondering if he ought to go in and put on a light. Or if she'd be spooked to come home and find a light that she hadn't turned on.

Serve her right if she was.

If she did come home tonight, perhaps it would spook her enough to make her leave "Uncle Tom" on the front porch—especially if she thought Mace was waiting inside.

With a grim smile, he got out his key and unlocked the door.

He put on a light in the kitchen and another small one in the living room. While he was there, he picked up the book work he had intended to get that Sunday, and then went to get the rest of his things out of the bedroom.

He crossed the room quickly, not letting himself look at the bed. He worked quickly and efficiently, gathering odds and ends, tossing them in the old duffel bag that was on the shelf. If Jenny and her date came back, he could say he'd just come to clean things out. He could brush past them without a word.

And if he just happened to knock Tom Whatever-His-Name-Was on his rear end as he was passing, well, those things happened.

There. He had everything. Tightening the drawstring on the duffel, he slung it over his shoulder and was starting toward the door when his gaze was caught by the photo on the top of the lingerie chest he'd built for Jenny three Christmases ago.

He knew what was in the photo. He didn't need to look at it. But he couldn't seem to help himself from going over and picking it up.

Faded now with age, it was an eight-inch-by-ten-inch color portrait of the two of them on their wedding day. God, they had been young. He couldn't ever remember being that young. But Jenny—Jenny didn't look like she'd changed a bit.

They had just come out of the church and were holding hands, and Jenny was smiling at him, her eyes filled with hopes and dreams, and he was grinning like he'd just won the world.

For a lot of years he really thought he'd won the world. But that was before being who he was had turned Jenny's dream to ashes. He felt as if a knife was twisting in his gut as he put the photo back on the dresser.

As he went out, he turned on the porch light. At least she wouldn't be coming home to a dark house.

He rode Chug up to the trees again. He didn't need to hang around. He was sure she wouldn't thank him for it—if she knew.

She wouldn't know.

He waited there in the dark. She was his wife—at least

for now. He was responsible for her. And if that meant waiting around to be sure she got in safely after a date, well, fine—he could do that.

He dismounted, loosened Chug's cinch and leaned against a tree to wait.

She hadn't left a light on.

Jenny was sure she hadn't left a light on. But when they came around the bend, the house was lit up like Disneyland.

What on earth?

One of her hands was clenched into a fist on her thigh. The other, wrapped loosely in Tom's, tightened slightly.

"Something wrong?"

She shook her head. "No. At least I don't think so. I...didn't remember putting on so many lights."

So who had? Mace?

Was he there? Waiting for her?

Her heart leaped and at the same moment her teeth ground together in irritation. God, it was exactly the sort of thing he would do—show up when she was out with someone else and put the lights on for her!

Did he intend to check out his successor?

"Well," Tom said cheerfully, "it's not likely to be a burglar. They usually don't go around putting on more lights."

Jenny managed a brittle laugh. "No, I'm pretty sure it's not a burglar."

"Want me to go in first and check it out for you?"

If it was a burglar, that would be fine. Not if it was Mace.

He might want only to check out Tom. On the other hand, memories of Taggart's bloody nose were all too clear.

The last thing she wanted was him punching out Tom's lights. And who knew what Mace would do these days?

She thought she knew him better than anyone. And now she was beginning to think she didn't know him at all!

"I'm sure it's fine," she said. "You don't need to check things out for me. I was probably so…flustered about our date, I just forgot."

Tom, having recognized and soothed her initial awkwardness, seemed to accept that explanation. "If you say so. But—"

"Really. It's not dangerous," Jenny said. Unless Mace was in there—and then she wouldn't guarantee she wouldn't give *him* a bloody nose! Now she gave Tom's hand a squeeze and smiled as he pulled up in front of the house.

"I had a lovely time," she said, hoping to get their goodnights said in the car. But he was already out and coming around to open the door for her. So she got out, too, and turned to say thank you there.

He took her hand and led her up onto the porch. His coat brushed her arm. She could feel his breath near her ear. He seemed closer than when their sleeves brushed during the movie. Was Mace watching from behind the window in the door?

She fumbled for her key and nearly dropped it, then gave a nervous laugh.

If he was, she swore she'd kill him.

"Here. Let me," Tom said when she couldn't seem to get the key in the lock. He took it from her and easily slipped it into the lock, turned it, then pushed open the door.

Jenny held her breath.

The room was empty.

She breathed again.

"See," she said brightly, turning to Tom who came in after her. "Not a burglar in sight." And if she said the words with uncommon loudness, just in case Mace was lurking in the bedroom, Tom would never know.

"I see," Tom said. But he didn't seem to be looking

around and noticing the absence of burglars. He seemed to only see her. He was looking at her with an expression both tender and intent.

Quickly Jenny averted her gaze, taking the key and making a fuss over putting it back into her bag. Whatever Tom wanted, whatever that look meant, she wasn't ready for it—whether or not Mace was planning to play jack-in-the-bedroom or not.

"It's really pretty late," she said. "I'd offer you a cup of coffee, but if I kept you out much longer, you might disturb the twins when you got back to Felicity's."

"And you're not ready to offer me a cup of coffee, in any case," Tom said, his voice resigned, his smile rueful.

Jenny raked fingers through her hair, then shook her head. She wasn't sure if she should be grateful or embarrassed that her discomfort was so apparent.

"You're right. I'm not," she admitted. Then she added quite honestly, "But it's not because I didn't have a good time tonight. I did."

"So did I."

"And I…just…want to remember the good time. I don't want to…to—"

"You don't want to go any further. I know," Tom said quietly. "I understand."

"Good." Jenny laughed a little nervously. "I wish I did," she muttered under her breath. She knotted her fingers together. God, she was bad at this. And thank God Mace wasn't watching her make a fool of herself. She edged Tom toward the open door.

"Did you have a good enough time to do it again?" he asked her.

She nodded. "Yes, I did. Yes."

"Then we'll do it again, shall we?"

She smiled. "Please."

"I'd like to please you, Jenny," he said. And then, before she realized what he was about to do, he closed the distance between them and pressed a light kiss against her lips.

It wasn't a possessive kiss. It wasn't at all the sort of kiss that Mace gave her. There was nothing of need or of passion or of love in it.

And yet it sealed something. It was an end...and a beginning.

Jenny gulped.

Tom stepped back and looked down at her, then trailed a finger along her cheek. "Night," he said softly.

Then he turned and went out the open door and down the steps. "I'll call you," he promised. Then, with a grin and a brief wave of his hand, he got in the car and drove away.

Jenny stood in the doorway, fingers touching her lips as she watched until the car went around the bend and out of sight. Even after she could no longer see it, she stood there—touching, feeling, fretting—in the cool stillness of the Montana night.

And then, in the silence, she heard a horse whicker in the darkness.

She heard more—the creak of saddle leather, the chink of the bit, the muffled sound of hooves on pine needles.

Her fingers curled into fists.

Damn him, he was watching!

Well, she hoped he liked what he'd seen!

"Spying, Mace?" she called softly into the darkness, knowing he could hear her as well as she'd heard him. "Show's over. Hope you enjoyed it."

Then she went inside and slammed the door.

Chapter Seven

No, thank you very much, he hadn't enjoyed it. Not one little bit.

He never minded if Taggart gave Jenny the occasional peck on the cheek or if Jed or Noah did likewise. They were his friends. He understood all about duty kisses among relatives. His brother, Shane, always enjoyed them a little too much for Mace's liking. But he tolerated it.

He had a hard time tolerating this.

Mace didn't like seeing Jenny kissed by another man. He didn't like watching a man he didn't even know bend his head and touch his lips to Jenny's as if he had every right to!

Even if he did have every right to, Mace reminded himself.

"Jenny's a free agent," he said aloud for the fiftieth time today, slamming the ax into the log he was theoretically splitting into firewood. He'd been working on it for two hours, and if he went on this way much longer, he could probably corner the world market in toothpicks.

But if a guy wasn't going to haul off and take a swing at somebody, he had to work off his aggression somehow.

Besides, in fewer months than he would like, it would be winter again. Never too late to start firewood.

"Hey." A voice behind him caused him to jerk upright.

He turned to see Jed on horseback, looking down at him.

Warily Mace picked up his shirt from where he'd tossed it over a fence post and mopped his sweaty face, then regarded Jed over the top of it. "Hey, yourself."

So Jed was talking to him now. Did that mean things were getting back to normal?

"What're you doin' up here?" Mace asked.

"Slummin'?" A corner of Jed's mouth lifted slightly, then drew down again. "What the hell you're doin' up here is a better question."

Mace rubbed the shirt over his face once more, then wiped the sweat off his chest. "Cuttin' firewood."

It wasn't the answer to the question Jed was asking, and Mace knew it. But it was all the answer he was going to get.

Jed raised one brow. "In July?"

"A guy can never have too much firewood."

"Or too many brains. Reckon you must've lost some of yours."

No, things weren't back to normal. Normal was Jed talking about the weather or their cattle or the price of feed. It wasn't a leading statement about Mace's mental health.

He turned back to his firewood. Jed ought to know better. A guy didn't stick his nose into other people's business!

He swung the ax over his head and brought it down with a solid thunk into the log. He'd been doing it so long already that muscles were quivering. He waited a second before hefting it again, hoping to hear the sound of Jed's horse moving away.

He didn't. Out of the corner of his eye, he could see its hooves. It didn't move an inch.

Gritting his teeth, Mace raised the ax and brought it down again. And again. And again. *Go on, damn it. Get!* he urged.

Jed stayed.

Finally, exhausted and furious, Mace jerked his head around. "Enjoying yourself?"

"It's educational," Jed said mildly, "watchin' you make a fool of yourself."

Mace brought the ax down with a hard thwack. "What the hell's that supposed to mean?"

Jed's shoulders lifted in a negligent shrug. "Always figured you had it together," he said conversationally. "Better'n most. Better'n me, anyway. Far back as I can remember you always knew what you wanted. This land. This ranch. To build a herd. Always went after it. Al—"

"Some things you can't have, damn it!"

Mace's sharp tone made Jed's gelding pull at the reins. Jed soothed him, but didn't flinch. Nor did he leave. He looked at Mace with brotherly concern and not a little irritation.

"Why can't she?" he asked.

Mace's mouth set in a hard line. "Don't interfere."

"Don't tell me she doesn't still love you and wouldn't be just as good a wife to you! Just because she's got the college bug—"

Mace frowned. "What college bug?"

Jed's eyes widened slightly. He got off his horse and came across the yard. "You mean, that ain't it?"

"What the hell are you talking about?"

"Jenny takin' classes down at Bozeman. English lit and

somethin' else. We thought that's what you were all het up about." Now it was Jed's turn to look confused. "It isn't?"

Mace drove the ax into the stump by the fence and jammed his hands into his pockets. He shook his head.

He should have taken advantage of Jed's misconception. He should have encouraged that mistaken notion as the reason for their divorce.

God knew, it could have been.

They'd talked about college now and then. He'd always known she wanted to be a teacher. But he'd never imagined they'd be able to afford all those years at university. And what good were two or three classes? he'd reasoned.

So, in the past, whenever she'd mentioned taking classes, he'd always asked, "What for?"

And then invariably he added, "College costs money, sweetheart. Maybe...when we've got an extra ten grand or so."

Then he would sweep her up in his arms and make love to her so she'd forget all about the big wide world out there where she might meet someone or something who'd take her away from him.

And she *had* forgotten.

Then.

Mace felt a tight heavy feeling in his chest. He sucked in a breath and felt it catch in his throat. He turned it into a cough.

"You all right?" Jed asked.

"Just breathed in a little sawdust."

"You didn't know about her takin' classes?"

Mace shrugged. "She might've mentioned it."

"But you didn't fight about that?"

"No, we didn't fight about that. Hell, Jed, what're you doing? Tryin' to hang out your shingle as a marriage counselor?"

The tan on Jed's cheeks darkened even more. He tugged

at the brim of his hat. "Course not. It's just...we been worried about you."

"I'm fine."

Jed glanced at the small cabin, then back at Mace. It didn't hold a candle to the place he'd left—the woman he'd left.

Jed let the silence speak for itself.

"I said, I'm fine. You got something you need?" Mace demanded. "If you don't, I do. I need to get back to work."

Jed scowled at him. "Brenna said to see if you wanted to come for dinner."

"So she can pick at me, too?"

Jed let out a harsh breath. "You really do have a burr up your ass, don't you? Hell, Mace, we're your friends. We grew up together! All I'm doin' is inviting you to dinner!"

"Like you and Tuck ever invited me to dinner before you got married," Mace said dryly.

Jed rubbed a hand against the back of his neck, a rueful expression on his face. "Yeah, well, didn't Madger always say I had no social skills?"

Madge Bowen, the social worker who had been in charge of deciding if Jed was a fit guardian for his nephew, had never given him very high marks in that department. Sometimes she seemed to think him totally lacking in brains, until he'd had the sense to marry Brenna.

"Thank you for the invitation. I don't think it would be a good idea," Mace said evenly now.

Jed shifted from one boot to the other, looking around at the cabin and the woodpile. "You think this is a good idea?"

"I think you've worn out your welcome," Mace said tersely, reaching for the ax again.

Jed backed up, holding his palms up and out. "No need to get violent."

Mace just cradled the ax and looked at him.

Jed shook his head. "I was only tryin' to help."

"Don't." Mace said the word through his teeth. Then he turned and began to swing the ax again. It thwacked into the log resoundingly.

Jed got back on his horse, but didn't leave. Instead he leaned against the saddle horn, watching Mace work.

Mace ignored him. Sweat trickled down his spine and dripped off the end of his nose. His arms began to tremble again. He finished chopping one piece of log, methodically stacked the wood, then began on another.

Still Jed watched. Finally he shook his head, straightened up and settled himself loosely in the saddle, ready to ride.

"Better cut a lot," he said in that slow, quiet way he had. "Reckon you're in for a long cold winter."

Jed was just the first.

Apparently since the cold shoulder hadn't shaped him up, his buddies had decided that more direct intervention was necessary.

Taggart took a different tack. He made sure that Mace knew that damn Tom Morrison was perfect for her.

Not that Mace had asked him.

It seemed to him that Taggart had taken considerable pleasure in conveying the news when they met at the welding shop in Elmer.

"You haven't been around much," Taggart said, giving Mace a cheerful smile, which was at odds with the scowl he'd fixed on his friend at the last bull-riding weekend. "You haven't even met my brother-in-law. Name's Tom. He teaches lit at some college out in Iowa. Nice guy."

Mace grunted a reply and turned to the man who was welding a crosspiece onto a gate. "If you haven't got time to do this hitch now, Loney, I can come back and pick it up."

Loney Bates, who owned Elmer's Welding, Feed and

Video Shop, pushed his safety glasses up on his forehead and scratched his nose as he regarded Mace, who was shifting from one foot to the other. "You got ants in them jeans of yours? Told ya I'd get to it next. You kin cool your heels, you know."

"Just thought I'd make it easier for you," Mace muttered. "I got things to do." And no desire at all to stand around and shoot the breeze with Taggart.

If Jed, who never said anything, had felt compelled to put in his two cents' worth, there was no telling what a guy who could recite the Gettysburg Address on the back of an eight-second bull could take it in his mind to say.

"Get a cup a coffee an' wait," Loney ordered, then dropped his glasses again and went back to work.

"Here." Taggart thrust a full mug of hot coffee into Mace's hands.

"I gotta—"

"You gotta drink this or you're gonna make Loney mad, and then you'll have to go all the way down to Livingston to get your hitch welded, the way you're already goin' down there for groceries."

Mace flushed. Did every damn person in the country know his whereabouts at every moment and the reason for it?

"Prices are cheaper," he muttered into the coffee. But he took the mug and held it with both hands against his belly like a shield.

Fat lot of good it did.

"They are," Taggart agreed. But his penetrating green eyes told Mace that the argument held no sway.

Mace clutched the mug in a death grip and felt like a B-Western movie cowboy trapped in a box canyon with sharpshooters all around. The hero always got out alive. Mace had the feeling he wasn't playing that part.

Taggart, oblivious to the melodrama going on in his

friend's head, hooked out a rickety folding chair and sat, then shoved one in Mace's direction. Mace looked at it warily.

"Sit down. I'm not going to badger you," Taggart said. "So relax."

Uh-huh.

Mace took a swallow of Loney's bitter, black coffee and waited for the assault, but Taggart had turned his attention to Loney and was watching him weld as if he was studying his competitors in a National Finals bull-riding round.

Finally Mace slumped into the chair. He didn't look Taggart's way. He didn't say a word.

"He teaches eighteenth- and nineteenth-century British lit," Taggart said, never taking his eyes off Loney. "Creative writing. Every now and then poetry."

It wasn't Loney he meant.

"I thought you weren't—"

"I'm not." Taggart's voice was hard. "I'm just telling you. So you'll know."

Mace sighed. Poetry. Swell.

"He teach Baxter Black?" The New Mexico veterinarian-turned-cowboy-poet was the only poet Mace knew.

"Likes his stuff." Taggart grinned faintly. "Doubt if he's taught it yet. Not sure they're that enlightened back in Ioway."

Mace shrugged his shoulders against the cold metal of the chair and watched the sparks fly off Loney's welding torch. "Your wife doesn't mind when you malign her home state?" he asked after a moment, easing his way into conversation carefully, as if it were a swift-moving river full of rocks and shoals.

Taggart shook his head. "I'm bigger'n her."

"But I bet she knows you're ticklish."

"Didn't take her long to find out," Taggart agreed. He

sighed, then stretched, arching his back. "Not that we have a lot of time for that sort of thing these days."

"Tell your company to go home," Mace suggested.

"It's not him. He's helping out, actually. Gives us time to breathe now and then. Takes a turn with a colicky kid. Keeps Becky out of trouble. No small task that," he added.

"Hey, don't pick on my shadow," Mace protested.

Taggart grunted. "Don't get me started on your 'shadow.' She's as contrary as they come these days. Never just does what you say. Has to discuss everything."

"She's growing up."

"You're telling me. And I hear it's going to get worse before it gets better."

"Be glad you've got her," Mace advised. He'd take her in a minute if Taggart was offering.

"I am. She just drives me crazy, that's all. But, if Becky is a handful, she's a piece of cake compared to twins." He tipped the chair back, balancing it on two legs, and scratched the back of his head, then readjusted his hat and sighed. "I reckon the workload increases geometrically every time you add a kid."

"I wouldn't know."

Mace's knuckles were white on the mug and he stared straight ahead, watching Loney work as if he was Michelangelo.

"Well, they are," Taggart continued, oblivious. "If one cries, the other cries. I don't know why it doesn't work that if one sleeps, the other sleeps. And then they spit up. And need changing. And have dirty diapers. And need changing again." He sighed mightily. "I hear things get better when they get older. But in fact, I reckon the problems just change—if Becky's any indication."

"My heart bleeds," Mace said. He gulped down the rest of his coffee and stood up.

"Wha—?"

But Mace couldn't listen any longer. He thumped the mug down on the cluttered desk and started toward the door. "I gotta go, Loney. I'll pick up the hitch on my way back. You don't know how damned lucky you are," he said over his shoulder to Taggart.

Then he banged out the door and he didn't look back.

Brenna found him at the grocery store when he came in to buy a loaf of bread. It was the one thing he'd forgotten on his trip to Livingston. He was in town for maybe five minutes Wednesday afternoon.

But there Brenna was.

"Do you know what you're doing?" she asked him in the checkout line.

"Buying a loaf of bread."

"Don't be a wise guy, Mace Nichols. You had the best woman in the world, and you're throwing her away."

Mace shut his mouth and opened his wallet. He paid for the bread and said, "I know what I'm doing," to Brenna and went on his way.

Tess got him at the dentist's. Noah tried his luck in the hardware store. Even Felicity said, "You'd better think twice, Mace."

One way or another, he figured he'd met them all now—all the people who had a stake in his past, in his marriage, in trying to rattle him, irritate him, provoke him—even unintentionally—but basically to make him change his mind.

He'd weathered them all.

He'd forgotten about Shane.

It was easy to forget about Shane. His younger brother by three years, Shane blew in and out of Mace's life like the wind. He was a professional rodeo bull rider, who rarely spent two nights in one place.

Mace would have hated his life-style. Shane loved it.

And the best part, he'd once told his older brother, was that it was just "one movable party goin' down the road."

Life was only worth living, in Shane's view, if he could be here, there and gone again. In Mace's view, only his brother's unpredictability was predictable.

So why was he surprised when a week after his encounter with Taggart in the welding shop, four days after running into Brenna at the grocery, three days after seeing Tess at the dentist and Noah at the hardware store, to have the door to the cabin burst open and Shane stand there, demanding, "What in hell do you think you're doing?"

"Mending tack," Mace said from where he sat at the table. He made no move to get up.

Another time he'd have shaken his brother's hand. He wasn't shaking hands with anybody who looked this wild-eyed.

"Mending tack," Shane spat. He said a short rude word. "Don't be an ass, Mace. I'm talking about the divorce! Divorce!" He spat that, too, and slammed the door for emphasis, then stood glaring at his brother. "What the hell are you doing, getting a divorce?"

"Who told you?"

"Who do you think?"

A barroom gossip, he'd hoped. Some nosey rumormonger Shane just happened to run into as he traveled down the road. But he knew from the hard look on Shane's face just exactly who his brother had been talking to.

"You saw Jenny."

If it had been the rumor mill, Mace could have done a little damage control, laid his own groundwork, told things his way. But there was no controlling the damage if the news had come from Jenny.

"She told me you moved out. I didn't believe it. Then she showed me the divorce papers some fancy lawyer sent and—"

"He's not a fancy lawyer. It's Anthony Hollis from Livingston. A standard, run-of-the-mill—"

"I don't care if he's F. Lee Bailey! What the hell are you doing, divorcing your wife?"

The small cabin wasn't big enough to contain Shane's intensity. He was like a self-propelled cue ball, caroming off the walls. Mace just watched him, not saying a word.

Finally Shane stopped and came to loom over him. "Answer me, damn it!"

Mace shook his head. "It's not any of your business."

"The hell it's not! I'm your brother!"

"And this is between me and my wife."

"Your *wife* doesn't act like it's her idea!"

"It's not."

"Then—"

"But it's for the best."

Shane slapped a hand against one of the cabinets, making the dishes rattle. "Whose best? Yours?" he sneered.

"Yes," Mace lied because Shane would never believe in his form of altruism. "And Jenny's." That, at least, wasn't a lie.

"She doesn't agree with you."

"Someday she will. She probably already does," he said after a moment's reflection. "She went out with somebody else, you know."

"What?"

"Felicity's brother."

"And you *let* her?"

Mace lifted his shoulders. "It's up to her."

Shane kicked a chair so hard it fell over. "You are seriously crazy, you know that? You divorce the one good thing that ever happened to you, and you act like you don't give a damn!"

Mace's jaw locked. He stared straight ahead and didn't answer.

Shane jerked the chair upright and plopped down in it. He didn't speak right away. In fact, he seemed almost to be tamping his emotions down, drawing himself together. Then, after a long moment, he rested his forearms on the table and stared across it at his brother. "Why?"

All the flame was gone from his voice now. The fire was banked, but no less intense. He fixed Mace with an intense stare, the one that demanded answers.

Resolutely Mace shook his head.

Shane made a grinding noise with his teeth.

"I don't understand why you're so upset about it," Mace said finally, not quite able to keep the edge off his voice. "I mean, it's not like you're some paragon of matrimony yourself. Hell, you haven't even come within a mile of getting engaged. You're always off running somewhere."

"That's *why* I care," Shane said. He pulled his chair closer and leaned toward Mace. "Because you an' Jenny are all the family I've got. Yeah, I run around. Just like you said, I'm always off somewhere. But when I go home, I come here." He paused, letting the words sink in. "To you. And Jenny."

"Might've known it was pure selfishness."

"Like hell it is. I want you guys to be home to me, but that's not all I want. I want what's best for you, damn it, Mace—and it isn't divorcing Jenny!"

Mace didn't answer. There wasn't anything to say.

Shane never listened, anyway. Never had. He just went off half-cocked and did what he wanted, thought what he wanted.

And he was the last person Mace could tell the real reason to. He'd spent the better part of his life trying to be an older brother that Shane could look up to—a real man.

He had a very good idea what his brother's opinion of a guy with a zero sperm count would be.

Shane just sat there staring at him. Minutes passed. Mace lowered his gaze, went back to repairing the bridle.

"You're gonna do it, aren't you?" Shane said at last. His voice was flat and fatalistic.

"That's right. I am."

"And you're never gonna tell me why."

"I'm never gonna tell you why."

"You are one cold son of a bitch."

Mace's fingers curled into fists. He forced himself not to react more than that.

Shane pushed himself up from the chair and stood staring down. Then he shook his head and walked to the door. There he turned and took one last shot.

"I looked up to you, Mace. All my life. We were different, yeah, but to tell the truth, I always thought you were better."

Mace's eyes flicked up to meet Shane's in astonishment.

Shane didn't even pause. "Someday, I hoped I could be like you," he said. "I thought if I was lucky I might find the right girl and settle down—be like my big brother."

"You never—"

"I did. But I'm sorry I did. Because frankly, Mace, now I think you're an ass."

"She went out with him again."

It was never ending.

He'd survived Shane, had thought that had to be the end of it. And now, two days later, Becky was back.

Mace fixed his eyes on the bridle he was still trying to mend, and didn't even look up.

"I know you think you don't want to hear it, but it's getting serious." Becky had turned a chair around backward and was resting her chin on her fingers as they gripped the chair back.

"You're right. I don't want to hear it," Mace said.

"They went to Livingston for lunch and to look at this new art gallery." Becky went on as if he hadn't said a word.

Mace's eyes focused on the leather. His mind didn't. He didn't want to know. Didn't. Want. To. Know.

"What art gallery?" Since when had Jenny taken up going to art galleries?

"Dunno. Some Indian art one. And tomorrow they're drivin' down to Yellowstone for the day."

Head bent, Mace pushed the awl into the leather.

"They're gonna go see Mammoth Hot Springs. And take a nature hike."

"Like we don't have nature around here?"

"That's what I said. Dad told me to mind my own business." Becky sighed. "I could go with 'em."

Mace frowned. "What? Why?"

The look she gave him said he wasn't too bright. "Because if I was there they couldn't, you know, do anything." There was a world of ten-year-old knowledge about adult behavior in those last two words.

It set Mace's carefully reined thoughts running wild.

"They aren't gonna—" His voice rose irritably, then fell. He sucked in a sharp breath. "It doesn't matter what they do."

He could say it in his sleep. It was getting to be a litany. *It doesn't matter what they do.*

"Of course it matters!"

"Not to me." He jabbed the awl through the leather and narrowly missed putting it through his own hand.

"You don't care?"

"I don't care."

"Liar, liar. Pants on fire," Becky chanted.

Mace's head jerked up, a scalding flush rising on his neck. "What?"

"You heard me," Becky said defiantly. "You do care. You just don't want to. You're a chicken."

"A chicken?" A ten-year-old girl was calling him chicken?

"Well, go ahead. Be that way." Becky got up and thumped the chair around frontward, then shoved it under the table. "See if I try to help you anymore. Sometimes I think maybe it'd be better if Jenny did marry Uncle Tom."

This time the awl did pierce his hand.

"Damn it to hell!" Mace dropped the awl and grabbed his hand to stanch the blood. "Sorry," he muttered at the sight of Becky's stricken face. For the language, he meant.

"'S all right. Daddy says worse than that when the twins start crying." She dug in her pocket and pulled out a Band-Aid. "Here."

"What'm I supposed to do with that?"

"Use it."

"I don't—"

"It's not sissy if that's what you're worried about." She thrust it in front of his nose. "Hurry up, before you bleed to death."

"I'm not gonna bleed to death." But he was sucking blood out of his hand and looking for some place to spit it.

"Spit in the sink. Then wash your hand."

"God, you're bossy." But Mace hauled himself to his feet and ran his hand under the cold water faucet.

"Use soap."

The only bar of soap, so far as he knew, was in the shower. His glance around the sink must have conveyed that notion.

Becky let out a long-suffering sigh, twisted the cap on the dishwashing liquid and squirted it on his hand. "Rub it in. Good." The last word wasn't approval; it was a command.

Mace tried, as best he could with one hand.

Becky sighed. "Here. Let me." She took his hand in hers, poked it under the water again and scrubbed it like she was sanding a floor.

"Ow!"

"Don't be a baby. You gotta get the dirt out." She cast a hard glance at the offending awl. "You don't know where that thing has been."

Mace knew exactly where it had been, but he kept his mouth shut as she gravely rinsed his hand under the faucet—hot, this time—almost hot enough to scald him. Then she towed him into the bathroom, where she got a clean towel and dried his hand with a gentleness that belied the rough scrubbing.

"Do you have any antiseptic?"

"I travel light."

She rolled her eyes. "Men," she said, disgusted. Then she took his hand and very gravely and carefully put the Band-Aid in place.

"Women," Mace said, gently teasing with the same tone of mocking disgust.

Becky's eyes flicked up to meet his, and a very elemental electric awareness arced between them.

All the years that they'd been friends—since the moment of her birth, practically—all the years he'd been aware of her crush on him, which seemed scarcely shorter than her lifetime—all the years he'd watched her grow and develop and had wished someday he'd have a daughter as wonderful—all her worrying about him and Jenny now seemed crystallized in this moment.

And the moment went on. And on.

Neither of them looked away.

Becky's eyes were awash with unshed tears. He found himself blinking back his own.

And then she surged forward, and her arms went hard

around his waist, and she hugged him so tight he thought she might squeeze the breath right out of him.

He decided it wouldn't be a bad way to go.

His own arms wrapped around her thin shoulders, hugging her, too. His lips rested atop her silky brown hair.

"Care, Mace," she urged fiercely into his shirtfront.

Anguished, he shook his head. "I can't, Beck."

"You got to." She looked up at him then, her green eyes beseeching. "Try. Please. Then it'll be all right. I know it will."

Do you? he wanted to ask. How?

He didn't ask.

He ought to have told her she was wrong. He ought to have told her nothing would make this all right. But he couldn't.

So he shut his eyes and prayed for the optimism of youth.

"Why don't you come to dinner here?" Jenny found herself saying when Tom called to ask her to go out on Saturday night.

It seemed like a good idea at the time.

She'd gone so many places with him in the past couple of weeks that she was afraid things were moving too fast.

They'd had a wonderful time at the art gallery. Other than attending Brenna's shows, she'd never really gone to one. It wasn't nearly as culturally daunting as she'd feared. And if Tom had taken the lead there, explaining things about art that she didn't know, a few days later when they went to Mammoth Hot Springs, it was her turn.

He seemed to enjoy the hot springs and the nature hike as much as she'd enjoyed the art gallery. They had things to teach each other, and on the way back to Elmer from Mammoth that afternoon, she'd said so.

And Tom had smiled over at her and said, "I have a lot of things I'd like to teach you."

Jenny might not have been on a lot of dates, but she wasn't entirely unused to innuendo.

She'd flushed scarlet, and Tom had laughed delightedly and squeezed her hand. "All in good time," he'd promised. "All in good time."

But when he called to ask her out for Saturday, Jenny didn't think that was the time for it.

"Why don't you come here?" she said.

She thought a casual dinner at the ranch house would be smarter—make them less of a couple, give them more space.

It was a mistake.

Chapter Eight

Mace was not having a good day.

"You start out with a chip on your shoulder," his mother always told him, "and it won't be long before someone knocks it off."

Mace didn't think of that at the beginning. At the beginning he simply showed up at Taggart's. It was a bronc-riding school Saturday. He'd weathered the cold shoulders of bull-riding school and then all the more active interference that his friends could throw at him.

What else could they possibly do?

It didn't take him long to find out.

He'd only been there half an hour, had just helped Jed and Tuck sort out the horses for the first round of rides while Noah was in the classroom with his students, when Taggart came out of the house with a man Mace didn't know.

Jed took a look at Taggart and the man who was accompanying him across the yard, took another look at Mace, who was just shutting the last gate, and said, "Uh-oh," under his breath.

"What? Didn't you get 'em all in?" Mace asked, glancing around for a stray horse.

But before Jed could answer, Taggart said, "Hey, come meet my brother-in-law."

The penny dropped.

Mace finished putting the chain through the clasp, then turned slowly to take his first good look at the new man in Jenny's life.

He had thought of him as "the professor." A sort of weedy, balding, goateed nearsighted jerk. And those were the kindest terms Mace had considered him in.

The guy beside Taggart was a little taller than Mace, an inch or so over six feet. Lean, not really weedy. Clean shaven, with a healthy head of straight, blond hair brushed back from his forehead. If he was nearsighted, he must wear contacts.

But as far as Mace was concerned he was still a jerk.

His jaw tightened. His gaze narrowed.

Taggart cleared his throat and gave him a steely look—one that warned him to act like a grown-up.

Mace tried.

Taggart smiled. "Tom, this is Mace Nichols whose ranch runs alongside ours. Mace, I want you to meet Felicity's brother, Tom."

Mace waited to see if Taggart would add, "The man who's dating your wife."

Taggart, occasionally the soul of tact, did not.

The two men stood assessing each other. Sounds of conversation around them rose and fell and stuttered...and stopped.

Tom stuck out his hand. "Mace. I'm pleased to meet you. I've heard a lot about you."

From my wife? Mace wanted to say.

He, too, could manage a bare minimum of tact. He gave Tom's hand a brief clasp. "Likewise."

And a damn sight more than he wanted to hear, that was for sure.

"Taggart says you've done the very nearly impossible, building a ranch up from scratch in this day and age." Tom's tone was warm and admiring.

Mace might have basked in it if he hadn't wanted to punch the guy's lights out. "I've done all right," he said grudgingly.

"You're doing very well," Taggart said.

Mace thought it sounded more like a comment on his present behavior than on his ranching ability. He shot a dark look in Taggart's direction and tugged his hat down a little tighter on his head.

He gave Tom a curt nod. "Gotta get some more horses moved."

"I'm glad to have met you," Tom said genially.

Mace grunted.

Taggart glared at him, but he ignored it and turned back to the holding pens. What was he supposed to do, say he was glad to have met Tom, too?

He wasn't that good a liar.

Obviously Tom was. He seemed to be everything that Mace was not. Civilized. Couth. Polite. Educated.

Fertile.

Mace slammed his boot against the metal of the fence. The resulting thunk was embarrassingly loud.

Taggart and Jed and Tom turned to see what had happened.

Mace felt hot blood rise in his face. He turned away, stumbling slightly to try to make it look like an accident.

Then, hauling himself up on the fence, he hollered louder than necessary at Tuck. "Open the gate and let those horses in!"

The day seemed to go downhill from there.

He stayed away from the stands during the rides. But all the while he worked, he was aware of Tom sitting at the top of the bleachers.

Halfway through the second round of rides, he was joined by Felicity, babes in arms. Tom scooped up the one who was fussing, jiggling it and bouncing it in his arms like that sort of thing came natural to him.

Probably it did, Mace thought sourly, because after a few minutes he couldn't hear its cries anymore.

So he was good with kids, too. Becky had said he was. He shot a glare in Tom Morrison's direction. Felicity saw him look that way and waved at him.

Gritting his teeth, Mace lifted a hand in return, then dropped his gaze and his hand and focused all his attention on the horses he was putting in the chutes.

Well, almost all.

Behind him, he could hear Mick Hamilton and Warren Crosser, a couple of Noah's bronc-riding students, in earnest discussion.

"Wouldn't mind goin' out with her myself," Warren said as he began to unfasten his chaps after his ride. "She's quite a filly."

"She is," Mick replied. "But you're too late. She's already got another fish to fry."

Mace wondered idly which buckle bunny was no longer available.

"Who's she goin' with?" Warren asked.

"Taggart's brother-in-law."

Mace almost slipped on the fence and bit his tongue. *Jenny?* They were talking about *Jenny?*

"Must be gettin' pretty cozy," Mick continued. "Larrabee saw 'em in Bozeman a couple of times and I hear tonight *she's* having him over for dinner."

Mace's fingers tightened on the rail at the top of the chute.

Warren made a doubtful sound. "How do you know?"

"Asked her out myself."

"I didn't even know she was gettin' a divorce until today," Warren said enviously.

"Neither did I."

Warren grinned. "Talk about fast workers."

Mick grimaced wryly. "Yeah, well, the brother-in-law was faster."

"Wish I'd known," Warren grumbled. "Had my eye on her for years. Thought she was hitched to Nichols for life." He finished unbuckling his chaps and snapped them against his leg to smack the dust out. "Just goes to show, I guess, ain't nobody in it for life anymore."

"Coulda blowed me over," Mick agreed. "If I was Nichols, I wouldn't let her get away. Hell, I'd've kept her barefoot and pregnant for years."

"Would you?" Mace's voice dripped ice as he glared down at them.

The two cowboys looked up for the first time.

"Oh, hell," Mick said under his breath. He swallowed helplessly. "Sorry, Mace, I didn't know you was—I mean, I didn't think—"

"We didn't mean nuthin' by it," Warren said nervously. "We were just talkin'."

"Were you?" Mace said pleasantly. He dropped over the fence and stood in front of them, his fingers curling into fists. "Well, I've got a suggestion for you—shut up."

There might be more space at home than there was sitting side by side in a theater or studying paintings at an art gallery and sharing a meal in a restaurant....

But somehow, Jenny discovered, it was also more intimate because it was more personal.

The ranch house living room was *her* space. Those were her books on the bookshelves. Her hand-knitted afghan on the back of the rocker. Her pictures on the wall.

Hers.

And Mace's.

Maybe that was the problem, she thought, as it seemed as if the walls of the room were closing in on her and Tom.

When she and Tom went out, Mace was there, but in the background. He was a factor—Mace always seemed to be a factor—but he wasn't everywhere they turned.

Here—in this house—he was.

His *Stockman's Journal* still sat alongside her magazines. His muffler, the one she'd knitted him for Christmas and that he wore every winter day when he went out to feed the stock, still hung on the hook beside the back door. The pictures on the mantel were not just of Jenny, but of Mace, too.

She couldn't help but see him: Mace on their wedding day, Mace on horseback, Mace bottle-feeding a newborn calf.

She turned her head and tried to pretend he wasn't there.

She tried to be casual and unconcerned, the perfect hostess, babbling a welcome, taking Tom's jacket, commenting on the weather, gulping in surprise when he proffered a bottle of wine.

She and Mace never bought wine like that, with a cork and not a cap that screwed on.

"I—I don't know if I have a c-corkscrew," she mumbled, feeling her cheeks burn.

"No problem." Tom dug a pocket knife out of his jeans and proceeded to open it with that. "You do have wineglasses?" he asked hopefully moments later.

They were on the top shelf of the cabinet over the refrigerator—and they were very dusty. More embarrassment. But she got them down, rinsed them and dried them and tried to pretend she wasn't embarrassed as she handed them to Tom.

He poured two glasses and offered her one.

She shook her head. "Not...yet. I—I don't drink while I'm cooking," she said. It was true. And tonight, of all nights, she needed a clear head if she wasn't going to burn the house down!

"You drink yours and keep me company," she said, "unless you'd rather sit in the living room and read a magazine."

Tom lounged against the refrigerator. "I'd enjoy watching you cook."

Jenny felt like a monkey in a zoo—or a butterfly pinned to a board. She wasn't used to being watched.

She started making the gravy, reciting the process in her head, hoping she wasn't forgetting anything.

Tom stood watching, talking to her while she made the gravy and tried to look like she entertained gentlemen in her kitchen all the time.

She wasn't that good an actress. But Tom, bless his heart, didn't seem to notice—or if he did, he didn't care.

He'd spent the day alternately watching Noah's bronc-riding school and reading a new biography of Henry Fielding. And he enthused about both while Jenny stirred and listened and prayed that the gravy would thicken.

It was a cream gravy for the chicken-fried steak she was keeping warm in the oven, and it had never failed to do what she expected. But there wasn't much you could count on these days, as she well knew.

So she stirred—and prayed—and tried to think of questions she might ask about Henry Fielding with what was left of her mind.

It turned out the gravy was more reliable than Mace.

Just as she was about to despair of it, the gravy began to thicken, and Jenny sighed with relief.

"Finished?" Tom asked.

"Yes."

"How about that glass of wine, then?"

She wiped damp palms down the sides of her trousers. "All right," she said, feeling more sanguine and a little braver, "why not?"

He handed the untouched glass to her. Their fingers brushed. She jerked back and the wine sloshed in the glass. Quickly she took a sip and then a swallow.

It was, even to her untested palate, a good wine, smooth and slightly musky. It warmed her and mellowed her, softening the edges of her anxiousness, making Tom's touch seem more acceptable, making the walls of the room recede a bit.

"It was amazing watching those bronc riders," Tom was saying with a smile. "I wouldn't get on a bucking horse in a hundred years."

"Well, a lot of those guys wouldn't read Fielding's biography in a thousand, so I guess you're even."

"I guess. But Taggart was telling me he had a student in his bull-riding school who plays first violin in some university orchestra."

"Scott Hunter." Jenny knew him. She set her glass down to ladle the gravy into a bowl. "Did Taggart tell you he's a pretty fair baseball player, too?"

"What is he? Montana's answer to the Renaissance man?"

She smiled. "Something like that. A lot of the guys are talented in a variety of areas."

"I met your husband this afternoon."

His words were as blunt as they were unexpected. "Ow! Drat!" Jenny dropped the platter she'd just distractedly grabbed with her bare hand. "You met Mace? At Taggart's?"

Why hadn't she considered that?

She groped for a pot holder, but Tom got it first and steered her toward the sink while he rescued the platter.

"Run your hand under cold water," he commanded. "Are you okay?"

"Yes." *Tell me about Mace.*

Tom put the rescued platter on the table, then took her hand, examining her reddened fingers for a moment. He stuck them back under the running water.

"Keep them there for a few more minutes. I don't think it's a bad burn."

"I've had worse," Jenny said. *What about Mace?*

"You still need to take care of it as soon as you do it. Heals faster that way."

"I know." *What did he say to you?* "How's Mace?"

The words came out fine, with none of the intensity and none of the desperation she felt. They sounded casual, normal.

Maybe she was a pretty fair actress after all.

"He seemed fine," Tom said equally casually. "Taggart introduced us."

Did he say, "This is Mace, the man whose wife you're dating? The one you're having dinner with tonight?"

Did Mace behave? Suddenly Jenny found herself searching Tom's face for signs of mayhem.

"He was pretty busy with the horses. Taggart said Mace used to ride broncs."

"And bulls now and then. But it was a long time ago."

"Taggart said he was good."

"He was." But he wouldn't go down the road with them. He wanted the ranch more, and he always said rodeo was too hard on marriages.

There were other things even harder, Jenny thought now.

She took her stinging hand out from beneath the faucet and dried it off.

"He told me you and Mace built up this ranch from scratch, that you built this house together." Tom looked around the small homey room appreciatively. "He said Mace felled the trees, put up the frame, made the cabinets, did the finish work. That's pretty renaissance, if you ask me."

"Mace can do a lot of things," Jenny agreed.

She wondered what Tom would think if she told him Mace had been lurking on the hillside after he'd brought her home last week. He'd better not be there tonight, she thought grimly.

"Taggart seemed to think a lot of him."

"They've been friends for a long time."

Tom smiled but didn't reply. He stood waiting while Jenny hung up the towel. Was he expecting her to say something? Did he want to know the reason Mace had left her? If he did, he was too polite to ask.

Still the silence went on for a few more seconds, as if he intended to give Jenny time in case she wanted to add anything else. When she didn't, he said, "The smell of that steak is making my mouth water. How does your hand feel?"

Jenny breathed again. "Fine." She wiggled her fingers. "Just fine. Come on. Sit down and let's eat."

It was the sideways glances that got to him.

The whispers. The hushed voices.

Were those snickers he heard?

Every time he came upon a gathering of cowboys, the conversation stopped. Every time he left, it started again. Murmurs. Mutters.

Yeah, those were snickers!

Mace felt his neck burn and his face heat. He wanted to

pound their faces into the dirt. Warren and Mick and all the rest of them.

Oh, after Mick's gaffe earlier in the day, he never caught another obvious reference to Jenny and him and Tom Morrison.

But he was no fool.

And even if he were, even a fool wouldn't mistake the sudden silences when he came near, the speculative looks and sly smiles that followed when he walked away.

"Poor Mace. Couldn't hang on to his wife. Let her get away, and she's going with a college prof now."

"Poor Mace. Stupid fool Mace." He didn't have to hear the words to know what was being said.

Damn them!

And they didn't even *know!*

What would they be saying—and snickering—if they did?

When Tom left the bleachers shortly after five, Mace was aware of it. When he came out of the house, all cleaned up, half an hour later, Mace saw him. When he got in his car and drove away, Mace almost put his fist through a fence.

"Hey, dreamer! Let's go. Move 'em up, for crying out loud!" Jed yelled at him.

Mace gritted his teeth and slapped the horse in the chute on the rump, trying to move her into the next one. "Keep your mind on business," he told her.

Which was what he ought to be telling himself.

He did the best he could for the rest of the day. He concentrated on the horses, ignored their riders, and refused to let himself think about Jenny and her intimate dinner that night.

It was almost nine by the time Noah let them go.

Mace's stomach was growling. He was dirty and sweaty

and aching, and there would be no hot, home-cooked meal waiting for him—just as there hadn't been last time.

Just as there wouldn't be for the rest of his life.

"Hey, Mace," Jed called from his truck as he and Tuck headed out. "Brenna's got lasagna in the oven. You want to come?"

His stomach growled, but Mace barely looked up. "No. Thanks." He kept on loading the tack he had promised to mend for Taggart.

When he finished, he opened the door of his truck.

"Hi."

He turned to see Becky standing at his elbow and realized it was the first time she'd been around all day. "Hey, shadow, where you been?"

"Me an' Susannah went to Bozeman with her uncle to see a movie."

"Have a good time?"

Becky's shoulders winged up and she scuffed the toe of her boot in the dirt. "Better'n stayin' around here."

Considering the day he'd had, Mace could go along with that. "What's the matter? Twin trouble again?"

"Dad trouble," Becky muttered.

Mace raised a brow. "That's a new one."

"I forgot to feed Digger. Daddy says if I don't remember to feed him, we'll have to get rid of him." There was a wavering note in her voice that sounded suspiciously close to tears.

Mace reached out a hand and touched her hair. "I don't reckon it will come to that, Beck. You're pretty responsible."

"I try to be. But sometimes I forget. *He* forgets," she said with annoyance. "*He* forgot to pick me up at Tuck's last weekend. I went down to spend the afternoon, and he was s'posed to get me before dinner, an' I ended up eating dinner there!"

A corner of Mace's mouth quirked. "Reckon I ought to suggest that if he doesn't remember you, he won't get to keep you?"

Becky considered that with rather more seriousness than he'd anticipated. "He'd prob'ly be glad to see me go," she said finally.

Mace tipped her chin up so she had to look at him. "Don't you ever say that, Rebecca Kathleen. You know he loves you more than anyone on earth."

"'Cept Felicity and Willy and Abby."

"Different than Felicity. Different than Willy and Abby. You and your old man go back a long, long way. Heck, you practically raised him while he was raisin' you. Nobody has the relationship with him that you do."

"Nobody'd want it," Becky muttered.

"Maybe not right now. But he'll come around. Give him time."

"Not if he gives away Digger!"

"He won't give away Digger," Mace promised. "If he even thought about it, I'd punch his lights out."

"You would? Really?" Becky brightened at once. The beginnings of a smile played around the corners of her mouth.

"Don't you go forgettin' to feed that dog just to test me," Mace cautioned, having seen that look before.

Becky shook her head. "I won't." She touched his sleeve lightly and looked up at him with wide, green eyes. "Thanks, Mace."

He winked at her. "Don't mention it."

They stood in silence a moment. Then Becky said, "Are you okay?"

He didn't pretend not to know what she meant.

"I'm all right," he said.

"Jenny an' Tom are—"

"I know."

"But—"

A group of rowdy bronc-riding students came out of the barn just then, laughing and talking as they headed for their trucks.

"Hey, Mace," one of them called. "You wanta go grab a couple beers with us?"

"An' a couple of babes?" another yelled.

Mace's jaw tightened. "Not tonight."

"You can eat with us," Becky said quickly.

He shook his head. "Thanks, but I gotta go on now."

"Where?"

Good question. Was he going to go back to the cabin to sulk and stew, knowing that Jenny was entertaining another man in *his* house?

Or did he plan to skulk around outside watching like he had the night Tom kissed her in the doorway?

Would Tom kiss her again tonight? Or wouldn't that be enough for him?

Would he make love to her?

"I gotta go to Bozeman."

Mace needed space and distance and anonymity.

He needed a few beers—or maybe more than a few. He needed a little whiskey. Or maybe a lot.

Chapter Nine

There was an elk on one wall, a moose on the other and a couple dozen jackasses in between.

The music was loud, the girls were pretty, and everybody wore a hat and boots, even the bartender. It was definitely the right place to come, Mace decided, settling in with a beer.

He leaned back against the bar and contemplated the crowd. It was clearly a Bozeman crowd—better heeled and younger than if he'd stayed closer to home.

There was no way he wanted to tip a glass with the likes of Warren and Mick tonight—or any of the rest of Noah's bunch at the Dew Drop back in Elmer. He'd considered dropping anchor in Livingston, but there was always the chance he'd run into somebody he knew there, too—somebody who'd take it into his head to commiserate or, worse, ask questions.

He wasn't likely to find that in Bozeman. The town had

grown so big over the past ten years it looked almost like a million tiny lights spreading out in the valley as he came over the pass. Every time he came to town he found more development—new houses, new businesses. New bars.

But Mace didn't want a new bar. A new bar would mean a horde of sandal-wearing students drinking special-label beer and playing pool and looking down their educated noses at him while the Grateful Dead improvised on the jukebox.

Mace wanted George Jones and Brooks and Dunn, a little honky-tonk music—old or new—to soothe his battered soul. He wanted the rough-and-ready, tried-and-true.

There was only one good place for that—so he parked his truck outside the Six Gun and went in.

The Six Gun had been around for years, probably since its clientele had packed 'em. It was, in a word, a cowboy bar.

Low-key during the day, with not much music at all. If there was, it'd be Patsy Cline or Jim Reeves singing an old lonesome tune, so the depressed, serious and unemployed could feel sorry for themselves while they drowned their woes in cheap beer and rotgut whiskey.

But at night, especially Friday and Saturday nights, it was a different story. Oh, the cheap beer was still available. So was the rotgut. But it wasn't quiet now. It was the hoppin'est place in town.

Cowboys and ranchers alike came in to blow off a little steam, find an old friend or two, and make the long, solitary hours spent on the range recede for a while. There was the requisite number of cowgirls, too, and a few buckle bunny hangers-on who made life interesting.

Mace reckoned his life was interesting enough at the moment. He didn't need the added complication a woman would provide, even though it'd serve Jenny right if he took one home with him.

The thought of Jenny made him tip his beer up and drain the glass, trying to drown out any notion of her. He realized pretty quickly that beer wasn't going to do it. He'd be all night if he was intent on drowning his sorrows in that.

He chased the second one with a shot of tequila.

Ah, yeah. That was more like it. It burned all the way down. The edges of his mind fuzzed a little. His toes curled. But the worst visions of Jenny in bed with Tom Morrison blurred a bit, and that was good.

He had another beer. And another shot of tequila. It helped. But not enough. He kept drinking—more than he ought to have had, but fewer than he needed to forget.

If he closed his eyes, he could still remember Jenny kissing Morrison in the doorway. And the wail of the steel guitar didn't drown out the replay of Warren and Mick's conversation.

"I'd keep her barefoot and pregnant—"

Barefoot and pregnant. Barefoot and pregnant.

Mace slammed his glass down. Damn it all, anyway!

"Nichols? Mace Nichols? Well, I'll be a son of a pot-bellied pissant! I reckoned it was you! What the devil you doin' here?" The long-forgotten, but still-familiar, twang jerked him out of his misery.

Mace turned and tried to focus on the cowboy grinning at him. "Rooster?"

The chipped tooth, broken nose and thatch of graying red hair that peeked out from beneath a battered cowboy hat proved him right.

"None other." Rooster Lynch grinned like the Cheshire cat and slapped him on the back. "Been years, ain't it? How the hell are ya?"

Mace had never known if Rooster got his name from his bright red hair, his bandy-legged gait or his quick temper. Whichever, it suited him.

He'd been a young cowpoke on the spread where Reese

Nichols had been working when Mace was a boy. He'd followed Rooster around a whole summer. In the fall, Rooster had left.

"Got himself a girl down in Cheyenne," his father had said.

Later Mace remembered hearing Rooster had married the girl.

Later still he'd met up with Rooster and discovered that the girl from Cheyenne was three girls back.

He'd been married and divorced three times by the time Mace and Jenny got married. He'd probably married three or four more since.

"Thing about marriage," he'd once told Mace over a bottle of gin, "is you can't take it serious."

Mace hadn't believed him then. Now he thought maybe Rooster had the right idea.

"Buy you a beer, Rooster?"

Rooster hoisted himself onto a bar stool. "Don't mind if you do."

The bartender slid one down in front of him, then sent another on to Mace, followed by a shot of tequila.

"I could use me one a those, too," Rooster said, eyeing the tequila. "I got woman troubles. Some of us ain't as lucky as you."

"I wouldn't say that," Mace protested.

"Me, I ain't got the stayin' power. Things get tough, ol' Rooster just up and runs." Rooster drained his beer in one swallow, then wiped his mouth on the back of his hand. "What's her name?"

Mace frowned. "Whose?"

"Your wife's! Who else?" Rooster looked at him impatiently.

"Jenny. But—"

"Ah, yeah. Jenny." Rooster's beaming grin melted into

a sweet, sad smile. "I had me a wife named Jenny once. You ever meet her?"

Mace shook his head slowly. "Don't believe I ever did."

"You'd a liked her. Pretty li'l redhead, she was." Rooster's face screwed up in concentration. "Leastways, I think she was a redhead. Maybe not. Maybe she was the blonde and Evie was the redhead. I disremember now."

Mace had a lot he wished he could "disremember." He supposed he should have said he was getting a divorce, too, but somehow his didn't seem at all comparable to Rooster's.

"Met her in Vegas," Rooster mused, then frowned. "I think." He stared into the tequila glass, then tipped the shot glass and gulped. His eyes shut tight, and he let out something close to a death rattle, then sucked in a deep breath. "But she ain't my problem tonight. Tonight my problem's Fifi."

And he started in on Fifi.

Mace let it all wash over him—the French cancan dancer named Fifi that Rooster had met and married in Reno three months ago, his ill-fated decision to take her up to the line camp with him for the summer, the startling revelation that Fifi wasn't thrilled to find herself spending months at a time in the middle of several hundred thousand acres of Nevada wilderness with Rooster and a herd of cows.

It didn't require any more than the occasional nod or grunt. Rooster could handle a conversation or a herd of cows all by himself, with equal capability and assurance. And if he fretted about one or yammered on about the other, it was more to hear himself tell a good story than because it really bothered him.

Tom Morrison in Jenny's bed really bothered Mace.

It bothered him so much that the more he thought about it, the more upset he got.

It was all well and good for Rooster to say you shouldn't

take marriage seriously, but hell, when you'd been married to the same woman for fourteen years, when you'd been completely faithful to her for longer than that, when, in fact, she was the only woman you'd ever made love with in your life, it did not sit well to think of her having another man in her bed.

In *your* bed.

Mace gulped his last shot of tequila and thumped the glass on the bar. "Damn it!"

Rooster stopped, mid-sentence, and looked sideways at him. "T'ain't that bad. She wasn't that great, I don't reckon."

"She was—*is*—the best damned woman in the world!"

Rooster's brow drew down. "How do you know?"

"I was married to her, damn it!"

Rooster choked, then burst out laughing.

"What the hell's so funny?" Mace demanded, furious.

"You ain't been listenin' to a thing I said, have you?" Rooster was still grinning his fool head off.

Mace's fists clenched on the bar. "I got things on my mind."

"No joke," Rooster said mildly. He considered Mace. "Your lady givin' you a few problems, too, is she?"

"No." Mace bit off the word.

"Pull my other leg while yer at it. That's why yer here, ain't it? In the bar? Drinkin'? Wondered when I saw ya. You wasn't ever much of a bar hopper as I recall."

"A man can change," Mace said through his teeth.

"No. He can't." Rooster seemed certain about that. "A man is what he is. Ain't nothin' gonna change him. B'lieve me, I know. Wasn't one a my wives didn't try to set ol' Rooster on the straight an' narrow, but it didn't work. I'm here, ain't I?" he said with a thump on his chest. "No, sir," he continued without giving Mace a chance to reply, "a man don't change his spots no more'n a leopard does."

He bent closer and poked his face close to Mace's. "You, fer instance."

Mace kept staring into his glass. "What about me?"

"You still love her."

It wasn't a question, so Mace didn't answer.

It didn't need an answer in any case. Rooster would believe whatever Rooster wanted to believe. And there was no arguing.

There was just hurt and loss and—suddenly—a burning, boiling over anger.

Mace dug in his wallet and threw down some bills and started pushing his way past inebriated cowboys and giggling girls toward the door.

"Hey! Mace! Hey! Where ya goin'?"

Mace didn't answer. He didn't stop. The anger that had been simmering inside him since the day he'd got the doctor's test results boiled over at last.

Damn it all, yes, he still loved her! With everything in him, he loved her! Always had, always would.

And tonight another man had her!

"Mace! Wait up." Rooster hastily gulped the remains of his beer, tossed down the shot, shuddered and scrambled through the crowd after him.

Mace still didn't stop. "I need some air."

Rooster caught up at the door and pushed it open. Out on the sidewalk, with the noise and heat behind them, he regarded Mace with a sort of foggy concern. "Well, here now. Ya got air. Breathe."

Mace breathed. He shook his head. It didn't do any good. It didn't cool him at all. He started to walk.

Rooster, torn, stood watching him, then hurried to catch up. "You're antsier than a polecat with chiggers tonight! You an' your lady have a fight or somethin'?"

"We didn't have a fight."

"Somethin's sure biting your butt."

"'M all right."

"Sure y'are."

Mace walked. Rooster almost ran to keep up. Up one street and down the other, fast and furious.

"You know where you're goin'?" Rooster asked, panting now.

"No. Don't know. Don't care."

"Why you walkin' so damn fast then?" Rooster panted.

"You don't have to come along."

"Reckon I do," Rooster said, loping beside him. "Your daddy wouldn't thank me if I let you get throwed in jail."

"I'm not gettin' thrown in jail."

Rooster looked at him with eyes of long experience. "Yet."

Mace didn't know how far they walked. He didn't even know where they walked.

If he was back at Taggart's he'd take on the roughest bull on the place. He needed something—anything—some sort of outlet for the cauldron seething inside him. He just didn't know what—

And then he saw Sherpa's.

One look at the bar, with its pseudo-rustic log exterior, its massive stone fireplace and beveled, leaded glass windows, and the sign by the door urging Paddle Your Own Canoe set Mace's teeth on edge. If the Six Gun was at one end of the Bozeman bar spectrum, Sherpa's was at the other.

As he stood staring, a tall blond man with a goatee held the door open for a lady. She smiled at him, batted her lashes, touched his arm. The tall guy grinned. He stroked his beard. He curled his toes.

Mace's gaze stopped right there. *Curled his toes?* By God, yes, he actually did. And Mace could see him doing it, because he was wearing a pair of damned sandals!

He stalked straight in after them.

"Hey! Mace, what in holy hell d'you think you're doin'?" Rooster stared after him, aghast. "We don't b'long in there."

Mace didn't even slow down. He had reached the edge. Sherpa's was where he jumped.

While no one had given him a second glance at the Six Gun, plenty of heads turned when he stopped inside Sherpa's heavy, wooden door. The room, though not nearly as noisy as the Six Gun, seemed to quiet further as the patrons looked him over from the top of his straw cowboy hat to his shiny Cody Rodeo bronc-riding buckle, down the length of his dusty Wranglers, to the toes of his well-worn boots.

No one said a word.

"What'sa matter?" he said loudly. "None of you ever seen a cowboy before?"

Rooster sidled up next to him. "This ain't a good idea," he said under his breath.

"It's a fine idea," Mace said loudly, not even glancing his way. His eyes locked on the blond goatee's gaze and never wavered. "Best idea I've had all night."

"Sir?" A nervous voice addressed him.

Mace wasn't even sure where it came from until the men at the bar parted a bit, and he saw the bartender eyeing him warily. "What?"

The bartender gave him a thin smile. "I think perhaps you've had enough."

"Enough? I haven't had any yet. I just got here."

"It appears that you had plenty before you got here," the bartender said in polite, but firm, tones.

"Not enough," Mace muttered under his breath.

"C'mon, then, an' I'll buy ya another," Rooster said, latching on to that idea with the same enthusiasm that he grabbed Mace's arm and tried to tow him toward the door.

Mace dug in his heels. "Buy me one here."

"Mace," Rooster protested in a low voice. "You don't wanta drink here."

"Why not?" Mace said. He advanced on the blond man with the goatee who sat on a bar stool with his arm around the woman he'd opened the door for.

"You think I don't belong here?" Mace said to him.

"I think you have a perfect right to drink in any bar you want to," the goatee replied smoothly and shared a conspiratorial smile with the woman.

Mace saw red. "Damn nice of you. Very liberal. But then, you university types are like that, aren't you?"

"We try," the goatee said. "Now, if you'll excuse me, you're interrupting my conversation." He gave Mace a dismissive nod and turned back to the woman. The bartender brought them each a fancy, private-label beer.

Mace's teeth went on edge. "Draft beer not good enough for you?"

"Mace," Rooster pleaded, hanging on his arm.

The goatee took a long swallow, then stood up and faced Mace squarely. "You know, fella, I don't know what your problem is, but I think the bartender was right. You have had enough."

The problem, Mace could have told him, was that he didn't have *any* of what really mattered! But he was beyond talk now, beyond reason.

In what was left of his rational mind, he knew the goatee had nothing to do with any of it.

His fight was with Tom Morrison, God and, above all, himself.

But Tom Morrison was home in bed with Jenny, God wasn't into bar fights, and Mace had done enough harm to himself.

All he wanted now was one thing he knew he could accomplish—to wipe that smug smile off this man's face, pound him into the ground and mop the floor up with him.

"Don't tell me what I've got," he said, and his fist came up, and his arm swung round as he aimed directly at the goatee's astonished face.

He put all of his force into that swing.

And ended up flat on his butt!

His head rang. His ears buzzed. He felt like a herd of buffalo had flattened him.

"Wha—?" It was all he could say with the breath he had in him.

The goatee stood over him, shaking his head.

"*Ippon-seoi-nage,*" the goatee explained, as if he'd just given a demonstration. "The one-arm shoulder throw. Judo." Then he reached down and hauled Mace, still gasping, unceremoniously to his feet.

"I called the cops," the bartender said.

"No!" Rooster yelped. "Don't do that! He didn't mean nothin'! He just had a little too much—"

"Way too much," the goatee said. He reached down once more and snagged something off the ground and handed it to Mace, who was still trying to catch a breath.

It was his hat. The crown was folded, the brim bent. But no worse than his pride.

"Let's go," Rooster pleaded. "Lemme get him outa here," he said to the bartender. "C'mon!" He snagged Mace's belt loop and began tugging him to the door. "He ain't always like this," he apologized to the crowd as they went. "Just had a hard day. Got kicked in the head.

"An' I'm gonna kick ya somewheres else, ya don't get a move on!" he added under his breath to Mace, propelling him toward the door. "He won't give you no more trouble," he called over his shoulder.

Then he shoved Mace out the door, dragged him down the street and pushed him up against a wall. "What in the name of Debby Deever's dirty drawers has got into you?"

"It ain't like you never got in a bar fight," Mace mumbled, holding his head and wincing. He could almost talk. His brain felt like mush.

"At least *I* ain't never lost one," Rooster retorted.

"He didn't fight fair!"

Rooster sniffed. "Huh." He grabbed Mace by the arm again and hauled him around the corner and down another street like a mother with a grip on a badly behaved child.

"What the hell are you doing?"

"Gettin' outa here. You said you weren't goin' to jail, remember? Well, if you're still here when they show up, you're gonna be tellin' that to the cops."

Mace, mortified from the top of his head to the toes of his boots, let himself be dragged.

His ears rang, his stomach whirled, and his butt still stung from the swift unexpected smack on the hardwood floor.

What the hell—?

Judo, the goatee had said. *Judo?* Who the hell used judo in a bar fight?

"I coulda took 'im if he'd fought like a man," he mumbled.

"Uh-huh." Rooster steered him into the parking lot outside an all-night gas-station-convenience-store and pushed him down on the curb. "Sit there."

Mace sat. He watched glumly, head in hands, as Rooster disappeared into the store.

What the hell was he going into a store for?

Minutes later Rooster returned with a giant paper cup of coffee which he shoved into Mace's hands. "Drink this. It'll make you sober."

Mace didn't know that he wanted to be sober.

Not now.

Maybe not ever.

Rooster hunkered down next to him and stuck his face in Mace's. "Drink. You're gonna be sorry if you don't."

Mace gave him a baleful look. "Why? You gonna beat me up?"

Rooster shook his head slowly. "Not me."

They got through dinner fine. The gravy was creamy and thick. The steak was tender and done to perfection. The mashed potatoes were smooth, the string beans were fresh, and the green chili corn bread Jenny had made at the last minute, more to absorb some of her nervousness than because they needed more food, had Tom coming back for thirds.

She was delighted.

The longer they spent at the table, the less time they'd have to fill after.

What did you do with a man you invited over to your house for supper after you'd finished eating?

She wished she'd thought of that before. Only one thing seemed to be racketing around her brain at the moment: *go to bed with him.*

Of course that wasn't the only thing you could do with him, but it was the first thing she thought of.

The most petrifying thing she could possibly think of!

What if Tom expected *her* for dessert?

Of course he wouldn't. But just as surely, she knew she wasn't sure of anything.

She didn't know anything about dating. Except about dating Mace whom she'd known and loved forever—whom she *would* have gone to bed with after a dinner she'd cooked for him.

Only she'd never had the chance. She'd lived at home with her parents until she and Mace were married. Her father would have shot him before he would ever have let Mace have Jenny for dessert!

But times had changed.

Everything seemed to have changed but Jenny.

I'm a dinosaur, she thought as she watched Tom polish off the last of the mashed potatoes and his third helping of beans.

"Have some more corn bread?" she said, holding out the plate.

He sat back in his chair and rubbed his stomach ruefully. "I couldn't eat another bite of anything."

Did that mean she was safe?

She set the plate down reluctantly. Tom smiled at her. It was a warm, comfortable smile. It was also an intimate smile—the smile of a man looking forward to more than going home tonight.

Hastily Jenny got to her feet and began to clear the table.

"I'll help you," Tom said. "We'll get done faster."

"Oh, I don't need any help. I can do it easier by myself."

"Nonsense," Tom said with a smile. "What would I do if I didn't help?"

Read the paper? Watch television? *Go home?*

Did she really want him to go home?

What she really wanted was to take things easy, to go slow. Very slow. This was all new to her. Way too new.

And still she wanted Mace.

It was insane, she supposed. After he had walked all over her feelings, after he had walked right out of her life—still she couldn't put him out of her mind, couldn't stop wishing it was Mace who had offered to help with the dishes, Mace who, afterward, would take her to bed.

She wasn't letting Tom Morrison take her to bed.

He was a very nice man. He might even make a good husband. Someday. But it was too early to even think about things like that.

Oblivious to all the furor in her head while she washed the dishes, Tom wiped the plates and silverware and talked about everything from the weather to the nature hike they'd been on in Yellowstone to the letter he'd got from his daughter.

"How is your daughter?" Jenny practically pounced on this topic of conversation.

Tom's eyes always softened when he talked about Katie. It was easy to see how much he missed her.

"She's fine. She sent me a picture from when we went out for her birthday." He reached for his jacket on the hook by the door as he spoke, then took out a snapshot and handed it to her. It was a lovely picture of father and daughter sitting side by side on the grass of a park, looking at each other and laughing.

There was, between them, the sort of rapport Jenny had often seen between Taggart and Becky. It was the sort of rapport she'd always thought Mace would share with a daughter. He shared some of that with Becky, she knew, but Becky had Taggart, so it wasn't the same.

Her finger brushed lightly over the photo. "She looks so happy," she said. "You both do."

He nodded, his expression wistful. "It seems like ages since I've seen her. She's probably grown a foot."

"It won't be long before you'll get to see her again."

"I know. But it won't be the same." His ex-wife had recently remarried. There was a stepfather in the picture now.

"Things change," Jenny agreed softly. She set the photo down on the counter and went back to washing the dishes.

Working together, they finished the dishes quickly, just as she'd feared.

"I'll make coffee," she said. "And I think there's a good movie on. Mel Gibson, I think. Why don't you try to get it on the TV while I do this?"

For a moment she thought he might see through her and object, but then he nodded. "I'll do that."

When she brought the coffee out, Tom had the movie

on. He patted the couch beside him, and carefully, leaving a few inches between them, Jenny sat down. He slid his arm behind her as they watched. Or rather *she* watched.

All the while she watched the movie, she was aware of Tom—watching her.

She leaned forward, concentrating on the movie. He shifted his weight toward her.

The couch dipped. Jenny tipped. Tom's arm slipped around her.

She stiffened.

"Relax," he said softly. "I don't bite."

Jenny gave a small nod. She drew a steadying breath. *Relax,* she echoed in her mind. *Relax.*

Oddly, as the minutes passed and Tom made no more moves, she began to do just that.

It felt comforting somehow to have his arm around her shoulders. She liked Tom. He was solid, dependable. There.

Unlike some people she could mention.

He wasn't pressuring her, either. Not really. The pressure was in her head, not in his.

Cautiously she slanted a smile his way. He returned it. They turned their attention back to Mel Gibson. Jenny found herself sagging against him a little, settling in.

"Sorry," she muttered, straightening up.

"Don't," Tom said softly and drew her back against him, snugging one of her hands inside his. They remained that way until the end of the movie.

It was late, Jenny thought. Time for him to go home.

She started to get up. Tom held her where she was. He turned her in his arms and touched her cheek with one finger.

"Are you still afraid of me?" he asked softly.

"Of course not."

Tom shook his head. "Don't lie. I won't do anything you don't want me to do. Okay?"

"Okay," she whispered.

"I want to kiss you," he said. "How do you feel about that?"

She smiled. "Nervous."

"Why? What do you think is going to happen?"

You'll take me to bed. But as she thought it, she knew it wasn't the truth. Tom wouldn't take her to bed unless she wanted him to.

"May I kiss you?"

She stared at him wordlessly, her lips parted.

"Yes or no?" he said softly. His mouth was bare inches from hers. She could look at it or at his eyes, not both.

She swallowed. "Yes," she said in a tiny voice. "I guess."

A smile crooked the corner of his mouth. And then she couldn't see his lips any longer. They were touching hers.

It was a kiss that began very much like the first one he had given her. It was gentle, nondemanding. Not threatening at all. A match flame. Not a forest fire.

But he didn't let the flame go out. He eased her closer, wrapped his arms around her, drew her into his embrace. His tongue flicked out to taste the lips he was kissing. The moist warmth of his mouth made Jenny's heart beat faster, made her head begin to spin. She opened her mouth under his and felt his immediate response. The kiss deepened. Tom's hands moved over her shirt, easing open the buttons. And Jenny felt...

What did she feel?

Before she could figure it out, the telephone rang.

She jumped. Her face was hot, her hair disheveled, her shirt half-undone. Hastily she scrambled up. "I'll get it."

She ran from the room like the devil was on her tail. How could she have let things go that far?

She snatched up the receiver. "Hello?" She paused, then frowned, buttoning her shirt as she spoke. "Rooster? Oh,

Rooster! Of course I remember you. I'm sorry, but Mace isn't here. He—''

She listened, her hand stopped buttoning. Her fingers tightened on the phone. Her eyes got wide, and her jaw dropped open.

''He *what?*''

She didn't believe it. So he repeated it again, word for word.

''I'll be right there,'' she promised and hung up.

She turned to see Tom standing in the doorway. ''Something wrong?''

''Yes. No. I'm sorry. I have to go.''

''Is it Mace?''

Jenny finished buttoning her shirt, then stuffed it in her slacks. She hesitated, then shrugged. He'd hear about it later, anyway. ''Yes.''

Tom's brow furrowed. ''Is he hurt?''

Jenny grabbed her car keys and headed out the door. ''Not yet.''

Chapter Ten

"**W**hat the hell?"

If three cups of black coffee, a north wind off the Bridgers and a sermon from Rooster on the evils of taking on judo experts didn't sober Mace up, the sight of the tan Ford pulling into the parking lot sure did.

"*Jenny?*"

Mace felt like he'd swallowed the plastic cup. He tried to lurch to his feet, stumbled and fell back down again. He stared wildly at Rooster.

Rooster shrugged. "I called her."

The coffee that was already battling the booze in his stomach threatened to make an unscheduled and unwanted reappearance. "You called *Jenny?*"

You got her out of bed with Tom Morrison? Mace didn't know whether to cheer or cry.

"I know ya prob'ly been fightin' with her," Rooster continued, oblivious, defending his action. "Couldn't see no other reason for you actin' like a jackass," he added bluntly. "But she's your wife, bud. Has been for years—" he shook his head in astonishment "—who else was I supposed to call?"

Mace folded his arms across his knees and buried his face in his sleeve. "Anybody," he muttered.

He heard the slam of the car door, then her footsteps on the pavement, coming toward them. He didn't move, didn't look up.

The footsteps stopped. "Rooster?"

"Yes'm. Rooster Lynch. Sure didn't wanna have ta call ya, ma'am, but the way he was actin'…well, when that ol' bartender called the cops, an' I reckoned he'd end up in the hoosegow 'fore long. Whooo-eee! You shoulda seen 'im. Walked right up to some per-fesser type an' took a swing. Too bad he picked the wrong one!" Rooster cackled cheerfully.

"Rooster!" Mace protested, agonized.

He looked up long enough to see Jenny looking down at him as if he were something better left under a rock.

"You're damn lucky I got ya outa there," Rooster said flatly, ignoring his protest. "That wasn't the Six Gun, y'know. A feller's only gotta look t' see they don't cotton t' bar fights in places like that 'un."

"Really?" Jenny said. "This wasn't your normal hangout then?" she said to Mace in an almost conversational tone.

He wasn't deceived, and he knew better than to tackle that one.

Rooster didn't. "Oh, no, ma'am. We started out at th'Six Gun, all right. Mace was pretty well tanked 'fore I got there, and—"

"Damn it, Rooster!"

"You was about six drinks down the trail to perdition," Rooster said firmly. "An' I reckon he'd a good half dozen to go," he added for Jenny's benefit. "T'ain't like ol' Mace, but well, I reckon sometimes even a feller like him gets woman troubles."

"Woman troubles?" Jenny echoed faintly.

"I don't—" Mace began.

"Had 'em myself often enough," Rooster confided. "Reckon ain't nobody immune. So I just thought I'd keep 'im company, like. Drink with 'im. Walk with 'im. I'd a prob'ly fought with 'im if he'd a picked a better place to do it. But, well, at least I got him outa there. It's what friends are for," he added modestly.

"You did the right thing," Jenny said.

Rooster's self-congratulation had gone on long enough. And the hole he was digging Mace into was getting deeper and deeper. Mustering all his strength, Mace gave one more shove. This time he made it to his feet and stood with his legs spread, the better not to tip over, and met Jenny's disdainful gaze.

"You didn't have to come," he told her.

She turned back to Rooster, holding out her hand. "Thank you for calling me."

"My pleasure, ma'am. I mean, under the circumstances it wasn't exac'ly a pleasure, but, well...I reckon you understand." Rooster gave Jenny's hand an awkward shake and then doffed his hat. The tips of his ears were pink.

Jenny gave him one of her gentle smiles—the sort that Mace knew she wasn't going to bestow on him. "I know what you mean."

They stood for a moment just smiling at each other.

Mace gritted his teeth.

Then Rooster set his hat on his head again, tugged it down and took a step back. "I'll just be on my way then. Let you get goin'. You'll wanta take care of Mace."

Jenny turned back to Mace. Their eyes met. "Oh, yes," she said ominously. "I'll take care of Mace."

* * *

It didn't do any good to try to talk to her, Mace thought glumly as the car hurtled through the darkness heading back toward Elmer, with Jenny at the wheel, staring straight ahead.

God knew he'd tried.

As soon as Rooster left, he stood weaving in the parking lot and said, "I didn't know he called you."

"I'll bet you didn't."

"You didn't need to come."

"I'm glad to hear it."

"You can go home again. I'm fine."

She didn't even deign to answer that. She just took his arm and bullied him toward the car.

He dug in his heels. "I got my truck."

"Like they're going to let you drive it in your condition."

She didn't stop moving, just kept towing him along. He didn't have enough purchase on the asphalt to make a stand.

"Take me back to my truck then, if you're so all-fired determined to take me somewhere. I can sleep in the cab."

"You can shut up, Mace. That'd be wisest," she said with a sweetness that belied her grip on his arm. She jerked open the door of the car.

He teetered.

Jenny gave him a shove.

He toppled in.

She didn't take him back to his truck. She ignored his arguments, his directions, his threat to jump out in the middle of Main Street. She kept her eyes on the road and got back on the interstate, heading east.

Defeated, Mace slumped in the seat beside her.

They drove over the pass, then took the county highway north. The night was black. His mood was blacker. Jenny turned off the highway onto the asphalt. The road grew narrower, bumpier. It twisted and curved.

The three cups of coffee Rooster had poured into him began to have an effect. It wasn't the desired one. The truce it had reached with the tequila and beer back in the parking lot was being renegotiated.

He shut his eyes and clenched his teeth.

It was beginning to feel like the truce had been called off.

"Stop the car."

Jenny flicked a glance in his direction. "I will not. If you think for one minute I'm going to let you jump out here and head back up to hide in the woods after I've driven all the way down—"

"*Stop the damn car!*" He was fumbling the door handle open even as he spoke.

Jenny stopped with a screech.

Mace flung himself out just in time to be sick all over his boots and the side of the road.

He retched and retched and retched. Tequila, beer and coffee. Not a good combination at the best of times. But now...he groaned and retched some more. It didn't bear thinking about.

Finally he sank back against the car tire and shut his eyes. His stomach still clenched spasmodically. He held his head and sucked desperately at the cool night air and felt the breaths come shuddering through him.

A hand touched his forehead, tipped his hat back, brushed against his clammy skin. "Here." She wiped his face with a clean handkerchief. It was cool and dry and smelled like Jenny. He wanted to cry.

"Are you all right?"

He swallowed. "Swell."

He heard her sigh. He opened his eyes just far enough

to see her as she knelt beside him, still stroking his face, brushing his hair away from his forehead.

"Oh, Mace," she whispered.

He heard despair and dismay and a hundred other painful emotions in her voice.

Emotions he'd put there. Emotions he couldn't deal with. Not in her, not in himself.

"Don't," he pleaded. All his strength was gone. All his reserves depleted.

He couldn't fight her now. He shut his eyes.

"Please. Just take me home."

She took him home.

To *their* home.

"No," he said, when the car stopped and he opened his eyes again to realize that they were parked next to their ranch house. "Not here. I didn't mean here," he said desperately.

"Home, you said."

"I meant—"

"This is home." She got out, ignoring his protests, and went around to open the passenger door. She stood there, waiting.

"Jenny," he protested.

She reached in and took hold of his arm. "You're home, Mace. Come on."

He looked like hell.

She'd thought that the moment she'd seen him sitting there on the curb, hunched over, his hands dangling between his knees, his head bent, while Rooster hovered around, flapping and clucking and almost pathetically relieved when she showed up and he could turn the responsibility over to her.

Not that Mace wanted it turned over to her. That was abundantly clear.

Well, she hadn't been having very many kind thoughts about him lately, either. And she'd thought of a thousand pithy things to say to him on the way to Bozeman.

She hadn't needed to.

Rooster and the judo expert Mace had picked to tangle with—God forgive her, how she would have liked to have seen him flip Mace on his butt!—and Mace's own body had said it all.

Now, as she stood in their bedroom and stared at him, sound asleep on his stomach on their bed, one bare arm flung up, one jean-clad leg bent, she felt a stirring of sympathy for him.

Mace's head was turned toward her, so she could see the rough, black stubble on his face that told her he hadn't shaved in a day or two. A day or two's beard always gave him a certain attractively roguish look. But tonight, beneath the whiskers, she thought his skin looked sallow, his cheeks sunken.

There were dark circles under his eyes. And even now, in sleep, his brows were knitted and drawn down as if he was in pain.

She knew how he felt.

They were both in pain; they had been for a very long time.

She stepped closer to watch the steady rise and fall of his back. There was a bruise across his ribs, and she wondered how he had got it. If he'd been home, she would have known. She would have touched it and soothed it, and at night when she put her arms around him, she would have kissed it to make it better.

Tonight he had sent her out of the room while he got undressed.

"I can manage," he'd said gruffly, turning his back on her when he'd finally made it.

Jenny had started to unbutton his dusty shirt, but he had shrugged away from her. "I said, I'll do it."

So she had left him alone.

He'd gone into the bathroom. She'd gone to the kitchen where she ran hot water to do the cups she'd left from coffee with Tom.

It seemed like a thousand years ago—Tom and the dinner and the wine and the movie, Tom kissing her, her wondering if Tom expected to take her to bed.

It didn't matter what he'd expected, she thought wryly. Neither of them had expected this.

And now, with Mace sound asleep on the bed, apparently, despite his claims, *not* able to manage, because he was still wearing dirty jeans and socks—one with a hole in it—what was she going to do?

It was the middle of the night. There was only one thing to do: go to bed.

She got her nightgown off the hook on the bathroom door and slipped it on. She brushed her teeth and washed her face, scrubbing it well, because she could still catch a hint of the perfume she'd put on for Tom all those hours ago.

Then with one last look at Mace, she shut off the light and went into the spare bedroom.

The children's bedroom.

She lay down in the bed. But even though she was exhausted, she couldn't sleep. In the moonlight she could see the cowboy-and-Indian-border wallpaper they'd hung.

"So Becky will feel at home when she comes over. So Tuck can stay if he wants," she'd rationalized when they were doing the room.

"For our kids," Mace had said, cutting to the chase.

She remembered that afternoon as clearly as if it had happened yesterday. It was as if the ghosts of who they were—the happy, dreaming ghosts of an earlier Mace and Jenny—were there to play it out for her.

They were arguing about, of all things, the color of the curtains.

"Blue," Mace had said. "For our half dozen boys."

"Pink," Jenny had countered. "For our half dozen girls."

"A half a dozen hussies like you?" he'd teased, putting his arms around her and starting to tickle her. "How will I ever defend them from lecherous men?"

"Like you?" she'd said as he nuzzled her under the ear and nibbled her neck.

"We're doomed," he'd murmured as she pulled out his shirttails and tickled his ribs.

And then they'd loved each other—right there in the spare room.

"Maybe," Mace had said in the aftermath of their lovemaking, as he held her in his arms and kissed her tenderly, "we can tell our son he was conceived in this bed."

Jenny got out of bed. She could not sleep here.

Not tonight.

She started toward the couch in the living room. She never got there. A noise from the bedroom stopped her.

Mace was muttering in his sleep. Hurt, angry sounds. Painful sounds.

She peeked in. Mace had wrestled with one of the pillows, and now had his face pressed into it, while he clutched it against his chest.

He muttered again, and she moved closer to see if he was awake.

His eyes were closed. The hand that wasn't clutching the pillow dangled over the side of the bed. His knuckles were scraped.

From his swing at the judo expert?

Probably. Mace had cowboy's hands—rough and callused, hardened by years of manual labor and bad weather. Sometimes their roughness embarrassed him.

"I shouldn't be touching you," he'd say when they lay together naked and touching. "You're so soft. I could hurt you, scratch you."

Then she would take his fingers one by one and kiss them. "You could never hurt me," she'd told him.

He never had—with his hands.

She reached down and touched them now. Instinctively his fingers curved around hers, and so surprised was she that she looked once more to see if he was awake.

Of course he wasn't.

If he had been, the last thing he would have done was touch her. On the contrary, he'd have yanked his fingers away at once.

In sleep he held on.

His muttering stopped. His breathing evened. When she started to pull away, he frowned.

"Ah, Mace."

It was a plea, but if she'd been forced to, Jenny didn't know if she could have said what she was pleading for— that he let go, that he hang on?

She ran her thumb lightly over his abraded knuckles, then knelt beside him and touched her lips to them. He turned his head toward her, and a slow, soft sigh escaped his lips.

Jenny lifted her head and turned to study him.

She had thought she knew Mace inside and out. She'd thought she had seen him every way there was—but there was a new raggedness in his features now.

It wasn't just the shaggier hair, the shadows in his cheeks, the bruise on his ribs and fresh cuts on his hands.

He looked older. Leaner. More tired. He looked like Mace. And yet—not Mace.

He was both her husband and a stranger. A man she

thought she knew as well as she knew herself, and even after all these years maybe, didn't really know at all.

That was what her mind told her.

But her heart? Ah, her heart was a different story.

She brushed a lock of hair off his forehead. He stirred, half smiled.

Jenny swallowed. She couldn't face that smile.

And yet she couldn't look away, either. So much of her life had been spent in this man's arms, in this man's bed, she wondered how a few hours ago, she could have contemplated sleeping with another man.

Had she actually considered it?

No. Not really.

It was only that she thought she ought to think about it, since she had been going out with Tom.

But Tom was gone.

And if the fact that there was a man in her bed was surprising, that the man was her stubborn, hardheaded, determined, proud, idiotic husband was the biggest shock of all.

And, Jenny thought ruefully, she was apparently just as big an idiot as he was, because—despite the letter from his lawyer on her dresser, despite his anger and his pride and his refusal to let her share his pain, despite the fact that he would probably divorce her whether she agreed or not—she was going to slip out of her clothes and get into bed.

With him.

For the first time in ages he was warm.

His body, which seemed to have been clenched against the cold forever, sensed the heat gradually. It was close, but not close enough.

He edged back toward the source. Yes. Ah, yes.

He could feel it now, right next to him, against him. Wrapping around him, holding him, drawing him in.

Warming him—at last.

The tension in his body, so intense he'd forgotten what it was like to be without it, gradually started to ease.

God, yes.

He moved, stretched, moaned. He rubbed his bare skin against hers.

Hers? Yes. Hers.

She was the source of his warmth. *She* was the fire he had been missing. *She* was the blanket, the protection he needed from the cold.

He'd been cold. So cold.

And now he was warm again. Alive again.

He felt himself uncurling, opening to the heat of her skin and the tentative softness of her touch.

He murmured encouragement. *Please, yes. Touch me. Warm me.*

She understood. Her touch wasn't as tentative now. It became surer, firmer, yet still gentle. Her hands sliding like silk along his back, making him arch against her. The subtle shift as they stroked and slipped and moved around to caress his chest made him breathe deeper so he could intensify the feeling of her fingers hard against his ribs.

Yes. Oh, yes.

Her breath was hot against his spine. Her mouth was wet as she kissed him. They were small fiery kisses that kindled corresponding fires wherever they touched.

Down his spine she went, one vertebra after another and then back up. She nuzzled the nape of his neck, nibbled him with her teeth, licked at him with her tongue.

He groaned. Desperate. Burning suddenly.

Not with heat, but with longing. He longed to become one with her, to absorb her heat and make it his own.

Without her he was cold. Without her he was lost.

With her—only with her—he was whole.

He turned and touched her then, tangled their arms and

legs together. He rolled beneath her and drew her on top of him. There he let his hands play over her soft skin, skimming over her arms, framing her narrow shoulders, tracing the curve of her back as he drew her down against his chest and wrapped himself once more in her warmth.

Her lips touched his face—his forehead, his eyelids, his nose, his cheeks. His mouth.

He'd never realized how thirsty he'd become. Never understood how parched his life had been. Until their lips met. Until her tongue touched his—mated with his—the way his body needed to mate with hers.

No longer cold. Now he was hot. Hot and hard.

No longer relaxed. Taut again. Tense. But with a different kind of tension.

At her touch his body had surrendered the hard shell of defensiveness, melting his feeling of his isolation, soothing his loneliness.

She warmed his soul and made it soft. She heated his body and made it hard. But this new hardness would not defend him, but expose him.

He was afraid. For a moment he knew a split second's hesitation, an instant's withdrawal.

And then it was gone. Swamped in the need to be a part of her, to share the warmth and the oneness that only the two of them could make.

He eased himself inside, feeling the welcome wetness that both eased and excited him. He wanted to slide out, to feel it envelop him again. He wanted to stay there forever, wrapped in the heat of her body, trembling in this most intimate embrace.

He had been so lonely and so cold and so empty.

And now he was not.

He loved; he was loved.

His body spoke words he'd forgotten how to say. Her body told him over and over again words he had never hoped to hear again. And when he shattered in her arms, when he felt her shatter in his, he knew peace and wholeness at last.

He stroked her sweat-slick back. He kissed her eyelids, wet with tears.

Tears?

"Don't cry," he whispered. But oddly, inexplicably, he felt like crying himself.

He didn't understand it. Couldn't get his mind around it. Should have been able to. Couldn't.

It didn't make sense. Nothing made sense—except having this woman in his arms.

He drew her tight against him.

They slept.

Chapter Eleven

Becky felt like somebody's mother.

She sat in her bedroom and looked out the window and watched and waited...and watched and waited...for Uncle Tom to come home.

And while she waited, she checked the clock and paced her room and hoped he wasn't doing what she was afraid he might be doing.

She thought long and hard about petitioning God for His intervention. After her prayers for Mace, years ago, she was leery of making any requests that might be misconstrued. But she finally decided she would have to.

She wasn't going to be able to handle this on her own.

Of course she might have been able to. At least she would have been able to do her best to see that things didn't get *too* romantic during Jenny's dinner with Uncle Tom, *if* her father had cooperated.

As usual lately, he did not.

Noah was still going over the last set of bronc rides, and Mace was still working with Jed, when she decided Uncle Tom had been with Jenny undisturbed long enough.

She tracked down her dad out by the corral where he was feeding Noah's school broncs and said she needed to borrow a book from Jenny.

He said, "No."

"But I need it!" Becky said. "You're always telling me to be responsible, think ahead. Like rememberin' to feed Digger. An' here I am, trying to, and all you say is no!"

"Jenny has company." Taggart didn't even turn his head. He went right on pitching hay.

Becky knew that, but she couldn't explain it. Not to her father. She liked Uncle Tom a lot—and if it were anybody else's almost-ex-wife, Becky would've been cheering him on. But a girl had certain loyalties.

Becky's were to Mace.

"It won't take long," she said. "Please." She gave him her best pleading look.

"Call and ask Tom to bring it home to you."

"But I need to talk to her."

He looked over at her. "Why?"

"Er, well, 'cause. Um…she knows how to card wool an' spin it an' weave it and stuff." Trust her dad to ask a question like that.

Taggart leaned on his pitchfork. "And…?" He wasn't making it easy.

Becky shrugged helplessly. "And that's what the report is about."

"So you're angling to get her to do it for you." He sounded disgusted.

Becky didn't know if she'd rather he thought that—which wasn't true—or if she'd rather he knew the real reason. She thought this might qualify as one of those situations where her grandpa had said, "You're damned if you do and damned if you don't."

"You have to do your own work," Taggart said firmly.

"I only wanted to talk about it. Do like Felicity says—consult a firsthand source. We don't have to go now. We could go later. After you're finished. I'd help you finish feedin'."

Later might be better, anyway. More chance they'd be interrupting something Mace would want interrupted.

"No."

"But—"

"You seem pretty desperate to get over there." Taggart gave her a narrow, assessing look. "You wouldn't be meddling, would you?"

Becky's eyes widened. "Meddling?"

"Pokin' your nose in where it doesn't belong." Taggart's finger tapped the tip of her nose. "Checking up on Tom and Jenny."

"Why would I do that?"

"Because you're you," her father said with a fatalism born of long experience. "And you've been known to stick your oar into water you got no business paddlin' in."

"Moi?" Becky said with all the innocence she could muster. It sounded better when Felicity or Miss Piggy said it.

Taggart drew a deep breath and let it out slowly. *"Oui, mademoiselle. Tu."* He fixed her with a warning look. "You let Jenny and Tom be. And just in case this is some misguided attempt to mess with Mace and Jenny, you let them work out their own problems."

"I wouldn't—"

"I mean it," he said sternly. "Messin' in *my* life was bad enough—"

"I didn't *mess* in your life," Becky said hotly, stung by his ingratitude. "I introduced you to my teacher—"

"By not doin' a lick of work," Taggart reminded her grimly.

"It was very hard work," Becky contradicted. "I didn't *want* to miss all those assignments. An' you're glad I did," she added. "You wouldn't have Felicity and Abby and Willy if I hadn't."

Taggart scowled. "I'd have managed on my own."

"In about a hundred years, maybe."

"Taggart!"

They both turned at the sound of Felicity calling from the porch. She was scanning the area desperately, with two crying, wriggling bundles in her arms.

"Finish this, will you, Pard?" Taggart thrust the pitchfork at Becky. He started toward the house, then turned back. "Just remember—you've done all the messin' you're going to. You behave yourself or else."

Becky, feeling annoyed and just a little reckless, said, "Or else what?"

Taggart fixed her with a level gaze. "Or else, *mademoiselle*, you're going to feel my hand on your *derriere*."

Then he turned and loped toward Felicity and the babies.

Becky watched him go. She watched Felicity smile and hand him one of the babies. Watched the four of them go into the house together.

She stabbed the pitchfork into the hay and sighed. That was what you got for trying to be helpful.

Who'd have thought her father knew that much French?

It was the finest sermon Reverend Wilson ever gave.

Jenny didn't hear a word of it.

The children's choir had never sounded better.

Jenny didn't even realize they were there.

The men's benevolent society was selling chances on a Harley-Davidson motorcycle.

She bought all they had left.

"You must really want to win, huh, Jenny?" Tuck McCall said admiringly. "Who'd a thought it? If you win will you give me a ride?"

"Of course," Jenny said absently.

She was walking on air. All around her parishioners chatted and smiled, said, "Good morning" and "Hope all is well."

For weeks she'd put on her best smile and had assured them it was.

Now she was—for real—smiling all over her face.

She wouldn't have left Mace this morning if she hadn't had to teach Sunday school.

It had been too late to get a substitute when she'd woken up this morning to find herself still snugly wrapped in her husband's arms. But oh, would she have loved to stay right there.

Still, maybe it was right that she'd come. She had some prayers of thanksgiving to say.

"So, what happened last night? Was Mace all right?"

Jenny blinked, then looked up to see Tom standing in front of her.

She tried not to smile her head off. "Oh, um, yes. Yes, he is, as a matter of fact."

"I'm glad," Tom said. He waited then, as if expecting her to explain.

She knew she ought to. She knew she owed him at least that much. Hadn't she practically thrown him out of her house last night in her haste over Rooster's phone call? Hadn't she been promising a threat of mayhem in the tone of her voice?

"He was...unwell," she said, picking her words carefully. "A friend called from Bozeman to tell me. I had to go down and pick him up."

"But he's all right now?"

"Fine."

More than fine. He was *home!*

Jenny had told herself she was being a fool last night when she slid beneath the quilt next to Mace in bed.

She'd told herself she was only going to hurt worse in the morning.

She'd told herself she'd regret spending the night lying next to him, wishing for things to be the way they once had been.

And as she'd lain there, stiff and aching, the minutes stretched out and so did the pain.

She thought she would have to get up and leave.

And then he touched her.

He moved back against her. At first she'd thought he was asleep, thought the slow steady inching of his body toward hers was nothing more than the natural movement of a man in a drunken slumber.

But then he'd turned and burrowed closer. He'd slipped his arms around her, had drawn her into an embrace she had wondered if she would ever know again.

And he'd loved her.

She'd relived every moment of it all night long—the urgent touch of his hands on her body, the desperate search of his mouth for hers. It was a stronger, sweeter, by far headier experience than the wine she'd drunk with Tom.

"So, it's not a problem, then?"

Jenny jerked back to see Tom's smiling face looking at her hopefully.

"Well, I—" She didn't know what to say.

What could she say that wouldn't sound as if she'd only been using Tom as long as Mace wasn't around?

It hadn't been like that. Not really.

She'd enjoyed his company. A lot. If Mace weren't her husband, she thought she might well be able to fall in love with a man like Tom. But Mace was her husband, and...

Her helpless stop brought out a ruefulness in Tom's smile.

"I know," he said gently. "It takes time."

He reached out and gave her hand a squeeze. "I'll call you later in the week. Maybe we can go ride fence or something."

Jenny smiled. She couldn't help it.

Maybe he and Mace could learn to be friends.

Mace had had the nightmare to end all nightmares.

He'd dreamed that he and Jenny were getting a divorce, that he'd left home—left her. He'd dreamed that their marriage was shattered, their hopes destroyed. He was alone.

And Jenny...Jenny had someone else.

He lay in bed, shaking and sweating, barely able to do more than thank God that he was awake now and the nightmare was over.

Still, it felt so real he had to open his eyes and look around to be sure.

He drew an unsteady sigh of relief at the sight of his dresser across the room, of Jenny's robe on the hook by the door.

He was here where he was supposed to be—in his own bed.

He sighed and stretched—and stopped.

His body hurt in places that had nothing to do with normal everyday riding horseback. His head ached. His mouth tasted foul—like beer and tequila and not just on a one-way ticket, either.

He hadn't felt like this since the morning after his bachelor party, when he and Taggart and Jed had got tanked on a couple of fifths of Wild Turkey and he'd met the flock going the other way the next morning.

He shuddered.

And then he remembered...the Six Gun, Rooster,

Sherpa's. The judo chopping college prof. The coffee. The car ride.

Jenny.

And then he realized that his nightmare wasn't a nightmare. It was his life.

He groaned and dragged himself to a sitting position, looking around for Jenny. Listening for her.

He heard nothing. She wasn't there.

And yet…a flicker of memory—of warmth—surfaced in his brain for an instant. It vanished.

He tried to focus on it, to drag it back. It was gone.

The effort to bring it back, to expand on it, caused a small shudder to run through him. He could hold a glimmer—the memory of love deep and intense and desperate.

But that was all.

"You're dreaming, Nichols," he muttered to himself. "It's called wishful thinking."

Because God knew it was.

"You're drunk." And God knew he was that, too.

Or hung over.

Carefully, still keeping one hand against his head, Mace hauled himself to his feet. God, yes, he hurt. His back. His butt.

He groaned and straightened and stumbled into the bathroom to turn on the shower.

It helped. But not much. Not nearly enough.

He stumbled out again, wrapped in a towel, to look for clean clothes.

There were none. He'd taken the rest to the cabin the last time he was here.

He put his grubby jeans back on. His shirt was too awful to wear. He opened Jenny's bottom drawer to find a sweatshirt he could wear.

There was a new one right on top. Bright blue. It said MONTANA STATE.

Mace pushed past it and pulled out an old gray one advertising the National Finals Rodeo. Once it had been his, but Jenny had taken it over. It had always been big on her, and he'd done his fair share of sliding his hands up beneath it to cup her naked breasts.

The memory tantalized him. He tugged the sweatshirt on over his head.

There was a pot of coffee still hot in the kitchen. The memory of last night's coffee made his insides clench. But he had to put something in his stomach, and Jenny made good coffee. Lots better than he made for himself. He poured himself a cup.

Then he carried it into the living room and stood, breathing in the pungent aroma, while he let his mind and his stomach adjust.

He was home.

Jenny had brought him home.

He stood now, gazing around the room, taking it all in, thinking how much he'd missed it.

He rubbed a hand over the rough stone of the fireplace he and Jenny and Taggart and Jed had built. They'd even gathered the stones themselves, packing them down out of the mountains and up from the rivers. It had been hard work, but worth it. His gaze lit on the rocking chair that had been Jenny's mother's. It was the one piece of furniture she'd brought from her family home, because she remembered being rocked in it when she was a child. Beneath it was the rug that Jenny had braided for three long winters. And it lay on top of pine floors that he himself had laid.

There was a world of memories in this room—in this whole house. Memories he and Jenny had made.

He walked around, cataloguing everything: the old oak table his grandmother had given them from her house, the old grandfather clock they had bought at an estate auction in White Sulphur Springs, the pink-and-blue afghan Jenny had knitted for the baby they'd always hoped for.

The baby they'd never had.

Mace swallowed hard against the sudden thickness in his throat as he remembered how young she'd been when she'd finished it.

Scarcely more than a child herself, bright-eyed and eager, she'd twirled it around her like a cape and danced in front of him, just out of his reach. Laughing, he'd snagged it and hauled her into his arms and kissed her senseless.

He picked up the afghan now and curled his fingers around it. It slid through his hand, a fine wool, soft and worn.

It had been washed plenty of times since that day. Somewhere along the years, it had ceased to be the "baby's blanket" and had become the one Jenny wrapped herself in when she sat on the sofa to watch TV or read a book.

He bunched it up and rubbed it against his cheek. It smelled of soap, of wool, of Jenny.

He shut his eyes, pressing the afghan against them, fighting the tears that pricked behind his lids, fighting the need, the ache, the desire.

If only…

Still holding the afghan, he turned and walked back into the kitchen.

If only…

But before he dared even think the only *if* that mattered, he saw the dishes on the counter where she'd left them.

Two plates. Two cups. Two knives. Two forks. Two spoons.

Not one.

Not only Jenny's.

Tom's and Jenny's.

Mace's fingers strangled the afghan. His lips drew thin. His heart ached.

He looked down at the counter and saw a photo lying there of Tom and a young girl, laughing.

He felt as if he'd been sucker punched. As if God didn't think he was bright enough to figure it out for himself and so had decided to spell it out for him.

Well, okay. He got it—Jenny wanted a family. Always had. Always would.

She could have it with Tom.

She *would* have it with Tom.

She'd brought Macc home because it was her duty. That was all.

Nothing had changed.

But damn it, Mace thought, giving up the fight and letting the tears slide down his cheeks, his only dream that mattered now was of her.

When would she ever learn?

It was like the refrain of the old song. And Jenny made herself sing it over and over as a penance.

When would she ever learn not to be so unfailingly sanguine? When would she learn not to trust that what she wanted, hoped for, dreamed about, was inevitably going to become her future?

When would she accept that her marriage to Mace was over, that while the physical side of their love seemed as bright as ever, the rest of it was dead?

"I'm like that donkey you have to hit on the side of the head to get its attention," she told Brenna in dry-eyed, toneless disgust the day after she came smiling her way home from church to discover that Mace had left without a word.

Brenna patted her hand and gave her a cup of tea and a dose of sympathy. But since she didn't know the bottom line, she couldn't do much more.

Jenny knew Brenna was being kind. She also knew there was nothing much Brenna could say.

Her life was up to her.

She had been a doormat long enough.

She had tried to keep things together. She'd had the door slammed in her face.

But what rankled more than anything—what made her mad enough to spit—was that before he'd slammed it, Mace had so liberally sampled the wares.

The very thought of it made her teeth come together with a snap. The mortifying memory of how eagerly she had loved him and how willingly he had accepted it—and then walked out!—straightened her up and stiffened her spine as nothing else.

Was she going to spend the rest of her life waiting for Mace to come to his senses?

No, she damned well was not!

She took out the last letter from his lawyer, the one in which Anthony had tried to respond to her nitpicky questions about the division of property, including the herd and the horses, the barn and the house and furnishings.

She had been stalling when she'd written it.

She'd been giving Mace time. Well, she was done with that.

Mace had had time enough.

"We did it. It's all set." Anthony crowed over the telephone.

"What?" Mace said.

Anthony made an impatient noise. "What did you hire me for, Nichols? The divorce!"

"Already?" Mace scowled. He'd thought it would take months. A no-fault divorce, Anthony had told him, meant they would have to live apart for 180 days. "What about the time requirement?"

"There's an exception," Anthony reminded him. "If you both agree that there's serious marital discord and nothing's going to change."

"There's no way things are going to change," Mace had said when he'd hired Anthony.

Jenny, in her response, had disagreed.

She'd urged counseling. Mace had said no. She'd urged a cooling-off period. Mace had declined. It didn't matter how cool he got, he was never going to have any sperm. What was the point?

"She's thrown in the towel," Anthony said cheerfully. "She isn't contesting it. In fact, I got a letter from her lawyer this morning saying she agreed. Great, huh?"

"Swell." Mace licked dry lips. "What about the division of property?" he asked Anthony. "I thought she was going to argue over the custody of every cow."

The last letter Anthony had received from her lawyer had made it sound like that.

"Apparently not," Anthony said. "Travis—that's her lawyer—said he was willing to come up with a 'fair and equitable settlement.' How about that?"

"So she's…she's just…giving up?"

"She's giving up," Anthony agreed wholeheartedly. "Seeing the light, if you will. There's no way she can stop it, and she's finally realized it. So she's agreeing, and she's saving herself—and you—some money. With no long court battles, things can be done relatively economically. You keep more of the cows, basically," Anthony said. "You gotta like that, pal."

Oh, yeah. Mace tried to work up a smile. "But I can't afford to buy her out right now."

"She doesn't want you to buy her out."

"She doesn't?"

"Says not." There was a rustling of paper, and Anthony said, "I'm sure Travis argued long and hard against it, but he says she wants to—and I quote—'Dissolve the partnership so that Mace can have the ranch.' Then Travis writes—'We are naturally counting on him doing the honorable thing.' You got it made, buddy!''

Mace let out a breath. "I guess." He hesitated. "Does it say what she's going to do?"

"Just 'getting out of ranching.' Can't blame her, can you?"

Mace's fingers were limp on the receiver. "Nope." He couldn't blame her at all.

She was getting out of ranching, all right. She was marrying Tom.

She didn't say so. She didn't have to.

He might not have a college degree, but Mace could read between the lines as well as the next guy.

"You don't find many women that generous," Anthony continued.

"No."

"You really picked a good one." There was a long pause. In it Mace heard the unspoken question "Then what the hell are you divorcing her for?"

He didn't answer it. He said, "Thanks for calling. Is that all?"

"I do the paperwork. You and I go to court and get it finalized. Piece of cake. A few days, a week or two at most—depending on the judge's schedule—and you're a free man."

A free man?

"Swell." Mace's voice was toneless.

He didn't bother saying there would never be any chance of that.

Tom called on Wednesday while Jenny was sitting at the kitchen table looking at the classifieds. "So, do you want to ride fence?"

"No."

"Well, of course we don't have to. I just thought if—"

"I didn't mean to bite your head off," Jenny apologized. "I just don't want to ride fence, because the ranch isn't mine anymore. Or soon it won't be. I'm leaving."

"Leaving?"

"Taking your advice, actually. Sticking my big toe into university life. Moving on. So if you want to do something with me today, maybe we could go for lunch and let me check out apartments in Bozeman?"

There were cattle that needed checking on the summer range.

Taggart couldn't leave. He had new twins and no time. It was the new equation of his life, he said. Jed thought he could spare a day or two, but he was reluctant to leave Brenna with her father, Tuck and Neile alone.

"I'll go," Mace volunteered.

It suited him fine. Being on his own, far away from anyone, sounded like the best of all possible worlds. And if, while he was gone, Anthony called to tell him when the court date was, well, that was too bad. They'd just have to reschedule.

A guy had his priorities. To a cowboy, the herd came first.

Mace told himself that a hundred times a day over the next five days as he rode the high country, checking on his cattle and Taggart's and Jed's. It was true. But it didn't make it any easier.

He had the most beautiful scenery on earth—and no one to share it with. Other summers Jenny had come with him. They called it their "vacation," since they never had the time or money to go anywhere else.

"Why should we?" Jenny would always say when he apologized for never taking her anywhere. "People come to Montana for their holidays, don't they? We just have a head start on them.''

When they came together it had always been a holiday of sorts.

They brought a small tent and used it on the rainy nights. But on the bright clear ones, they slept out under the stars. Jenny would snuggle against his side, and together they would watch the stars.

Invariably attention would turn to things closer at hand. She would touch his rough-stubbled cheek and wonder how his scratchy beard would feel against her skin.

And he would show her.

He would wonder if her lips were as soft and moist as they looked.

And she would kiss him.

She would wonder if his fingers were as clever as they looked.

And he would touch her.

And...

And that's why he was going quietly out of his mind right now.

It didn't help that a bear scared some cattle and it took him half a day to round them up and bring them down out of the woods. It didn't help that a half dozen cows ate larkspur and there was nothing he could do to save them.

It didn't help that once the rain started, it never wanted to stop.

Montana, any cowboy could tell you, was pretty arid country. They got rain, sure, and snow, you bet. But a good year was a year they didn't have to irrigate much.

This year they'd be lucky not to have to build an ark, Mace thought.

The first day he got a short rain shower. He ignored it and went on with his work. The second day was lovely, bright and cold, with a wind coming down from the north-west. The third morning, he was awakened by rain in his face.

He hadn't brought a tent. That had always been a concession to Jenny. When he was alone, he used a fly.

The fly didn't help him when the rain came in horizontally beneath it. Grumbling, he made himself a fire to dry out a bit before he started work. He used up the last of the dry firewood.

If Jenny had been with him, she'd have cooked breakfast while he wrangled more wood. She'd have made lunch and had it ready when he came back from circling that afternoon. She'd have made dinner when he came in wet and tired.

But Jenny wasn't there.

Never would be.

He was on his own now.

On his own.

He didn't bother with a fire that night. He ate a granola bar and an apple and tried to tell his still-growling stomach that things would be better in the morning. It would have stopped raining by then, and he could once more treat it right.

But by next morning the rain hadn't stopped. Cold, wet and bone weary, he tried to find dry wood to make a fire. He sneezed as he was making the coffee.

He cursed at the scratching in his throat.

He worked all day, and the rain never stopped. He came back to camp weary and cold. He'd used all his firewood at breakfast. His shoulders ached; his head throbbed; his nose ran.

If Jenny had been there, she'd have had a fire going and supper ready.

If Jenny had been there...

"Damn!"

He ate his dinner cold, not wanting to heat it. Then he

rigged the fly, opened his bedroll and turned in. The rain would stop, he promised himself, and he would feel better in the morning.

By morning the rain had turned to snow. The ache had moved from his shoulders to the rest of his body. His head still throbbed. His nose still ran. And he started to cough.

It was hell.

The prettiest damn hell on earth.

The snow made everything a wonderland. Jenny would have loved it. It would have been a pain to work in, but she would have hugged him and tackled him and rolled them both in the snow, making him laugh and forget his misery. She would have made things all right.

It wasn't all right now.

It wasn't all right at all.

He kept working. He got sicker. The snow turned back into rain.

Three more days the rain kept up. He couldn't believe it.

Finally he gave up and headed back down. His eyes were streaming, his nose was running. He was coughing and aching. His teeth were chattering and his body was burning.

He needed a warm fire, a hot meal and about a hundred cups of coffee. He needed a heavy blanket, a dry bed and about twenty-four hours of uninterrupted sleep.

He was cowboy enough to see to his horse before he stumbled up the steps to the cabin.

He opened the door—and found a man he didn't know.

Chapter Twelve

Mace stopped, only his hand on the doorknob keeping him upright.

"What the—? Who the hell are you?"

The man, an older guy, sixty or so, with graying hair that might once have been red, looked just as startled as Mace. He was sitting in the chair by the fireplace with a book in his lap.

He shut it, then he said mildly, "You must be Mace."

Mace straightened slightly, his eyes narrowing a bit. "That's right."

"My name's Ian MacLeod." The man set his book on the small table and got to his feet, then held out his hand. Mace let go of the doorknob unwillingly, but managed to stay upright long enough to shake it. He was still trying to figure out who the hell Ian MacLeod was. The name was vaguely familiar, but the man was not.

"Taggart told me you'd be up on the summer range another week or so," Ian MacLeod told him. "That's why he told me I could use the cabin."

"Use the cabin?" Mace croaked. He coughed to clear his throat.

Ian smiled. "He obviously wasn't figuring on the weather we've had. Sorry about that. I didn't intend to disturb you. I've been staying with Noah and Tess for a little while—sort of regrouping—and I thought I might give them a break and myself a little space. So I asked if they knew a place I could do a retreat, and Taggart suggested here."

"Retreat?" Mace echoed. He was confused, light-headed. The fever was getting to him. The only kind of retreat he could think of was the kind he'd seen in old Western movies. "As in...cavalry?"

"As in 'spiritual,'" Ian MacLeod said with a gentle smile. "I'm Maggie Tanner's father."

It took Mace a moment to put it together. Maggie Tanner...Tanner's wife...Noah's sister-in-law's...father. The grieving uncle of Susannah's that Becky had mentioned.

"I'm a minister," Ian MacLeod said.

Mace's teeth came together with a snap.

Damn Taggart and his meddling, anyway! How dare he send up some minister to meddle in his life and tell him what to do!

And then he remembered that Taggart had thought he was gone. Taggart was simply doing Maggie's dad a favor—a favor he had every right to do.

This was Taggart's cabin. Mace was the one who was squatting, not Ian MacLeod.

The vision that had kept him going, the promise that had sustained him through the bone-chilling, rain-soaked ride back this afternoon—the fire, the warmth, the bed—rose up one last time, then vanished beneath the wave of knowledge that Ian MacLeod had far more right to the cabin than he had.

He backed toward the door. "I'll go."

"Of course you won't go," Ian said. "You're living here."

"Not now. I'm not supposed to be now." Mace shook his head. He coughed again.

Ian reached out and caught his arm. "There's plenty of room at this inn. We'll share."

"You'll want to be alone."

"I've been alone for the past five days here. I'm going to be alone the rest of my life," he said wearily. "I think I can stand a little company."

But Mace didn't think he could. Once more he said, "No."

"We can talk about it later. Over a bowl of chili. How about it? I made it from scratch this morning."

Mace could smell it. The delicious aroma was making him weak. His stomach was growling. "Maybe a bowl."

Ian dished it up.

Mace barely ate half before he fell asleep.

It was the oddest thing Jenny had ever done—apartment hunting.

She felt like a fraud. Yet it was the most realistic thing she'd done since Mace had walked out on her. She had to do what she'd told Travis, her lawyer, she was going to do when she'd asked him to write Anthony and tell him she would agree with Mace's petition. She was going to move out, move on.

Still, looking at apartments felt almost like an out-of-body experience. Well, not quite out of body.

More as if she was in a body, all right, but someone else's.

After her initial burst of bravado, when she'd suggested

it to Tom, Jenny shrank from actually getting out the classifieds and seeing what was available.

The very thought terrified her. Like nothing else she'd done since Mace had left her, it made "life after divorce" seem real.

She didn't want to do it.

She thought maybe she could move into Elmer. It wouldn't be such a big step. Surely she could find something closer. She might even be able to rent a room from Alice Benn. Alice had a big house.

She would have called her, except by the time she thought of it, Tom had arrived with the classifieds in hand.

"I found four apartments near the campus and two farther away."

"I don't know about this," Jenny began hesitantly.

Tom gave her a sympathetic smile. "Scared?"

"Actually, I am."

"It's a big step. I know."

He did know. He'd done it. And he'd survived. Jenny took heart from that.

"Come on," he said. "You've just got to dive in. You might not float, but I guarantee you'll learn to swim."

Jenny desperately hoped so.

All the apartments were small and expensive and jammed together. Jenny, not used to having people living right on top of her, rejected every one.

"Hey," Tom chided her when they got back in the car after Jenny had turned down everything in less than an hour, "give 'em a chance."

"But I don't like all these people around. I like space."

"Maybe you shouldn't be looking for an apartment at all, then," he said. "Maybe you ought to look for a house." He opened the classifieds again and spread the paper out against the steering wheel.

"I can't afford a house." Even the cost of the apartments seemed prohibitive.

"How about a room in a house?"

"I was thinking about Alice's."

Tom frowned. "Who's Alice?"

"A retired teacher. She lives in Elmer in that great big, green, two-story house behind the Laundromat."

"You don't want to live in Elmer," Tom said firmly.

"I don't?"

"Not if you want a fresh start. If you stay in Elmer, you'll always be looking over your shoulder wondering where Mace is. Is that what you want?"

Jenny shook her head. No, she didn't want that.

He scanned the paper. "Here's one. 'One room in older home close to downtown. Ideal for single. Kitchen facilities available.' Want to look?"

Jenny nodded. "Let's look."

They looked. They looked at three others Tom suggested. Only one, a room in a two-story brick house near the post office, was a possibility. It was small but clean, and Jenny liked the older woman who would be her landlady.

Still, she couldn't bring herself to say yes. It was so small, and the only view was of the house next door. She told the woman she would think about it.

"You'll have to let me know this week," the woman said. "I'll have students calling, wanting to rent."

"I know I'm being picky," Jenny told Tom when they were in the car again and heading home. "I can't help it."

Tom shrugged. "You're going to have to live there. Be as picky as you want. It's another two weeks until school starts. Maybe there will be others tomorrow or later in the week."

"Maybe," Jenny said. But she was sure she would never find anything that came close to the house she and Mace had built with their own hands.

"We can check the paper again tomorrow."

"Yes," she said with as much determination as she could muster. "All right."

After he fell asleep over the chili, there wasn't any arguing about him staying on.

The warm fire, dry clothes and good food all conspired against him. When he finally jerked his head up, embarrassed, Ian ignored his protest and fetched a blanket from the bedroom.

"But—"

"No *buts*. I will only make one concession to my venerable age." Ian smiled. "You can take the couch."

Mace could have slept on the plank floor and never known the difference. He coughed most of the night, but the next morning his fever was down, and the aching was gone. He felt more rested than he had in days. And breakfast was on the table.

He stared, dazed, at the bowl of oatmeal, the plate of eggs and bacon. A small part of him wondered if he'd died and gone to heaven. Given his track record, it didn't seem likely.

"Reckon you're spoiling me," he said to Ian.

"Sometimes," Ian said easily, "a guy needs a little spoiling."

It should have been the other way around, Mace thought as he dug into the meal. Ian was the grieving widower. He was the one who should be looked after. But when he said as much, Ian just went on dishing up his own bowl of oatmeal and shook his head.

"I've been fussed over enough. Thought Maggie'd smother me when I was with her and Tanner. That's why I left." He smiled wryly. "It's not that I didn't appreciate it. I did. And she needed to do it," he added. "But after a while, well, I needed some time on my own."

"You're not on your own," Mace pointed out. "I'm here."

Ian lifted one brow. "I trust you're not planning to fuss and smother."

Mace shook his head. "No."

"Then I think we'll get along just fine."

To Mace's surprise, they did.

At first he expected Ian to bring up the divorce. Surely a minister would have plenty to say about a marriage falling apart.

But Ian said nothing. He didn't mention Jenny. In fact, he didn't seem to know that Mace was married at all.

He spent a fair amount of time reading and writing and just staring off into space with a faraway look in his eyes. But he was also eager to help Mace with the everyday work.

"I don't know much about cowboying," he admitted. "But I'm willing to learn."

And because he was still feeling a little weak from his cold, Mace was glad of the help. They worked together in companionable silence a good part of the time. Sometimes, though, Ian's faraway look prompted him to apologize for his lack of attentiveness. And then he usually explained why he'd drifted off.

He reminisced. He told Mace stories. The stories invariably were told on himself. They were funny and wise and self-deprecating, and very easy to listen to. Many had to do with his wife, Fiona, a woman Mace grew to know and respect through Ian's tales.

It was easy to see how much Ian missed her. She was the reason for the faraway look. She, as much as his faith, Ian told Mace, was the rudder of his existence. He hadn't been able to face staying in Torre de León, the South American town where she died.

"Had to get out of there. I couldn't face it," Ian said,

watching as Mace braided a horsehair bridle. "It wasn't the same without her. It hurt too much. And I was angry, too."

"Angry?"

"I told her to come home when she found out about her heart problem. She'd have had better care here."

"Why didn't she?"

"Because she said our work was there, our lives were there. She said she wouldn't leave me. I said we could both come back, but she said, no, we were needed there. We talked about it. Talked, hell!" Ian shook his head. "We argued about it for days. She said it was what we'd decided on together—the mission work, our life down there. So we stayed. And she died...and now I'm here."

His pain was almost palpable. Mace could feel it the way he felt his own.

"God, I miss her," Ian said. "You can't imagine how much."

"I think I can," Mace answered.

Then for the first time, he mentioned Jenny.

If Ian was surprised Mace had a wife, he never said so. If he wondered where she was now, he never asked. He simply listened.

There was a certain release in being able to talk about her. Over the next few days saying her name became easier.

One night they were playing checkers in front of the fire, and Ian told him about checker games he'd won against Fiona.

"I used to win a kiss for every man I got." Ian smiled. "I thought I was so clever, getting all those kisses. It never occurred to me she had a vested interest in being a terrible checker player."

"Jenny and I used to play checkers at her house before we got married," Mace told Ian. "We didn't have the money to go out, and her dad said we weren't just going to go sit in the truck. He never let me get away with anything," Mace grumbled.

Ian puffed on his pipe and smiled slowly. "He let you marry her."

Later when Ian told him about meeting Fiona at a freshman mixer and understanding the meaning of "love at first sight," Mace talked about the first time he saw Jenny.

"It wasn't love then," he said. "I was too young. Too dumb. But from the beginning she wasn't like any other girl I ever met. She had this sparkle, this eagerness, this sense of life."

And sometimes without Ian mentioning Fiona at all, Mace found himself talking about Jenny.

He told Ian about Jenny's faith in him, her willingness to give up her scholarship, her plans for college, to marry him.

"She didn't have to. She wanted to." He shook his head. "She could have had so much more if she hadn't married me."

He talked about the years they'd struggled, the cattle they'd bought, the winter storms that had taken their toll, the mother cows and calves they'd lost.

"I wanted that herd more than anything. It was going to provide our future," he said. "It was going to be the security we could depend on. No getting fired. No getting let go. I wanted to give her and our kids what my dad could never give us. And she agreed."

He talked about the house they'd built, the home they'd made.

"It wasn't much to start with. I cut the logs myself, me and Taggart and Jed. Got a mill to do the finishing, then we built it ourselves. Jenny made all the curtains. She hooked the rugs. She even helped shingle the roof. Got frostbite on her fingers we were so late getting it on that year. And she never complained a bit."

He talked about realizing his dream. "The herd's getting pretty good-size now. It's still touch-and-go. Probably always will be. No money in ranching these days. But it's there. It happened. It's real. Because of her. She gave up everything she wanted for my dreams."

Mace stared into the fire a long time before he said, "Now it's my turn." He looked at his hands, not at the fire, not at Ian. "She wants a family and I can't…have kids. There's no way I can give her her dream." His mouth twisted and he slanted a glance Ian's way. "That's why I've been living here. After I found out, after we got the tests back and knew there was no hope, I moved out. Filed for divorce. It's better that way," he said firmly, looking once more at his hands. "When I'm out of the picture, she'll be free to marry again…somebody who can give her kids—who can give her her dream."

He was surprised at the words that had come out of his mouth, words he'd never expected to say to anyone. But then he realized he was expecting Ian to tell him what to do, to give him an answer—to take away the burden.

Ian sat in the rocking chair, puffing on his pipe and staring into the fire as he always did. He made no judgments. He asked no questions. He gave no answers.

Mace slumped back on the sofa and stared at the dying fire. Ian's rocker creaked. Outside, the wind soughed through the trees. Nearby he could hear crickets chirping, up on the mountain the sound of a coyote calling.

Then the rocking chair stopped creaking. Slowly, as if he felt every one of his sixty-odd years, Ian rose to his feet and started toward the bedroom.

As he passed, Ian touched Mace's shoulder lightly. "You'll miss her, son. You'll miss her."

It was all there in black and white.

The herd, the land, the house. The assets of the fourteen-year marriage of Jenny and Mace Nichols. Along with Travis's recommendations for an equitable split.

"Not by any means what you deserve," he'd written. "But at least enough to get by adequately."

Even so, she knew it would hurt Mace's prospects. She wasn't sure he could keep the ranch, even if she tried to give him every break she could and still have something left for herself.

"You don't owe him a thing," Travis had told her during their first meeting.

But Jenny knew she owed him the happiest years of her life.

"Try to see that he gets the ranch," she'd told her lawyer, who stared at her, dumbfounded and in horror. "Just see that I get a minimal amount to live on. I can work. I'll manage."

It would actually be salutary, she thought now as she waited for Tom to pick her up for another trip to Bozeman. If she was forced by her circumstances to keep herself busy, she wouldn't think about everything she had lost.

She'd think about important things—like keeping a roof over her head.

This time she was more realistic.

She knew she wasn't going to get much room for her money, and she knew it was going to be expensive. She knew she didn't want an apartment. Living in a human equivalent to a chicken coop didn't appeal.

"I'd go crazy," she told him when he suggested they check out another new building on the edge of town.

"You could at least see the mountains from your deck," he argued.

But Jenny was adamant. "It would be worse. I would see what I was missing."

So they narrowed their search to the new listing of rooms available in houses near the university.

The room she had turned her back on last week began to look like a palace compared to the ones she saw this time. But, just as the landlady had predicted, that room had already been snapped up.

"Wish you'd called me Wednesday," the landlady said when Jenny stopped back. "I'd rather have had a nice quiet girl like you."

Jenny wasn't sure how the lady could tell she was such a nice quiet girl just by looking at her and said so as they walked back out to the car.

Tom smiled and lifted her hair away from her cheek. "Trust me. It shows." His fingers lingered longer than they needed to. But his touch was gentle. He was kind. He even had a dimple in his cheek when he smiled.

Jenny managed a smile, too.

He laced his fingers through hers. "Come on. We'll find something."

They spent all afternoon going from one place to another. They went, Jenny said later, "From bad to worse."

She was sure there were lovely places to live in Bozeman. But none of them were for rent that day. By the time they had exhausted and rejected all advertised possibilities, even going back to take another look at a few of the less crowded apartment complexes, Jenny was even more depressed.

"Things might look better over a piece of pie and a cup of Java," Tom suggested.

Jenny shrugged, then mustered a smile because it wasn't Tom's fault things weren't working out. Maybe it would be a good idea—a chance to step back and consider things. "All right."

He took her to a small café downtown. "What kind of pie do you want?" Tom asked after the waitress seated them.

Jenny didn't want any pie. She wasn't hungry. But she said, "Raspberry."

"Make that two," Tom told the waitress. "And two coffees."

The coffee gave Jenny something to hold on to. The pie gave her something to fiddle with while she considered her options.

What options? she thought.

The apartments depressed her. The rooms were tiny and looked out onto trash cans or worse. Maybe Taggart's parents wouldn't mind renting her a room. They lived in Bozeman now.

But did she want to foist herself off onto people she'd known all her life? Did she want to see their concerned faces, sense their worry, hear the silence of things unsaid whenever she came into a room?

No, she couldn't ask Taggart's parents. She poked at her pie and tried to think of something else.

"I have an idea." Tom had been so quiet she'd forgotten he was sitting across the table from her.

"You know someone in Bozeman with a room to rent?"

"Not in Bozeman."

"Belgrade, then. Or even Manhattan."

"I was thinking maybe Des Moines."

"What?" She stared at him.

"I was thinking you might consider moving to Des Moines."

"*Iowa?*"

"That's where it was the last time I looked."

Jenny shook her head. "Why on earth would I go to Iowa?"

"Besides the fact that I'm there, you mean?" He took a long swallow of his coffee, then set the cup down and faced her squarely across the table. "Think about it," he said.

"Why shouldn't you go? You want a fresh start. What could be fresher?"

"But I don't know anything about Iowa! Other than you and Felicity I don't even know any*one* from Iowa. I don't have a place to stay. What would I do? Where would I work?"

"Well, I'd invite you to stay with me...but I know you wouldn't do it," Tom said even before Jenny could open her mouth to protest. "And you'd be right," he continued. "It's too soon. But you know I'm interested. You *have* to know I'm interested." His gaze leveled on her, making her face warm. "Don't you?"

Jenny shifted uncomfortably. "We've...gone out." She mashed a raspberry with her fork.

"And I'd like to keep going out. I'd like us to get to know each other better. But I have to go home next Saturday." He had already extended his stay once, Jenny knew. But the college where he taught began school before Labor Day. He was cutting it close as it was.

"I—I'd like that, too," she began carefully. "But I don't think..."

"If you were closer we could take things slower," Tom said. "But at least we'd be 'taking things.' You could stay with my parents at first, if you didn't find a place you liked right away. They have a big house. They would love to have you."

"They don't even know me."

"They have always welcomed my friends and Felicity's and my other sister's. They'd like to have you. I'd like you to meet them. I'd like you to meet Katie."

His daughter, he meant.

"Oh, Tom."

"I think you'd like her," he said quickly.

"I'm sure I would."

"And I think she'd like you. There are jobs. If you

wanted to work as an aide again, I'm sure you could find something. And if you just want to take classes, well, there are plenty of colleges. You could go to Drake or one of the other area colleges. You can go where I teach if you want. I'd like to teach you.'' The innuendo was mild, but she heard it. The smile he gave her then was gently teasing.

Jenny shook her head.

"Too soon," Tom said. He sighed. "All right. Too soon. But it would be a start. You'd have a place to stay. I could show you around, teach you the ropes. Help you get settled. What do you say?''

"I don't know what to say." Jenny still couldn't quite imagine it.

Tom, on the other hand, seemed to have imagined it very well. In fact, he seemed to have it all worked out.

"And—'' he reached across and took her hand in his "—you wouldn't ever have to worry about running into Mace."

No Mace.

No mountains.

No cabin.

No looking at things and thinking about what might have been.

"You get a chance to make things happen," Tom said softly. "Not just regret what didn't—and never will."

Jenny's mind was a whirl. She shook her head, trying to settle things down, sort things out. "I don't know," she said at last, staring into her coffee mug. "I don't know."

Tom squeezed her fingers in his. "I know you don't. But think about it. I'm going home on Saturday. You could come with me."

Jenny lifted her eyes and stared at him.

"You could," Tom repeated. "Just think."

Mace heard the truck coming up the hill long before it got within sight of the cabin. When he saw Noah, he wondered if he'd forgotten to go down to help out at one of the schools or if something had happened to Jenny.

His heart lurched. He was down the steps and halfway to the truck by the time Noah climbed out.

"Ian here?"

Mace nodded, relieved. Noah wasn't there to see him at all. He tipped his head toward the house.

"Thanks." Noah walked past him up the steps.

At the sight of him, a smile wreathed Ian's face. "Well, look who's here. You running away from your responsibilities, too?"

Noah shook his head, his mouth twisting. "Maggie called this morning. She asked me to come up and tell you—" he hesitated "—there's been a bad earthquake at Torre de León."

Mace, his hand braced on the doorjamb, saw Ian's face go white.

Now Ian asked, "How bad?"

Noah shook his head. "Don't know for sure. Reports are just coming in, and frankly not a lot of them are coming in here. We're not thought to have a big interest in that part of the world. But," he added quietly, "from what Maggie said, it sounds pretty rough."

For a long moment Ian didn't move. He shut his eyes and simply stood there, bleached, drained.

And then he opened his eyes again and drew a breath. Mace could see his chest expand, could see his spine straighten.

But he still looked old. He still looked tired, even as he exhaled sharply and nodded. "I'll get packed."

Mace followed him into the bedroom. "I thought you weren't going back there. You don't have to, you know."

"Yes, I do." Ian was taking his clothes out of the dresser as he spoke. "I'm needed."

"Yeah, well, you're needed here, too," Mace said lightly, wanting to ease his pain. "I can always use a good hand."

Ian turned, his mouth curving into a smile. "Thank you for that. It's good to know I could make it as a cowboy. But I'll be a better hand there. It's what I'm called for. It is, as Fiona always said, my life. *Our* life," he corrected himself quietly.

Mace hesitated. "You're sure? I mean...on your own?"

He had heard enough over the days they'd been together to know that Ian and Fiona had been a team. They'd been so much a part of each other in their work, in their lives, in their love, that her death had come close to crushing him. He was doing all right now. Mace didn't want to see him go back and be destroyed.

"I won't be on my own," Ian said. "I thought I would be. That's why I came back—because I couldn't face being there without her. But I'm not ever going to be without her wherever I am. She's here." He tapped his chest lightly, then touched his head. "Inside. Always will be."

He drew another breath, an even deeper one, and let it out slowly, settling in, gathering strength.

"I don't like what happened. I never will. It doesn't seem fair her dying and me still being here. But no one ever said life was fair, did they?" He smiled wryly.

"No, no one did," Mace said, his voice hollow.

"Fiona knew that. Even when it ended sooner than we wanted, she wasn't sorry we'd stayed. I was. I was angry. But now, well, I can put my anger to use, perhaps. Work it off. I have to go back. Fiona and I have work to do."

Fiona and I. As if she really was still with him. As if she was a part of him. As if he was a part of her. Two parts of a whole. Always.

A marriage that even death couldn't break.

Ian tossed the rest of his belongings into his duffel bag and slung the strap over his shoulder.

Then he straightened and met Mace's eyes.

"For better or worse, isn't that in the ceremony?" he said. "I forgot for a while. You might have, too."

They looked at each other. Then Ian took a step forward and gave Mace's shoulder a squeeze. "Think about that."

Chapter Thirteen

Becky had been waiting for this day all week.

Actually she'd been waiting all month—not that she was ready for school to start. Becky was *never* really ready for school to start.

But she was ready to climb the mountain with her dad.

It was a tradition.

Every year, on the Friday before school started, she and Taggart would climb this peak just north of Flathead Pass. She didn't know if it had a name. She and her dad called it Tiptop because when Becky was five she hadn't thought there was any place higher you could go.

They'd been climbing Tiptop since the year she'd started school—since she'd had to stop going down the road from rodeo to rodeo with him and stay, instead, with her grandparents at home.

He'd taken her that first time because he'd wanted to show her where he was going.

She hadn't been very big, and her legs hadn't been very long, and Taggart had had to piggyback her almost as much as she'd walked. But it had been worth it.

When they finally got to the top, the world was spread out at their feet.

It went on for miles and miles—as far as Becky's eye could see.

Taggart had set her down and then hunkered down beside her and pointed. "See that road?"

She'd nodded. She could remember it stretching like a silver thread across the valley until it disappeared into another set of mountains.

"That's the road I'm traveling. It's the same road we took when we went to Spokane last month. The same one we took to go to San Francisco. And Vegas. They all connect. So I'm not gone. I'm just down that road somewhere. And if you ever need me, I'll take it right back to you."

He'd turned his head, and his face was so close to hers she could feel his breath on her cheek. His hat shaded them both from the sun. "Got that, Pard?"

She remembered her throat had felt so tight she could barely get her voice up past it. But she'd nodded because she knew he wanted her to.

He had to go. It was his job. But that didn't mean she wouldn't miss him.

"Got it," she whispered when she finally dragged her voice up from the toes of her boots.

She remembered how he'd nuzzled her cheek with his nose then. She hadn't wanted to giggle, but it tickled, and she couldn't help it. It was just a tiny giggle, but she was glad after she'd done it, because it made him smile.

"I don't want to leave you any more than you want to stay," he told her as he sat down on a rock and pulled her back against him, between his knees, so that the two of them could sit spoon-fashion looking out over the valley to the end of the world.

"But things aren't always the way you want them to be. Life changes. You got to go on, though, you know?" He had a hand on her shoulder and he'd given it a gentle squeeze.

"I know," she said, finding her voice easier now. She wrapped an arm around his thigh and leaned her cheek against his knee. "It's okay, Daddy."

And it was.

Mostly.

He'd called her every night. She told him all about school and her teacher and the dumb boy who cried when his mother left him every day.

"She should've taken him up on the peak," she'd told her father. "Then he'd know she was just down the road from him."

The knowledge had sustained her until her father's car accident. Then, for a time, the very thought of roads had been a scary place. But after the accident, he hadn't gone out rodeoing anymore. He'd stayed home with her. And things had been good.

Mostly.

For her, anyway, if not for him.

And that was when they'd met Felicity.

Taggart was happier since they had Felicity. Becky knew that, and she was glad. After all, hadn't having Felicity for a mom been her idea in the first place?

Well, actually she supposed it had been Susannah's.

But Becky had done the dirty work. She was the one her dad had yelled at when things went wrong. She deserved some credit.

Last year she'd got some credit. Last year had been the best year of her life.

Mostly.

Both Taggart and Felicity had climbed the peak with her. They'd stood there, the three of them, as a family, and they'd faced the world together.

And now they had the twins.

Becky didn't know how her father planned to get them up there, but she was sure he'd manage. She was even willing to help carry one of them, preferably Abby, who didn't pee on you, if he wanted her to.

She got out of bed early because she knew it would take longer this year and he'd want to get back before the twins needed a nap.

Taggart was sitting at his desk going over some breeding charts. When she came down the stairs, he didn't even look up.

"So," she said, "what time are we going?"

He looked around. "Going where?"

"Up the peak."

He blinked.

Becky felt a lead ball start to form in her stomach. "It's Friday," she reminded him. "School starts Monday. We have to climb Tiptop."

Taggart rubbed a hand down his face. "Aw, hell, Pard. I can't do that today."

"Why not?"

"I've got to go over these charts before Robertson calls. We're buying new stock."

"But after—"

Taggart rubbed his face with his palms. "After, I've got chores, Pard. And then I want to take a nap."

Becky looked at him, horrified. *"A nap?"*

"I'm bushed. I got—" he considered for a moment "—three and a half hours' sleep last night. Four hours the night before. Less the night before that."

"I didn't keep you awake," she said frostily.

"Not this week. You did your fair share of it when you were their age," he said.

She dug the toe of her boot into the rug. That wasn't fair.

Did she remind him of his failures as a dad? Did she mention the time he let her get sick at the rodeo from eating too much junk food? Did she bring up how he'd missed winning her that big, stuffed rabbit in Cheyenne because he was so busy ogling some slinky cowgirl he couldn't have hit the broad side of a barn with a handful of rice, let alone a target?

No, she did not. She scowled at him.

He didn't notice. "Besides," he said, "Uncle Tom is leaving today. We're having dinner first, at Grandma and Grandpa's in Bozeman."

"We could be back by then."

"No. Not today. There isn't time," he said in his annoying, patient-father tone. He rattled the breeding charts. "I've got work to do."

"You could've done it yesterday!"

"I didn't have time yesterday."

"You never have time anymore!" She felt tears welling and sniffed them back hard. She wasn't going to cry! She hadn't cried when he'd left to go down the road—and she'd been little then—she wasn't about to cry now.

"We'll go another time. Tomorrow. No," he said wearily, "not tomorrow. I'm helping Jed cut hay tomorrow. Sunday? Maybe we can make it Sunday."

"Sunday?" she said doubtfully.

Upstairs she heard one of the twins start crying and Felicity's footsteps going down the hall. In another minute, Becky knew, the other one would yell. Yep, there it was. Right on cue.

"Taggart?" Felicity called. "I'm feeding Willy. Could you change Abby?"

Taggart looked at his daughter as he got to his feet. "See?"

Becky stepped back and watched him pass, standing still under his absent ruffle of her hair. Then she turned to stare at his back as he slowly climbed the stairs.

"Yeah, I see," she said.

Jenny was packed.

Her clothes. Some books. The afghan that her mother had knitted her. Pictures.

She hesitated over those.

A woman starting over with a new life probably shouldn't take pictures of the old. But as she turned the pages of the albums she had put together over the years, she knew she couldn't leave them behind.

There were so many good memories in them. Of the ranch. Of the mountains. The cattle. Taggart and Felicity and Becky. Jed and Brenna, Tuck and Neile. Noah and Tess and their children.

Mace.

She sucked in a deep breath and shut the album, then packed it away at the bottom of her case.

She walked around the house, going slowly from room to room, saying goodbye.

To the bed where she and Mace had made love so many nights—and a few days—for so many years.

To the stove where she had burned the roast the first night they'd moved in and where she'd baked the Christmas cookies that Mace was always trying to nibble before she got them decorated.

To the fireplace which they had built together, stone by stone, and in front of which one night last year they had loved one another all night long.

To the children's bedroom—she refused today to call it

the spare room; it would be a lie—where they had hoped and dreamed and lost it all.

She wasn't sure when the tears started. Maybe they'd been rolling down her cheeks for days. Sometimes it felt like it. Sometimes it felt like inside she'd been crying so long she would never stop.

But then she heard the car coming up the road, and she swiped determinedly at her face.

"You'll be fine," she told herself. "Fine."

She hoped someday it would be true.

Watching her dad walk up the steps to change Abby after he'd just told her there was no way he could climb Tiptop was bad enough. Banging her fist against the barn door and getting a jagged splinter in it just added insult to injury. Having to dig it out with a needle by herself because Taggart and Felicity were double-twinned only added fuel to the fire.

But when Becky finally got the splinter out and put the antiseptic on it and then discovered that they were out of Band-Aids, well, that was the last straw.

It was a small thing.

It was her life in a nutshell.

"Damn it," Becky said, and didn't even care if they heard her.

It wouldn't matter, she thought grimly. They wouldn't notice if they did.

There were *no* Band-Aids.

Felicity always bought Band-Aids. Felicity's belief in Band-Aids was one of the things that had made Becky sure the quality of life in the Jones household would improve when Taggart married her. And it had.

For two years they'd had Band-Aids.

And now?

Becky sighed as she sat with her arms wrapped around

her knees and stared out across the valley from the top of the mountain.

Now they had twins.

Mace didn't realize how much he'd come to count on having Ian there until Ian was gone.

He'd gone back down the mountain with Noah, and silence seemed to fill his place. The rocking chair sat empty. The pipe smoke faded. The cabin seemed to echo.

There was no one to joke with. No one to talk to. No one to listen to. No one to share a meal with.

All there was, was time to think.

Mace thought. He thought about Ian and Fiona. About their marriage. Fiona's illness. Ian's anger. Not at her. At life.

He thought about Fiona's insistence that they stay. About Ian's reluctance. About Fiona's persuasion. What had Ian said she'd told him?

"It's not just *my* life. It's *our* life. We're married. We're in this together."

And Ian had agreed with her. They'd stayed. She'd died. He'd been angry again. Hurt still.

And yet…he went back.

When Noah came and told him about the earthquake, he didn't even hesitate. "We have work to do," he'd said. "Fiona and I."

And he went to pack.

Fiona was with him. Inside him, where he'd never lose her. For better or worse.

As Ian had told him to, Mace thought about that.

He thought about the other marriages he witnessed every day. He thought about Taggart and Felicity. About Jed and Brenna. About Noah and Tess. He thought about Maggie and Tanner and about Noah's other brother, Luke, and his wife, Jill.

Things hadn't been easy for any of them. And yet you couldn't think of one without the other. They were—like Ian and Fiona—two parts of a whole.

One of the guys—he couldn't even remember which one—had once said to him, "She makes me whole."

Once he'd have thought that about Jenny and himself.

Once, in fact, he'd have put Jenny and himself at the top of the list—the strongest, the happiest, the most resilient of couples. They'd done everything together. Loved and laughed. Fought and made up. Struggled and coped.

Together.

Until this.

This.

His infertility. *His.* Not hers.

"It's *my* problem," he'd yelled at her when she'd told him they would deal with it.

"It's *our* problem," she'd countered quietly.

But he hadn't believed her then. He'd been too caught up in his own pain, his own feelings of inadequacy, his own rage at the injustice of this affront to the very essence of his masculinity.

He hadn't had space in his heart to allow her to share his anguish. He'd shut her out, denied *her* pain, rejected the notion that she had as much at stake as he had.

And now?

Now he wanted her more than he'd ever wanted her in his life.

In the void Ian had left, he had nothing.

No hope. No future. No one.

Ian didn't have Fiona anymore, either. Not physically. But he would always have her in his heart.

"I'll always have her," he'd said to Mace one night when he was staring into the fire. "We're together one way or another until the end."

"I thought we were in this together," Jenny had once said to him.

Mace hadn't believed her then.

He wanted desperately to believe her now.

Becky heard the footsteps coming.

She didn't turn around. It would be more hikers. There were a lot more hikers this year than five years ago, when she and her dad had first started climbing the peak. It wasn't special anymore.

And wasn't that the truth? she thought glumly. Though she had to admit she was glad she'd come.

It was hard to feel the world was really pressing down on you when you got up above it this way.

It was hard to feel that Willy and Abby were the worst things to ever happen in the universe when the universe was so big and Willy and Abby were really pretty small. It was hard to blame Felicity for forgetting Band-Aids when Becky thought about all the things her stepmother did do. Felicity had a whole house to run and babies to look after and book work to help Taggart with. And she had bought Becky a new shirt with a really cool bull rider on it just last week and it wasn't even her birthday.

It was even hard to hold a grudge against her dad when she remembered the good times. And when she thought how really, really tired he looked.

"Hey, Pard."

The soft words behind her made her almost jump out of her skin.

She jerked around to see her father coming up the last few steps to the top of the mountain. He looked beat. Worried. Worse by far than he had that morning.

She hadn't told him where she was going. Why should she? she'd rationalized. He wouldn't care. He probably wouldn't even notice she was gone!

"I thought you didn't have time to climb today," she said, squelching her initial guilty start and marshaling what little defense she could manage.

"I was wrong."

Just that. Nothing else.

She looked up at him. He sat down beside her, but he didn't look at her, just sat with his knees drawn up, his elbows resting on them as he stared off into the valley. At the road that had taken him away from her years ago.

Did he remember what he'd told her then? About the roads all connecting? About him just being on down them somewhere, but always close enough to come if she needed him?

He must, Becky thought, her throat tightening, because he'd come.

"I'm sorry if I scared you," she whispered, edging closer to him.

He turned to look at her. But he didn't just look.

He reached for her and put his arms around her. He pulled her up onto his lap and hugged her hard, pressing his face into her hair and rocking her the way he hadn't rocked her since she was a really little girl.

"I'm sorry, too, Pard." His voice was muffled against her neck. She felt something wet touch her ear.

She reached up and touched it wonderingly. Was it a tear?

She pulled back to look at him. "I wasn't running away," she told him urgently, needing to make him understand now that he was here. "I was coming back. I just needed...needed to do this."

"We both needed to do it." He smiled a little crookedly, a little sadly. "Your going on your own just pointed it out to me."

"I was mad."

"You had a right to be. Things have been...a little rough

lately. I realize that. I didn't mean to turn you down. I *never* want to turn you down, Pard. I just—just—I'm stretched pretty thin these days.''

Becky laced her fingers through his. She was surprised to see that there was less difference in the size of their hands than she remembered. "I know. I understand. It's okay."

He shook his head. "It's not. Lookin' around for you today when we were about to set off for Grandma and Grandpa's and not findin' you just about scared me spitless."

"I didn't mean to scare you."

"Best thing you could've done," he admitted with a heavy sigh. "It woke me up." He brushed a hand over her hair, let it linger, as if he needed to reassure himself that she was really there.

Becky snuggled a little closer, liking the feel of his arms around her. She'd forgotten just how much.

"Thank you for coming," she said in a small voice.

He pressed a kiss against the side of her head. "My pleasure, Pard. It will always be my pleasure. For a long time it was just you and me, and I guess I sort of took it for granted. I thought having Felicity just made it better."

"It did make it better," Becky said, worried suddenly that he might think she was sorry he'd got married. "I love Felicity."

A corner of his mouth tipped up. "I do, too."

Becky breathed a sigh of relief. She didn't want to ever have to think about him getting another divorce. She knew, even if he'd never said, just how much the first one had hurt. "Good," she said. "That's all right, then."

"It will be," he promised. "It won't always be this hectic. Willy and Abby will grow up. They won't demand as much time." He shook his head. "I never counted on twins."

"They're okay," Becky allowed after a moment.

"They're an adjustment," Taggart said. "Sometimes they drive me nuts."

Becky's eyes widened. "They do?"

"I love 'em. I wouldn't be without 'em," her father assured her. "But it takes a hell of a lot out of you just keepin' up with them."

"At least there's two of you," Becky said. It didn't seem quite so bad once she knew her father didn't feel all jolly all the time he was having to deal with screaming kids. It made her own feelings seem a little less awful.

"There's two of us," Taggart agreed. "And, like I told you the first time we came up here, things change. In this case I think they'll get better. We'll have more time. But if we don't, remind me about today. Will you?"

Becky nodded. "It's a promise."

"And we'll try to adjust," Taggart said. "That's a promise, too."

Taggart's arms tightened around her, and he gave her a long, hard hug. Becky hugged him back. "Love you, Pard," he said.

"Love you, too. Always." Then she swiped at her eyes and grinned at him.

He grinned back. Then, lifting her and setting her on the ground, he got to his feet and held out his hand.

"We'll come again," he said as he started down. "Next year."

"All of us?" Becky asked as she followed.

"If we can," Taggart said. "I'd like that. Would you?"

"Yeah, I think I would. I think Willy and Abby are gonna need to see that the world is bigger than them."

Taggart stopped and turned his head to look back at her. He smiled.

Suddenly she heard a thin, wailing sound. "What's that? Is that a baby? Who would bring a baby up here?"

"Felicity."

Becky stumbled. "What? She brought them? Here?"

"She's waiting down where you left your horse. She wanted to come all the way, but I said no. I thought this one was between you and me."

He met her gaze and held it. This was her dad—the dad she'd always known, the dad that was there inside the one who had so much more to cope with these days.

"It was," Becky said after she thought about it. "But," she added, "it's not just you and me anymore, is it?"

Taggart shook his head.

Becky slipped an arm around his waist and felt his go around her shoulders as the trail widened and the two of them could walk together. "Then I guess we better go back down and help Felicity out."

Her stepmother was waiting in the truck, nursing Abby. She had her thumb in Willy's mouth, letting him suck. But she didn't seem to be paying much attention to either one of them.

Her gaze was on Becky and Taggart.

As they came down she opened the truck's door and handed the babies to Taggart, then wrapped her arms around Becky and hugged her tight.

Wordlessly Becky hugged back. Then she stepped away and said, "I'm sorry," because she knew Felicity had probably worried even more than her dad.

"So am I," Felicity said. "I'm glad you're all right."

"I'm fine," Becky said. "Better than fine." She looked at her dad, holding both crying babies, and smiled. Then she looked at her stepmother and said, "You better get back and feed her."

"Yes." Felicity took Abby from Taggart. He was left with a squalling Willy. He looked from the baby to Becky's horse which he needed to put in the trailer before they could start back down.

"I'll hold him," Becky said.

Taggart lifted his brows in surprise.

But Becky held out her arms, and carefully Taggart put Willy in them.

Her brother was much bigger than the last time she'd held him. He wiggled more. He held his head up. He waved an arm and smacked her in the face.

She started in surprise, then laughed. "Not bad," she told him, looking over his head to meet her father's eyes. "But I think there's still a few things I can teach you."

He would go see her in the morning.

Before church. He would catch her before she left and he would say...he would say...

He didn't know what he would say.

What could a guy possibly say to the woman he loved and had left? How could he explain the pain he felt? How could he admit that he had never really considered hers?

Of course she knew that. It was obvious.

He shouldn't go.

There would be no point.

But there was a point. He understood something now he hadn't understood before. He understood about marriage being a give-and-take between two people. He understood that even though it was *his* infertility, he was *her* husband. What they did about it should have been a choice both of them made.

He could tell her that.

If she would listen.

And he could tell her now as well as he could tell her tomorrow. There was no point in waiting.

He was halfway down the mountain when he saw Becky coming his way on her horse. He slowed when she waved frantically at him.

"What's up?" he asked.

"You gotta stop 'em!"

"Stop who?" He wasn't stopping anyone or anything, not until he talked to Jenny. "Twins givin' you trouble again?"

"No. They're fine. You gotta stop Jenny. She's leavin' tonight with Uncle Tom. She's going to Iowa!"

Chapter Fourteen

The words hit Mace like a sledgehammer to the heart.

He couldn't find his voice. He could barely find his breath.

"You're sure?"

"That's what my dad says. An' my mom. We were s'posed to have dinner with him tonight at my grandparents'. But we didn't go 'cause, well, I climbed Tiptop and...and my dad came after me." She ducked her head a moment, and Mace got the feeling that there was a lot more to the story than that.

He'd hear it sometime. Not now.

"What's that got to do with Jenny going with Tom?"

"Uncle Tom was gonna meet us at Grandma's. But when Daddy called Grandma to tell her we'd be late, she said Uncle Tom would be late, too, because he was stopping to pick up Jenny! And I told Daddy I couldn't go to Grandma's," she said urgently. "I had to come and tell you."

Mace shut his eyes. He took a deep breath, but when he opened them again Becky was still looking at him, the same desperate expression on her face that he felt deep inside.

"Maybe she was just going along to...to say goodbye."

He was grasping at straws and he knew it. He didn't want to believe—wouldn't let himself believe—and yet in his gut he knew it was true.

"Maybe," Becky said, but there was no doubt in her voice. She said it only to humor him. "But I don't think so. Come on, Mace. I bet you can catch her if you hurry."

Still he hesitated. Obviously Jenny had made her decision.

Or...had he made it for her?

"What time does the plane leave?" he demanded.

Becky beamed. "I knew it! I knew you loved her!"

Mace stared at her.

"Daddy thought I shouldn't come. He told me not to meddle." She wrinkled her nose to tell him what she thought of that idea. "But I told him you had a right to know 'cause I was sure you loved her. And then he said since he'd come to his senses today, he guessed you oughta have a chance to do it, too. So, have you?"

Mace, not following entirely, said, "Have I what?"

"Come to your senses. Realized you don't want a divorce."

"I don't want a divorce," Mace said. He just hoped it wasn't too late to convince Jenny.

"Good," Becky said. Then, "Why did you?"

He knew Ian would never mention what he'd told him. He was not so convinced about Becky. But it was a question he was going to have to face if he got Jenny back.

"I can't have kids," he told her.

"So?"

He stared at her. Did the words that had sounded so

monumental in his head sound small to her? Well, of course they might. She wasn't affected by them.

"Jenny wants a family," he explained patiently. "She's always wanted a child. And I'm—" he forced another word out "—sterile. I can't have any."

"So get one." She gave him an impatient look.

"It isn't that simple. You don't just drop into a supermarket or the hardware store. You can't get a family at Kmart."

"You could adopt one."

"It isn't the same."

"Why not?"

Why not? The question was so simple. The answer so...so...

"You don't think Jenny could love a kid that wasn't hers?"

"Of course she could!" Mace had no doubt about that.

Becky shrugged. "Then, what's the problem? I know you can."

He stared at her, not following her logic. His confusion must have been written on his face for she spelled it out.

"You love me."

It was that simple, after all.

But just in case he didn't get it, Becky was willing to elaborate. She eased her horse up as close to the truck window as she could and leaned forward in the saddle. "And I love you, Mace." She met his gaze squarely, and he recognized the gift she was giving him. "If I was married to you, it wouldn't make any difference if you couldn't have kids."

"It wouldn't?" But it wasn't really a question, because he could see the truth of her statement in her face.

She answered him, anyway. "Of course not. I'd be sad 'cause I'd want 'em to look like you and prob'ly they wouldn't. And Jenny would prob'ly want that, too. You're pretty good-looking, you know.''

His mouth twitched at that.

"But," Becky added, "she'd prob'ly be glad in another way."

"How's that?" Mace asked.

"If she was lucky, they wouldn't be as pigheaded stubborn as you are, either.''

God, he hoped Becky was right.

He was staking his life on Becky being right.

He drove as fast as the road would allow.

If she hadn't left yet, maybe he could talk to her. Maybe he could tell her—convince her...

But when he drove around the bend and saw the house, it was dark.

He ran up the steps, anyway, calling her name, hoping against hope. But the house was dead quiet. There was no clutter. No dishes on the drainboard. Not even a dirty glass in the sink.

He checked the bedroom, yanked open the closet door and saw exactly what he'd feared to see: her side of the closet was empty now, too.

She was gone.

And the airport was a good hour away.

He ran back to the truck, jumped in and pressed the accelerator all the way to the floor.

Montana didn't have a daytime speed limit.

It did, unfortunately for Mace, have a nighttime one.

He was frantic. Desperate. Furious when he saw those flashing red lights coming behind him. He was tempted to not stop. When he did, and the cop did a slow Western amble from the patrol car, he was tempted to gun the engine and drive off.

But if he did, with his luck he'd get caught and hauled off to jail, and there would be no Rooster to call Jenny and no Jenny to come and bail him out.

He sat and fumed while the cop wrote him the ticket. He gnawed his knuckles and tapped his fingers on the wheel.

"Where you off to in such an all-fired hurry?" The cop tore the ticket off and handed it to him.

"The airport."

"Right." The cop nodded and waved him on his way. "Just don't fly until you get there."

He parked in a no-parking zone. He practically vaulted over a couple coming out of the door. He ran all the way to the desk.

"The flight to Minneapolis?" he gasped.

The desk attendant pointed. Mace turned to see a plane hurtling down the runway and lifting off.

The adrenaline that had got him down the mountain and over the pass drained right out of him.

He felt weak. Dizzy. Sick.

"I can get you a seat on the first flight in the morning," the attendant offered.

Mace shook his head, watching as the plane rose higher, grew smaller, banked as it began to turn.

"No," he said, his voice as hollow as he felt. "It's too late for that."

He was numb as he walked back to the parking lot. His chest felt as if one of Taggart's bulls was sitting on it, pressing down, squeezing the air, the breath, the life right out. He stopped on the curb and tried to steady himself, to draw a breath, to move on.

In the twilight he could see the lights of the plane as it completed its turn and headed east, taking Jenny away.

Out of his life.

And into Tom's.

His eyes blurred; his throat tightened. He sank down on the curb and put his head in his hands.

He wasn't aware of the footsteps until they stopped right in front of him. Even then, he didn't look up.

"Mace?" Her voice was soft, hesitant, worried. Astonishing. Familiar.

His head jerked up. *"Jenny?"*

He lurched to his feet, stunned and self-conscious. He dragged a hand over his face. "What're you doing here?"

She smiled faintly. "I was going to ask you the same thing."

She stood looking at him warily, a suitcase in her hand, another at her feet. She pressed her lips together nervously, looking at him, then away, then back at him again.

Waiting. For him.

And so he told her.

The words weren't pretty. He'd never be an orator. He stumbled over them, trying to explain the hurt, the pain.

"You asked to talk. You wanted to talk. But I couldn't. Not then. All I could feel was the pain. It wasn't just being told I couldn't do the main thing that makes a guy a man. That was bad enough. Hell, it was terrible. But just as bad, maybe worse, was that I also knew I'd failed you."

"You didn't—"

He cut her off. "I thought I had. I believed I had. I knew how much you wanted children. It was your dream—"

"*You* were my dream."

"Children with me, maybe," he allowed. "But when I couldn't have any, I assumed you wouldn't want me. I was scared you wouldn't want me," he corrected himself. "So I took the decision out of your hands. I told myself I was being almighty generous letting you out of our marriage." His mouth twisted with self-recrimination as he said the words. He bowed his head. "What I was doing was being an almighty coward. And I was failing our marriage, too."

He stopped talking then. And the silence seemed to go on and on. He felt it grow around him like the onset of a Montana winter—hard and deep and numbingly cold. He couldn't look at her.

And then he felt the warmth of a hand against his cheek. A soft touch. A gentle stroke. A lingering.

He lifted his head.

"I was so hurt," she said softly, her hand still on his cheek. "When you left, I wanted to die. I didn't know how to reach you, how to get you to trust me enough to keep our lives together. I thought I could wait you out. I thought you would come to terms...realize it was important, but not *most* important. But you never did. You asked for a divorce!"

Mace listened. For the first time he heard it all from her point of view. He understood now the pain she felt had nothing to do with his not being able to have children.

"Even after we made love that night," she whispered, "you left again."

"I saw the picture," he told her. "Of Tom and his daughter. I saw the dishes."

"Dishes?" She wasn't following. He couldn't blame her.

"I thought you wanted him," he said simply.

"And I thought, fine, if that's the way he feels, I'll go," she said. "Tom's a good man. A kind man." She dropped her hand.

He said tonelessly. "I know."

And he knew if she went to Tom—after all he'd done to drive her away—it was no more than he deserved.

"I was going with him," she said in a low voice. "I packed. I got all the way to the airport. I couldn't get on the plane." She lifted her gaze and met his. "He's a good man, but he's not *my* man. When I married you, Mace, I married you for ever and always. In all ways," she added fiercely. "I'll never love anyone else the way I love you."

It was more than he deserved. It was more than he dared hope for. It was everything he would ever want—Jenny's love—for the rest of his life.

"I came after you," he said brokenly. "I wouldn't blame you if you said it was too late. I would understand if you told me to go to hell. But I hope to God you won't. Ever." He pulled her into his arms then, and held her close, his forehead resting on hers, her lips touching his own. "I know I hurt you. I know I wrecked our marriage. Help me put it back together again. Help me make it right."

Jenny's eyes were shining. Her smiling lips were trembling. "You mean it?"

Mace nodded. "I mean it. There's nothing I can say that will change what I did, except what you already know—I was selfish. I was foolish. I was wrong. I'm sorry. And...I love you, too."

It was December.

The night was crystal clear and cold. The snow was thick on the ground. But it wasn't snowing now. The runway was clear. The plane would be landing soon.

They stood, Mace's arm hugging Jenny's shoulder, Jenny's arm around his waist, as they watched and waited.

The phone call had come three months ago on a crisp fall day. Mace had finished moving the cattle down that afternoon. They were going to be shipping on Friday. Jenny had taken the day off school to help sort and shape up the herd. She was even going to miss her lit class at the university tonight so she could help.

Mace had told her she didn't have to.

She'd said, "I want to."

And that was why she had still been at home when the phone rang.

Mace had answered it, heard the crackle of a long-distance connection, the lag and then the faint, "Mace? Is that you? Ian here."

He stood watching the sky now, waiting to catch the first glimpse of tiny blinking lights—lights that meant a plane was coming—and he remembered how delighted he'd been, how glad he was to hear Ian's voice, how eager to tell Ian he'd come to his senses, that he'd realized what Ian had—that marriage was for better or worse—and that he and Jenny were together again.

But Ian already knew.

"Talked to Maggie last week," he'd said. "I have to say, I'm glad. I also have to say, I'm not surprised."

And then he had got to the point.

"Now that you're back together, I wonder if you're considering a family?"

"I can't have kids, Ian. Remember?" It still wasn't easy to say, but he managed it.

"I remember," Ian said gently. "But there's more than one way to have a family. That's why I'm calling. I have three children here I'd like to see become yours."

Mace stood dumbfounded, unable to say even one word.

"Shocked you, have I?" Ian chuckled. "Never considered it?"

"Yes." They had, just these past weeks. They'd gone so far as to start checking out agencies. "But...th-three?"

Mace remembered that he'd almost lost his grip on the receiver then. His mouth had gone dry, his stomach flip-flopped. He'd looked wildly around the room.

"What's wrong?" Jenny asked. She was looking at him worriedly from where she was making spaghetti sauce at the stove.

Mace couldn't answer. Ian was talking, anyway—explaining—and it was all he could do to listen.

"A family I knew quite well," Ian was saying. "The

parents were killed in the earthquake. They left a boy who's seven, a girl, five, and another boy who's not quite three. They have a grandmother here, but she can't raise them. She's not all that well. So I've been talking to her, discussing alternatives.''

"Alternatives.'' Mace managed a barely credible echo.

"And she'll let them go...*if* I tell her they'll have parents who will love them...*if* I can promise they'll go to a good home.'' He paused. "I can't think of anyone who'd be a better father and mother than you and Jenny, Mace.''

Mace hadn't known what to say.

He'd looked at Jenny, who was still looking at him with a quizzical, slightly worried expression on her face.

"Are you all right?'' she asked.

He nodded numbly. He cleared his throat and swallowed hard.

"Let me talk to my wife, Ian. I'll call you back.''

Then he hung up and told Jenny what Ian had said. Jenny didn't believe him.

"Children? *Three of them?*'' She shook her head. "That isn't funny, Mace.''

No, it wasn't funny. It was exhilarating—and it scared him to death.

"He means it, Jenn,'' he said with a sound somewhere between a sob and a laugh.

"Call him back,'' Jenny demanded. "Tell me about these children. Tell me more.''

Mace called. He and Ian talked. Then Jenny and Ian talked. Then he and Jenny talked all night. For the first time in memory, with shipping only three days off, Mace didn't even think about shaping up the herd.

"It would mean a huge change,'' Jenny said cautiously. She looked like she didn't want to hope.

"Yep,'' Mace agreed.

"It wouldn't be just the two of us. There would be *five* of us—all at once."

"Yep."

"That's pretty daunting."

"It is." He was smiling all over his face.

She looked at him as if he'd lost his mind.

"Buying the ranch was pretty daunting," he reminded her. "Starting the herd was a risk. Building the house was a commitment."

"It's not the same," she said.

But he knew what she wanted. It was the same thing he wanted. He didn't look away.

She swallowed and gripped his hands hard. "Are you sure, Mace? What do you really think?"

"I think I love you, Jenny. I think—I know—you love me. I think we are being given what we've said we wanted for years. We've got enough love to spare, enough to share." He leaned forward and laid a kiss on her lips. "And any kids who get to call you Mom are going to be the luckiest kids on earth."

She had smiled then.

And, drawing her close and holding her tight against his heart, so had he.

Still, there were some scary moments. Nightmares of inadequacy. Perfectly realistic feelings of having bitten off more than they could chew. There was lots of red tape. There were bureaucratic stalls and governmental snafus.

As the days became weeks and the weeks became months, sometimes they thought they would never see the children. At those times the photos Ian sent of three black-haired, brown-eyed urchins—Marcos, Pilar, and Antonio—seemed like no more than paper dreams.

Finally, a week ago, Ian had called again.

"I'm not going to preach this year," a voice said without preamble. "I'm playing Santa Claus instead."

Mace, who'd been kicking snow off his boots and shaking it out of his hair, took a moment to connect. "Santa Claus? Ian? Is that you? What are you talking about? Santa Claus where?"

"In Bozeman. Christmas Eve. Be at the airport at seven. Santa's bringing you a couple of sons and a daughter."

And now he and Jenny pressed their faces against the glass, their arms around each other, their hearts in their throats as they waited.

Behind them, Mace knew, were their friends.

"Do you mind if we come along?" Felicity and Becky had stopped by to ask them yesterday.

"We have to come," Becky said. "Some people go to stables. Other people go to airports," she explained. "It's what Christmas is all about."

And so they were there—all of them: Felicity, with Taggart holding Willy, and Becky with Abby in her arms; Tess and Noah with their three, Susannah, Clay and Scott; Jed, holding Neile, next to Brenna, and Tuck with Brenna's father leaning on him; Taggart's parents; Maggie and Robert Tanner and their little boys, Jared and Seth and Nick, and Maggie's two brothers, Duncan and Andy. All of them had come to pick up Ian and meet the new arrivals.

Even the middle Tanner brother, Luke, whom Mace barely knew, was there. He'd brought his family to spend Christmas with his brothers. He and his wife, Jill, and children, Keith and Katie and brand-new baby Jack had come to the airport, too. So had Jenny's sister, Teresa, up from Cody for the holidays, and—Mace's biggest shock of all—his rolling stone brother, Shane.

"It's Christmas," he'd said this morning, when Mace had looked astonished at opening the door to find him standing there. "Where else would I be? Besides—" Shane had grinned and punched him lightly on the arm "—a fat guy in a red suit left a lot of toys in my truck and I had to bring 'em to somebody. I don't get to be an uncle every day of the week.''

"There it is." Jenny's voice was so quiet in the midst of the hubbub that Mace almost didn't hear her.

But then her fingers dug into his ribs, and he felt her tense against his side, and he pressed his nose against the glass and looked where she was looking, and, yes, there it was!

Blinking lights in the distance. Coming closer. Lower. And then the plane touched down.

"I'm scared," Jenny whispered. "Are you scared?"

"Terrified," he admitted.

"We could turn and run," she said in a small voice.

Mace shook his head. "Been there. Done that. It doesn't work." He turned and drew her fully against him. "But we can do this. Together." He looked deep into her eyes. "Can't we?"

Jenny raised herself just enough to touch her lips to his. "Yes," she said. "Oh, yes."

Then the tunnel door opened and the first passengers began to appear. Grandmas and grandpas. Aunts, uncles. Brothers, sisters. Families and friends—home for Christmas—were all swooped down upon by eager relatives. Bundled off amid laughter and hugs and kisses.

And then there was quiet.

And then, at last, there was Ian.

He came out of the doorway with a little girl clutching one side of his coat, a boy clutching the other and a smaller, sleeping boy in his arms.

He stopped when he saw them, his eyes meeting first Jenny's, then Mace's. And then his gaze dropped to the children. The older boy looked worried. The girl looked scared.

"My children," Mace heard Jenny whisper, awed.

The family she'd always wanted. The family *he'd* wanted more than he'd ever dared admit.

"Our children," Mace corrected her softly. Their fingers squeezed together. Their hearts beat as one.

Together they walked toward Ian and the children.

With tears running down her face, Jenny held out her arms, and Ian settled the sleeping toddler in her embrace.

Mace brushed a finger across Antonio's still-baby-soft cheek, and then he hunkered down until he was on eye level with his brand-new son and daughter. They looked apprehensive, scared, but hopeful.

He felt apprehensive, scared, but hopeful...and as if he'd been given the best Christmas present in the world.

He felt his own tears brimming and did his best to blink them back as he held out his hands to Marcos and Pilar.

"*Bienvenidos, mis hijos,*" he whispered, and if his voice broke, suddenly it didn't matter at all. He gathered them in—his son, his daughter—and held them next to his heart. "Welcome home."

* * * * *

Don't miss the next CODE OF THE WEST
book by Anne McAllister. The irrepressible
Shane Nichols meets his match in
THE COWBOY STEALS A LADY,
coming to you in 1998 from Silhouette Desire!

Dear Diary

  MACE is a DAD!! How about that? I think its pretty amazing him and Jenny getting 3 kids that way. Pretty cool, too—except he sure doesn't have the time he used to. But he's <u>lots</u> happier now—he and Jenny both. And yesterday he told me not to worry, that he would always have time for his best friends. And then he said "Like you, SHADOW!" and he hugged the stuffing out of me.

  Later my dad said "You are a good friend, Pard" and Felicity said, "The best" and Abby smiled and Willy burped. They love me. I love them too—even when it's hard cause like Felicity says, love is like that.

                                                    Decky

Ps: I'll always love MACE—even when I'm 80 and he's 103!!!

Daniel MacGregor is at it again...

New York Times bestselling author

NORA ROBERTS

introduces us to a new generation of MacGregors
as the lovable patriarch of the illustrious MacGregor
clan plays matchmaker again, this time to his three
gorgeous granddaughters in

THE MACGREGOR BRIDES

From Silhouette Books

Don't miss this brand-new continuation of Nora Roberts's
enormously popular *MacGregor* miniseries.

Available November 1997 at your favorite retail outlet.

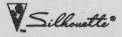

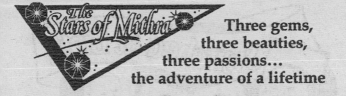

The Stars of Mithra

Three gems,
three beauties,
three passions…
the adventure of a lifetime

SILHOUETTE·INTIMATE·MOMENTS®
brings you a thrilling new series by
New York Times bestselling author

Nora Roberts

Three mystical blue diamonds place three close
friends in jeopardy…and lead them to romance.

In October
HIDDEN STAR (IM#811)
Bailey James can't remember a thing, but she knows
she's in big trouble. And she desperately needs private
investigator Cade Parris to help her live long enough to
find out just what kind.

In December
CAPTIVE STAR (IM#823)
Cynical bounty hunter Jack Dakota and spitfire
M.J. O'Leary are handcuffed together and on the run
from a pair of hired killers. And Jack wants to know
why—but M.J.'s not talking.

In February
SECRET STAR (IM#835)
Lieutenant Seth Buchanan's murder investigation takes
a strange turn when Grace Fontaine turns up alive. But
as the mystery unfolds, he soon discovers the notorious
heiress is the biggest mystery of all.

Available at your favorite retail outlet.

by two of your favorite authors

Penny Richards and Suzannah Davis

Four strangers are about to discover the true bonds
of brotherhood...with a little help—and love—
from four terrific women!

THE RANGER AND THE SCHOOLMARM
by Penny Richards (SE #1136, 11/97)

THE COP AND THE CRADLE
by Suzannah Davis (SE #1143, 12/97)

LITTLE BOY BLUE
by Suzannah Davis (SE #1149, 1/98)

WILDCATTER'S KID
by Penny Richards (SE #1155, 2/98)

Thirty-six years ago, in a small Texas hospital, four
adorable little boys were born. And not until they were
all handsome, successful, grown men did they realize
they were SWITCHED AT BIRTH. Find out how this
discovery affects their lives. Only in

Silhouette ® SPECIAL EDITION ®

ELIZABETH AUGUST

Continues the twelve-book
series—36 HOURS—in
November 1997 with
Book Five

CINDERELLA STORY

Life was hardly a fairy tale for Nina Lindstrom. Out of work and with an ailing child, the struggling single mom was running low on hope. Then Alex Bennett solved her problems with one convenient proposal: marriage. And though he had made no promises beyond financial security, Nina couldn't help but feel that with a little love, happily-ever-afters really could come true!

For Alex and Nina and *all* the residents of Grand Springs, Colorado, the storm-induced blackout was just the beginning of 36 Hours that changed *everything!* You won't want to miss a single book.

SILHOUETTE WOMEN KNOW ROMANCE WHEN THEY SEE IT.

And they'll see it on **ROMANCE CLASSICS**, the new 24-hour TV channel devoted to romantic movies and original programs like the special Romantically Speaking—Harlequin™ Goes Prime Time.

Romantically Speaking—Harlequin™ Goes Prime Time introduces you to many of your favorite romance authors in a program developed exclusively for Harlequin® and Silhouette® readers.

Watch for **Romantically Speaking—Harlequin™ Goes Prime Time** beginning in the summer of 1997.

If you're not receiving ROMANCE CLASSICS, call your local cable operator or satellite provider and ask for it today!

ROMANCE CLASSICS

Escape to the network of your dreams.

See Ingrid Bergman and Gregory Peck in *Spellbound* on Romance Classics.

Share in the joy of yuletide romance with brand-new
stories by two of the genre's most beloved writers

DIANA PALMER
and
JOAN JOHNSTON
in

LONE STAR CHRISTMAS

Diana Palmer and Joan Johnston share their favorite
Christmas anecdotes and personal stories in this
special hardbound edition.

Diana Palmer delivers an irresistible spin-off of her
LONG, TALL TEXANS series and Joan Johnston crafts an
unforgettable new chapter to **HAWK'S WAY** in this wonderful
keepsake edition celebrating the holiday season. So
perfect for gift giving, you'll want one for yourself...and
one to give to a special friend!

Available in November at your favorite retail outlet!

Only from

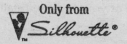